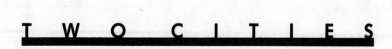

TWO CITIES

ALSO BY ADAM ZAGAJEWSKI

TREMOR: SELECTED POEMS (1985)
SOLIDARITY, SOLITUDE (Essays) (1990)
CANVAS (1991)

TWO CITIES

On Exile, History, and the Imagination

ADAM ZAGAJEWSKI

Translated by Lillian Vallee

FARRAR • STRAUS • GIROUX • NEW YORK

Translation copyright © 1995 by Lillian Vallee
All rights reserved
Originally published in Polish under the title *Dwa miasta*
in 1991. Copyright © 1991 by Adam Zagajewski
Printed in the United States of America
Published simultaneously in Canada by HarperCollins*Canada*Ltd
Designed by Debbie Glasserman
First edition, 1995

Library of Congress Cataloguing-in-Publication Data
Zagajewski, Adam
[Dwa miasta. English]
Two cities : on exile, history, and the imagination / Adam
Zagajewski ; translated by Lillian Vallee. — 1st ed.
p.   cm.
I. Vallee, Lillian. II. Title.
PG7185.A32D8913 1995   891.8'547—dc20   94-18883 CIP

"Drohobycz and the World" was originally published in Harper
and Row's *Letters and Drawings of Bruno Schulz* and is used
here with the permission of Jerzy Ficowski and Jacob Schulz.

Contents

CONTENTS

TWO CITIES

TWO CITIES

Rain fell for four days. Heavy, dirty clouds drifted over the city, hurried and impatient as unending cargo trains transporting the ocean to the east.

Finally the sun broke and the rooftops, damp and steaming, became instantaneous mirrors shining carefree and triumphant.

If people are divided into the settled, the emigrants, and the homeless, then I certainly belong to the third category, although I understand it very soberly, without a shadow of sentimentality or self-pity.

Settled people die where they were born; sometimes one sees country homes in which multiple generations of the same family lived. Emigrants make their homes abroad and thus make sure that at least their children will once again belong to the category of settled people (who speak another language). An emigrant, therefore, is a temporary link, a guide who takes future generations by the hand and leads them to another, safe place, or so it appears to him.

A homeless person, on the other hand, is someone who,

by accident, caprice of fate, his own fault, or the fault of his temperament, did not want—or was incapable in his childhood or early youth of forging—close and affectionate bonds with the surroundings in which he grew and matured. To be homeless, therefore, does not mean that one lives under a bridge or on the platform of a less frequented Metro station (as for instance, *nomen omen*, the station Europe on the line Pont de Levallois-Gallieni); it means only that the person having this defect cannot indicate the streets, cities, or community that might be his home, his, as one is wont to say, miniature homeland.

In my case a certain (perhaps too simple, too obvious) explanation suggests itself, for I spent my childhood in an ugly industrial city; I was brought there when I was barely four months old, and then for many years afterward I was told about the extraordinarily beautiful city (Lvov) that my family had to leave. So it is not surprising that I looked upon real houses and streets with a semicontemptuous air of superiority and that I took from reality only the bare necessities.

And this is why—at least this is why it seems to me—I became notoriously homeless (I am trying to say this in a way that does not elicit pity, but, at the same time, neither do I wish to pride myself on this peculiar characteristic).

My parents' life was cut in two: before they left and after they left. And my life, too, except that my four months spent in that breathtaking city could in no way equal the experience of many years of mature existence. Yet no matter where one cuts and divides life, one cuts and divides it into two halves.

If I had lived only eight months, mathematicians would have been content. Because, however, events took a different turn, the mystics can be happy instead, because those first four unconscious months blaze with the light of an epiphany.

Homeless, but not at all unhappy. Nevertheless, the worse city offered me various humble riches, beginning with a roof over my head.

And sometimes there were even more generous gifts. Once, for example—I was probably around sixteen at the time—one of my classmates sold me some records he had lifted from a student club for a song. (This club had been partially destroyed by a fire, so my classmate wasn't exactly guilty of theft.) These were Deutsche Grammophon Gesellschaft recordings and they contained the following works: Igor Stravinsky's *Petrouchka*, Beethoven's String Quartet op. 59, no. 3 (the last of three quartets dedicated to Rasoumovsky), Mozart's Piano Concerto no. 25, and "Spring," part of Haydn's oratorio *The Seasons*.

The selection of records was arbitrary. I imagine that, though he was not exactly a thief, my classmate must have been in a hurry when nabbing the records. For me, however, this completely random collection of works became the basis of my musical education.

Connoisseurs will undoubtedly ask: But where's Bach? Monteverdi? Where is Gregorian chant, Schubert, and Wagner? Unfortunately they were not in the student club. And besides, Wagner had compromised himself politically. There weren't many classical records in the stores. It seems that Wladyslaw Gomulka, the man running Poland at the time, placed no great value on music (which took its toll—his governing was highly unmusical).

No, there was no Bach or Monteverdi among the recordings. But there was the brazen, rakish, challenging trumpet of *Petrouchka*, there was the meditative wealth of the opus 59 quartet, there was one of Mozart's late piano concerti, and, finally, there was Haydn's paean to the earth opening up to spring.

I have one of the records to this day and it is before me: the

Third Rasoumovsky Quartet. Its parts: 1. *Andante con moto* —*Allegro vivace,* 2. *Andante con moto quasi Allegretto,* 3. *Menuetto: Grazioso,* 4. *Allegro molto.* Performed by: the Koeckert Quartet. Yellow label on an ebony disk.

Music was created for the homeless because, of all the arts, it is least connected with place. It is suspiciously cosmopolitan. Why do sections of a musical work have Italian names? Why was Beethoven born in Bonn and why did he die in Vienna? Why did he dedicate three violin quartets to a Russian aristocrat? Why do the Chinese play Chopin's nocturnes? Why did Handel go to London and Rossini to Paris?

Painting is the art of a settled people who enjoy contemplating their native haunts. Portraits confirm the settled in their conviction that they are really alive (because they are visible). Only still lifes—and not all—reveal the absolute indifference of things, their cynicism, lack of local patriotism. The pitchers painted by Morandi have nothing in common with Bologna; they are frail, thin, and full of air. In Vermeer's paintings, the interiors belong to Delft, but the windows open upon nothingness (that is, light).

Poetry, meanwhile, is befitting emigrants, those unlucky ones who stand over an abyss—between generations, between continents—with their miserable belongings. Their lips move sometimes—some of them grind out awful curses, others poetic stanzas.

Sociologically, my family is entirely representative of that chimerical social stratum called the intelligentsia: it derives from the petty gentry, which lost its property long, long ago, and for almost the last two hundred years has been undergoing the most diverse metamorphoses and experiments, most frequently ending up as notaries or schoolteachers, who keep traces of their noble ancestry—coat of arms and the name of the last remnants of their estate—in the very bottom drawer.

In addition to this, my father was raised in a home where Josef Klemens Pilsudski, the socialist, was admired, while my mother grew up in a family that was loyal to Roman Dmowski, the nationalist.

In October 1945, our foursome, that is, my parents, my sister, and I, endured a two-week journey from Lvov to Gliwice. The family graves stayed in the east. The household spirits probably hesitated before they decided to accompany us on that uncertain journey in a cattle car. The spirits of notaries, schoolteachers, doctors, defunct gentry, most often leading an uncertain existence, eating someone else's bread.

Some emigrated, seeking their fortune in Western Europe —for example, the one who was not a notary or a schoolteacher but a potter and who settled in the bilingual Swiss town of Biel/Bienne and opened a tile factory.

My grandmother's cousin, Leopold Zborowski, emigrated to Paris and became an art dealer. Soutine and Modigliani were among his painters; he had the reputation of a dealer who took tender care of his artists and did not exploit them. He was probably also a poet. In a museum in Houston hangs a portrait of him by Modigliani (it is not his best painting). The museum note informs the viewer that the portrait is of Leopold Zborowski, "a Polish poet."

He was a handsome man. He lived beyond his means and died young and bankrupt, in spite of the fact that the artists he promoted entered the history of world painting. He was one of the better-known personages in Montparnasse. In one photo an elegantly dressed Zborowski sits at a café table in southern France, absorbed in reading the news; the photo is black-and-white, but one feels the presence in it of Provençal sunlight, softened by a canopy of plane trees. A brief moment of peace, rest, and also a brief moment when it seems the subject of the photo is saying, "But of course, I belong to this moment, the light of the south is my light, the leaves of the plane trees are my favorite sunshade, and I always learn about the world from this newspaper."

It is hard to know how to evaluate human careers and destinies. Does longevity count, or the number of offspring, or a bank account, or the traces left on the face of the earth? If one considers that last criterion, Leopold Zborowski can hardly complain.

Sometimes just one trace remains: for example, my grandfather's brother, Emil, died very young, but he left a pamphlet in which he discusses the problems of education. This pamphlet can be found in many libraries; it is a frail monument to my ancestors because most of them were teachers, in elementary and secondary schools, trade schools, and gymnasia in Lvov and the vicinity, Stanislawow, and Sniatyn (Emil lived in Przemysl).

It is difficult for me to imagine how their homes, furniture, and gardens looked. Sometimes I wonder what the atmosphere of their lives was like and what sort of moral air they inhaled. I think that often it was an atmosphere of unfulfillment: disrupted careers in a partitioned country, an uncertain future. But perhaps it wasn't like that at all. Ruling the empire was robust Franz Joseph, who lived so long he almost became a freak of nature, like an ancient linden tree. My ancestors were schoolteachers, so they lived modestly but securely, and it is likely that throughout their careers they knew what sort of retirement pension they were due.

They were able to hang on to what remained of their old homes and furniture through war and deportation: a wicker armchair, Polish highlander kilim, watercolors and paintings, and photographs that depicted ladies in enormous hats and beloved, long-dead cats and dogs. The family was close-knit; they liked their Sunday and, especially, holiday dinners and suppers, during which they were able to secrete a peculiar hormone of familial, fraternal warmth, intimacy, and trust. They discussed matters of hearth and country. During these never-ending meals, all that was distant and alien became insubstantial; only the familial and intimate existed. Owing to the properties of the Polish language, whose specialty is exquisite diminutives, they bore double first names. To the world at large, to the authorities, their names were Jan, Boguslaw, Wladyslaw, Tekla, Teresa, or Maria, but, in fact, only the endearing family diminutives really counted—As, Myszka, Musia, Renia, Adzio, Tolo, Bogus. It was as if there were two currencies, two languages, two systems of denotation: one for outsiders and one for the family.

Families, bastions of fraternity and self-help, were the real frames of reference; familial clans embarked upon relations with one another or competed with one another, high up in aristocratic spheres as well as much lower, in the spheres of the modest intelligentsia. It was difficult for strangers to be accepted into these circles. Around 1910 one of my grandmother's cousins married a lovely, intelligent, and energetic woman who hailed from a family of Jewish intellectuals. The process of accepting her into the clan lasted for decades. She did receive a family diminutive, Auntie Busia, but a considerable segment of the clan boycotted her in the beginning. And even her own family censured her and broke off all relations. She lived to be almost a hundred years old. I knew her well, visited her often in Cracow, where she lived first with her husband, my Uncle Jozio (cousin to Eugeniusz Kwiatkowski, the prewar vice premier of Poland), and later, after his death, as a lonely, indomitable old woman.

When I praised the newly arisen Solidarity movement in 1981, she gave a hostile snort, saying, "What! Why, they're socialists!" I realized that her political opinions had been formed before the First World War, and I dropped the discussion.

She was proud, independent, self-reliant. Uncle Jozio remained completely in her care. And she was always in love with him because Uncle Jozio, a quiet, shy, and elegant bank official, was a good-looking man. In my family, one said, "Almost as gorgeous as Uncle Jozio." Even as a completely gray-haired man with a white beard, he was still handsome. People said he had "the distinguished look of a senator."

They spent the First World War in Vienna, "just in case." Auntie Busia told me that, when leaving their Lvov apartment, she put a jar of apricot preserves on the table, in the hope that the eventual trespassers who came to loot the apartment houses would stop at the apricots. I also know that when my aunt and uncle returned from Vienna, the jar (and quite a few other things) was gone.

During the Second World War they hid in a village, for obvious reasons. It seems that this time they did not even consider leaving apricot preserves. Nor could Vienna be considered a safe haven.

When she was very old and unable to care for herself, the entire family diligently looked after her. Thus she was accepted seventy years later. It wasn't easy to get admitted to a clan, to a large family, even though it must be said that membership in this close-knit institution brought few special privileges; it didn't even give one access to material riches (what riches— not manors but apartments; not grounds but gardens, currant bushes, raspberry canes) or to power. It all boiled down to diminutives and moments of intimacy, of peace, when after dessert the talk ceased, bees hummed in the garden, teaspoons stopped their clinking, butterflies dozed on branches of lilac.

My aunts . . . My uncles . . . There was also a Protestant branch of the family—Pastor Kubaczka, who lived in Goleszow, near Cieszyn.

There was Aunt Berta, a music teacher. After the war she moved to Cracow, where she occupied a corner in the home of distant relatives who would allow her to unfold a cot in the kitchen at night but would not allow her to be there during the day. She roamed the city waiting for nightfall. She deposited her only treasure, a piano, in a Cracow conservatory, because she certainly couldn't carry it around with her during her endless walks along the streets of that city.

My aunts . . . More important than my uncles. My uncles didn't usually live as long; they vanished into banks or schools, silent, absorbed in reading newspapers or books, while my aunts ruled their families, long before the triumphs of feminism, as Queen Victoria had ruled the United Kingdom, except perhaps a bit more ruthlessly.

My aunts, emerging from the kitchen, vanishing into the garden, bent over sewing machines in the evening, wearing spectacles reflecting orange lamp shades. My aunts, the Fates.

In 1945 almost my entire family was packing suitcases and trunks, getting ready to leave Lvov and vicinity. At the same time countless German families, who were told to leave their homes and apartments in Silesia, Danzig, Stettin, Allenstein, and Konigsberg, were also packing. Millions of people were forcing resistant suitcases shut with their knees; all this was happening at the behest of three old men who had met at Yalta.

In October of that year we found ourselves in the worse city, Gliwice. The Red Army was still garrisoned there, and in the evenings one often heard shots fired from a *pepesha* into the dark streets (or so I was told later).

My aunts and uncles, their friends and friends' cousins, families, clans and tribes, all of them, left Lvov and met— not all but most of them—on the streets of Gliwice.

What sort of city was it? The worse one of the two. Smaller. Unpretentious. Industrial. Alien.

But one had to live there. And oh, wonder of wonders, here too there were sunrises and sunsets, and the same seasons of the year passed through calendars and municipal parks. A wooden replica of the Eiffel Tower, the transmitter of a prewar radio station, loomed over the city. Occasionally the setting sun hid behind it. Exactly at the moment it was supposed to slip beneath the comforter of the earth, the enormous red-hot ball stopped of its own accord and relished a moment of pure immobility, which drove astronomers crazy—they'd press their fingernails into their palms and shout, "Faster, faster," as they watched their chronometers.

The new city was alien. The evenings were the hardest. On a peaceful summer day a sunset is like a caress, and the spot touched by it is filled with tenderness. What should one do? The calculated indifference toward the new city, typical of newcomers, was put to a severe test in the evenings. From a certain hillside the ugly city looked quite alluring. Church spires shot out from the crowded tenement buildings, and on each spire rose a green hood of verdigris. The windows glowed scarlet. Tin rooster weathervanes fluttered cheerfully in the breeze.

The gentle pastel hills deceived the emigrants. A fringe of dark woods deepened on the horizon. Fog meandered through meadows. The elevator shafts of coal mines amid orchards and gardens looked like menorahs. Rooks gathered in the sky and, concentrating in a black, boiling cloud, flew north.

The radio station drew my interest. I found out that the Second World War began there (this was the paradox of our migration: as a direct result of the war and Yalta, my parents were deported from their city to the source of the misfortune). This was the so-called provocation at Gliwice, an attack of soldiers of the German Sicherheitsdienst (SD) dressed in the Polish uniforms of the watchmen of the radio station. The organizer of this bit of theatrics was Reinhard Heydrich, on the personal orders of Hitler himself, who, as a reader of La Rochefoucauld, knew that duplicity is the homage paid by crime to virtue, and in the autumn of 1939 he wanted to appear in the role of Poland's victim, not its aggressor.

At that time I was convinced that in some mysterious way the radio ruled the world. I heard about the nature of radio waves; I knew that they were invisible but that one could catch them with the help of an antenna web. My father wrote scholarly articles and books about radio waves. I later wrote a poem about them. The slender tower of the radio station reigned over the city. All this was connected. The radio spoke, whispered, sang, and went hoarse. On short waves there were signals full of anger. It was here that all the anger of the world found an outlet; Radio Moscow battled London and Munich.

The medium waves, however, were full of gravity and music. Schubert's *Lieder* and Chopin's waltzes replaced short waves full of political hatred. On Sundays at four-thirty a Chopin concert was broadcast, and from behind every curtain, from every window, from every home came the chords of the funeral march, pam pam pa pa, pamparampa pa pa pa.

The new inhabitants of Gliwice reminded one of Europeans only superficially. The majority of them were deported from the east. They were fresh emigrants; but it was not the emigrants who had left their country, it was the country that had simply shifted to the west, that's all. And they along with it. Also, almost all of them could put the prefix *ex* before the names of their professions, vocations, and existences. They were *ex*-judges, *ex*-officers, *ex*-professors—not to mention *ex*-children—deprived of their former careers by a new system that subjected the past of each citizen to severe scrutiny (if the citizen had a past; but even the poorest folks had some sort of past).

Thus, for example, at the farmers' market on Bytomska Street, the vegetable vendors, dressed in winter jackets, sweaters, sheepskin coats, and knit gloves revealing red, frozen fingers, spoke in a singsong, eastern accent. They greeted certain clients with added courtesy: Dr. So-and-So, they said to an old man in a threadbare, prewar fur coat; the attorney So-and-So, they said to a tall old man leaning on the arm of his middle-aged daughter. Will the professor have eggs or chicken wings today, asked another vendor of an old man who was hard of hearing and could not return her courtesy, especially since her courtesy was the rule and was only partially linked to the moment. For the second half of the greeting glided into the past, went back a decade, and pertained to the same, but

considerably younger, professor, who shopped at another market, in another city, in another epoch, in another currency.

These people at the farmers' market on Bytomska Street
were only partially real and of the moment; beyond that they
seemed more like shadows. Living shadows, emigrants in their
own country: ex-professors of a university that no longer existed; ex-officers of an army that no longer existed, with eastern
accents of a no longer extant East; ex–city council members
and ex-lawyers or civil service ranks that belonged to a different
era, with twice-darned coats, shoes of prewar leather, and faded
hats bearing the labels of companies that were now defunct.

Only eggs, tomatoes, and cherries were ordinary and real,
trivial and palpable.

My parents belonged to the younger generation at that time;
they did not have to change outfits, or perhaps did so only to
a minimal, unavoidable degree. Those exiles, however, who
ended up in Gliwice in middle age had not the strength to
change anything in their clothing, manner of speaking, or
thinking. They carried their past around like mothballs. Old-
fashioned suits, summer jackets with short sleeves, creases
pressed for all eternity into fine wool trousers, shoes from
twenty years ago. They walked in them gingerly, so as not to
damage the soles or nick the leather. They walked in the tree-
lined lanes of the park, rested in the shade of post-German
chestnuts and beeches, professors and attorneys, cobblers and
janitors, officials and tram operators. They grew bored, lived
on skimpy pensions, roamed the streets of the city, treading
the post-German sidewalks with dignity.

I did not realize that this roaming of the streets was a slow
dying. They walked the streets, looking with amazement at
the Prussian bricks of the tenements. They were absorbed with

dying and taken aback by the place in which they were to die. They died distrustfully because they did not know this place, this air, this land very well. Some hurried; others tried to put death off for later, so they could have a good look at their surroundings, so they could get to know the local trees and herbs, so they could like this land.

They lost their memories—usually for biological reasons, because of old age, although some appeared to crave sclerosis and oblivion and voluntarily chose to live in a fog, merging epochs, people, dates.

In my family, too, there were old people who were losing their memories—both of my grandmothers and my grandfather. I accompanied them on walks. They would lean on me, and I explained where we were and where we were going. I, who knew nothing yet, put my memory at their disposal! They, who could have told me so much about their long lives, weren't capable of gathering their wits about them.

In losing their memories they returned to their lost city. Paradoxically, by losing their memories they recovered them, because it is clear that loss of memory in old age means loss of control over the most recent layers of memories and a return to old memories, which nothing is capable of eradicating. They returned to Lvov.

Thus I walked the streets of Gliwice with my grandfather —because it was he I accompanied most often—but in fact we were strolling two separate cities. I was a sober boy with a memory as small as a hazelnut, and I was absolutely certain that in walking the streets of Gliwice, among Prussian secessionist tenements decorated with heavy granite caryatids, I was where I really was. My grandfather, however, despite his walking right next to me, was in Lvov. I walked the streets of

Gliwice, he the streets of Lvov. I was on a long street that would certainly have been named Main Street in America but here bore the sneering name Victory Street (after so many defeats!) and joined a small square with an equally small railroad station. At the same time my grandfather was strolling down Sapieha Street in Lvov. Later, for a change, we walked to Chrobry Park (the Polish king was supposed to polonize the German trees), but my grandfather, of course, found himself in Lvov's Jesuit Garden.

My grandfather was bilingual—his mother had been German. In his youth he had translated the poems of Polish modernist poets into German, and when I began to advertise my first attempts at poetry, he felt I was continuing the interests and work of his youth. He was an indefatigable walker. He spoke in a loud voice that often embarrassed those he was with, as he had the habit, during the German occupation as well as in Stalinist times, of expressing his political views on the street or in the tram. He belonged to that breed of men who pushed their glass to the center of the table upon drinking their tea, in the expectation that someone—servant or wife— would take and rinse it. He had probably never boiled an egg in his life nor washed a single plate. He smoked half cigarettes tucked into metal holders.

People in town assumed he knew all languages. He even taught himself Dutch in midlife. Before the war, he had been a secondary school teacher and had taught German. In his old age, in Gliwice, he opened a small office as a certified translator. He was good to me, but I felt there was something severe in him. Once I witnessed a scene in which a poor man came to him to have something translated and told my grandfather upon entering that he had no money. My grandfather threw him out. To this day I remember how I hated him for this, for a while. This was the severity of a bourgeois who knows that he cannot relent in business matters. Softness is appropriate at home and in church, but in the store or the office or when performing official duties, one had to be uncompromising.

My grandfather was short, stocky, and bald and wore glasses. His mother had died early and his father sent him to be raised by his mother's family. He progressed diligently in life along the rungs of a modest career, which brought him to the position of head administrator of the school superintendent's office. In Gliwice his old acquaintances—true to the Austrian obsession with title and rank—continued to address him as "Director." He remained the director, although in the end merely the director of our family, over whose meetings he presided until his memory failed him.

Afterward he dozed all day in an armchair and, because of this, could not sleep at night. He was always waiting for guests to arrive, but whenever they did, he would fall asleep. But this was not until he was eighty-eight years old.

All his life he kept records of his expenditures. There are notes from his youth where next to expenses listed for room and board dinners, and writing materials is the notation "luxuries." What these luxuries were neither I nor anyone else has ever found out.

Even if in some ways he was the unyielding bourgeois with dictatorial inclinations, then I should be the last person to judge him because he was very good to me, as I have mentioned. I saw the process of his aging, weakening, softening, stretched over the years. At the beginning he was like the Colossus of Rhodes—powerful, majestic, arbitrary. Then his authority, his might slowly crumbled; he gave up more and more of his prerogatives; he grew smaller, I grew bigger; he weakened, and finally became an old man I helped get from bench to bench because he no longer had the strength to walk great distances. From as far back as I can remember, he walked with a cane, but at the beginning his wooden cane was one of the many aspects of his might—just like the silver chain on the watch whose lid opened at a thumb press—until he needed the cane more and more, finally leaning on it desperately.

Passionately interested in political events, he listened to the radio and read foreign-language newspapers, which made sense considering his knowledge of languages. The more difficult task was getting these newspapers, especially in Stalinist times. During that period he had to content himself with the Communist *L'Humanité*, a paper he loathed, but he tried to decode the truth about events from the falsified commentary.

He kept up a correspondence with relatives in Switzerland —the descendants of the tile setter who had settled in Biel/ Bienne—and I know from my cousin, a pastor in Zurich, that he assessed the situation at the time soberly, that is, pessimistically. It's a good thing the UB—the secret police—never read them.

He liked painting. On the door to the room where he received clients and guests he hung a small reproduction of Rembrandt's *Nightwatch*. It was probably the first painting I studied, peering at the dark tones of the reproduction thumbtacked to his door. He liked Dutch painting the most, including Ruysdael and Vermeer. Particularly still lifes and landscapes appealed to him and matched his passion for concrete objects, ordered yet autonomous. His enormous desk, always neat and dust-free, was a ready model for a still life. It always held the same books: dictionaries and encyclopedias that occupied their designated row and never trespassed beyond it. Sometimes a colorful postcard from Switzerland leaned against them or a postcard bearing a reproduction of a Giotto or a Fra Angelico. In the middle was an inkwell, like a small pool in the center of a meadow, and next to it a pen and a few pencils. Lastly there was a small slender flask of blue-and-white porcelain that often held the curving stem of a single rose or carnation, along with scissors, letter opener, and stick of sealing wax, smelling of the post office and distant journeys. Because the window of the office, which also served as the place in which the entire family gathered each Sunday, faced north (and the tenement building opposite), it was often in semidarkness, like an old painting. Under the window was the armchair in which my grandfather read and later, in his final years, did nothing but sleep.

Afternoon teas and informal visits took place on the other side of the narrow corridor, in the kitchen where my tiny bent grandmother bustled. It was here that Grandfather lit his half cigarette. Sometimes a stranger passed through the corridor— a subtenant my grandparents had taken in in order to meet the demands of their budget (the office of a certified translator wasn't a very profitable enterprise). The subtenant lived in a small room that faced the courtyard, and my grandparents were always unhappy with him. He was radically strange. He never stayed put for very long. When he appeared in the corridor in pants and an undershirt, he was the very personification of strangeness to me as well. Walking around in an undershirt was something we simply did not do. Of course I didn't know it at the time, but usually the subtenant was someone from outside our impoverished but conceited social class. We were the intelligentsia (that is, the bourgeoisie minus the money), and we knew foreign languages, read books, studied paintings. And we were homeless, we had come from Lvov. Even though he was barely tolerated by my grandfather, the subtenant appeared to me to be more at home in this reality, stronger, and on more intimate terms with our surroundings. Alien.

My grandparents lived in a tenement house that was an eight-minute walk from the building in which we lived. I knew exactly how long it took to walk from one place to the other because as soon as I got my first watch, I tried to set a new record for myself, measured in minutes and seconds, whenever I went there alone. The street joining the two addresses was called Czestochowska Street at first, but in the early fifties it was changed to Klement Gottwald Street. In spite of this, that is, in spite of this hardly metaphysical name, it was the avenue of the angels for me; at that time we ate Christmas Eve supper at my grandparents' place, and after supper we went back home where, in a cool room (the window was left open, evidence of the angel's visit), a Christmas tree awaited us and beneath it presents. I don't know why I never noticed that my father always left my grandparents' apartment fifteen minutes before we did. Along the way I saw angels slipping into other homes, hurrying, silent, diligent, floating gently in the crisp, cold air. The snow squeaked under our feet; Christmas tree candles flickered in other people's homes.

The presents were modest. My parents could not afford great expenditures. My father taught at the Polytechnic and wrote books about radio waves, but his salary was ludicrously meager. He had no desk comparable to the piece of furniture in my grandfather's office. He worked at an ordinary table picked up somewhere at a bargain. Because the table was too low, Father raised it by nailing four metal food cans to its legs (as if he were shoeing a horse). In class I belonged to the poorest pupils, but I was shielded by the umbrella of intelligentsia illusion: my father was a professor, and at home book spines crowded one another on the shelves. The mechanism of my love of self is reminiscent of the psychological reflexes employed by my ancestors, the déclassé gentry, provincial teachers. After October 1956 my non–Party member father became the vice president at the Polytechnic. I was eleven then and experienced a moment of triumph when the school director, a perfect conformist, asked me how my father was doing, how he liked his new position, and so forth.

We were poor but we had something like a half servant, a half nanny, probably because it cost almost nothing. She was an older woman, a German named Czolga, who eventually became almost another member of the family and our closest friend. Later she emigrated to West Germany, but for a long time afterward she sent letters full of homesickness. It was she, or perhaps her successor, who talked my parents into buying a live goose that spent a few weeks in a makeshift coop in our kitchen.

Objects were divided into three categories: aristocratic, bourgeois, socialist. The aristocratic came from Lvov. Because the deported families did not have the means to take everything, they took only what was most valuable: silver (and most certainly gold, but my parents had no gold), paintings, rugs, kilims, watercolors, family keepsakes, rare books, period furniture. I call them aristocratic because generally speaking they served no purpose and had a sentimental rather than a market value. Paintings hung on the walls played the role of keepsakes.

The same with the watercolors, professional or amateur portraits of long-deceased members of the family or sketches of Lvov churches and squares. In everyday speech we called them "prewar."

Meanwhile bourgeois objects were called by an adjective created expressly for this purpose: "post-German" (just as later one would speak about "postmodernist" art). In leaving their homes the Germans must have been governed by the very logic used by Lvov inhabitants when leaving their city, that is, they took their aristocratic objects—their silver, gold, paintings, antiques, watercolors, treasures—and they left behind many utilitarian things—stoves, Singer sewing machines, Erika and Continental typewriters, tools, bicycles, cheap silverware. The precious metals came from Lvov, the cheap ones were post-German. Of course, the Germans also left their houses, apartments, gardens, trees, birds, and clouds.

I am sure that no one will believe me, but the things brought from Lvov really did smell different from the local post-German things. I don't know if I could do it now, but then I could recognize and classify objects with my eyes shut, by smell alone. The steel of sewing machines covered with black shiny paint that made the gold Singer letters stand out smelled completely different from the silver ladle engraved with my grandmother's initials. The German Nordmende radio retained its stubborn German smell in spite of the fact that Polish announcers spoke through it.

Articles fished out of the gigantic junk pile of wartime arsenals made up a separate subcategory: pieces of handguns, bullet shells, rusty bayonets, and army-uniform buttons. I knew them more from legend than by sight. They were highly valued by boys.

Later, socialist things were produced by the incompetent

postwar Polish People's Republic. Sometimes, rarely, something promising turned up—a blender or a graceful motorbike—and this immediately elicited a short-lived enthusiasm that "we are already managing to make such things," that "this is being made here," and then an amazement undermined by doubt and a growing skepticism, because experience taught us that only ugly things could be found in the stores, that nice ones vanished like lightning and never appeared again.

All these objects had to live with one another, touch one another, inhale their various smells, constantly mix, as was appropriate in a classless society. But slowly rust appeared on some of the things; others became worn from excessive use, transparent, sick.

Meanwhile, the old people continued to roam a city they did not understand. Old ladies wore hats fashionable forty years before, and they covered their faces with a thick layer of powder. Right next to them walked old men who no longer heard anything. In old suits. In ties that fed tribes of ravenous moths.

They spoke about things lost. About the lost city. The hills of that city. About a certain day, long ago. About delicate and ripe raspberries. About Germans and Russians during the war: who was worse. About hunger. Siberia. About a certain servant who stole but who was so nice and helpful otherwise that she was forgiven. The city they had left was the loveliest in the world.

They addressed each other as Mr. Engineer, Mr. Councilman, Mr. Editor, and Mr. President. They simply did not want to accept the fact that they had ended up in a difficult, strange, ugly city. They considered themselves still in Lvov. Mr. Attorney, Mrs. Wife-of-Doctor So-and-So. They were incapable of moving to Gliwice. Indifferent, whether they had lost their memories or not, they pretended that nothing had changed. The entire city was transformed into a theater. Mr. Major, Mrs. Wife-of-Professor So-and-So. Certainly we will return, they said in brief moments of relative lucidity. We will never return, said the few realists. But they were not heeded and the theater took up its frenzied activity, roaming, pretending, using antiquated titles. There were bridge parties, teas, name-day celebrations, dinners, and funerals. There was a dancing school in which the maître spoke through his nose almost like a Frenchman.

Our neighbor who lived on the floor below hated the Communists so much that he did not leave his dwelling at all. Sometimes he appeared in the courtyard in blue pajamas. He also had come from Lvov. He belonged to the radical wing of the community of transplants and refused all contact with the new world. He went out into the courtyard in his pajamas so that no one would think that he had quite left the house. These were a prisoner's exercise walks in the prison compound. I did not understand him then, and he made me laugh; now I think about the suffering of someone who sentences himself to a house arrest lasting for years and who lives amid unpacked trunks, post-German walls, in semiobscurity. He was an old man, full of hatred and despair. He probably returned to the bygone days in his dreams, to the city he had to leave. Perhaps that is why he always wore pajamas. He lived in dreams, only in dreams; his pajamas were a diving suit in which he descended into the past like a frogman.

We did not know him; he refused even to meet his neighbors. We were not in his dreams, and he did not want to know us when he was awake. He was unreconciled, dreamy, alone (although he lived with his wife, who worked and ran the house; I sense, though, that he probably didn't say much to his wife either). I know nothing about him. I can only imagine his bitterness, his internal monologues, and the light in his dreams. And the moments, when he awoke, without hope. Shadows on the walls, the building next door outside his window, and, next to it, yet another gray building.

The spire of the neo-Gothic church. The ruins of the municipal theater, bombed by the Russians or the Americans in the final months of the war. Steel foundry and coal mine. A middling pond in which I tried to catch fish on a primitive rod made of stiff bamboo. In one of the parks, a palm hothouse. An African humidity always filled it (and goldfish lived there, but they were pink rather than gold). My old aunt playing with the silver coins she brought from Lvov. Tins full of treasures.

And tenement buildings. And in them, besides the newcomers, were Silesians and post-German Germans. I knew little about them, and almost never ran into them—if I don't count Czolga. I belonged to a large theater troupe which, having transported its infants and old people as well as an enormous surplus of props and decorations, appeared one day in this city and pitched tents in it.

There was also a local airport, hosting, in my time, a few old biplanes called *kukuruzhniki* and an enormous fleet of docile white gliders (it was hard not to like them; they skated along the air softly, without a rustle, doing harm to no one). There was, outside the usual railroad, also a narrow-gauge train. Its winding tracks led south, to a place that was barely twenty kilometers away. The small cars moved slowly, so slowly that one could stick a hand out of the train and touch the passing trees, telephone posts, air, branches. Along the tracks were miniature train stations, and in one of them, in the waiting room, swallows wove a nest beneath the ceiling and no one was allowed to shut the door for fear the nestlings would starve.

A certain kind of symbolic opposite of this train (sluggishness vs. speed) was a highway running through a neighboring city, one of the attainments of the civilization of the Third Reich. For many years after the war, there were so few cars that the highway was usually half empty. Cows and goats crossed it, and heavy horse-drawn carts rolled down it in heavy autumn fog. Sometimes there wasn't a soul on it except for the ants roving north to south and back again. Sometimes the only ones to take advantage of the highway were cyclists (and, among them, bent over the handlebars, yours truly).

There was also something else: a new political system. Today it has been thoroughly described, unmasked; entire libraries are devoted to it, hundreds of doctoral theses. Everything is clear; we now know we were dealing with the Communist variety of totalitarianism, characterized by this . . . and that . . . But at the time, there were no doctoral dissertations or libraries, no analyses or scholarly colloquia. One recognized the new system by the following symptoms: fear, blood draining out of the face, trembling hands, talking in whispers, silence, apathy, sealing windows shut, suspicion of one's neighbors, signing up for the hated Party membership.

On the first of May there was a parade along Victory (or, rather, Defeat) Street. Athletes, students, and workers passed by the May 1 reviewing stand. Beautiful girls waved red scarves as a greeting to the idiots gathered on the tribunal. Trucks carried enormous puppets depicting class enemies and, especially, Truman, who smoked a cigar that was about a half yard long. I despised him; he was the personification of evil. His name had grave connotations.* To this day, when I think about Truman (something I do rarely) I have to separate the old layer of grave and sinister associations from a rational historical analysis.

On May 1 the older generations, all those smart and unreal ladies and their deaf beaux, disappeared from the city streets, seeking refuge at home; they left the stage to make room for the other theater. They probably listened to London, which broadcast good or bad—but always real—news.

In the city of my childhood Plato's two great beasts came together. One was, naturally, organic to a considerable degree, practically covered with real animal fur and, actually, if left alone, if not irritated by the Jews or the Ukrainians, was good-natured and languid. The other had artificial but sharp teeth, fake skin, red banners, and loudspeakers instead of a larynx. One came from Lvov, the other from Moscow. Two conformities. One molded by centuries, formed by many generations of gentry and pharmacists, shoemakers and doctors; the other constructed in a hurry by Lenin and his guillotined friends.

The totalitarian beast was a very strange creature; this was a conformity without conformists, as it was actually rather difficult to come across zealous proponents of the new system, if one did not count the functionaries who were paid for their enthusiasm with a pension and a relative sense of security. Nor was there a dearth of poets or writers, praising the terrible beast; in our city, however, there was only one poet, no writers.

The struggle for life and death was on. It took place everywhere—in the schools, factories, offices, and government bureaus. Only the old people who had lost their memories or

* The Polish word *trumna* means casket. —Trans.

pretended they had lost them were excluded from it. All others had to participate in some fashion. Sometimes the sun shone so intensely and the leaves glittered so brightly that both sides forgot for a few or a few dozen hours about the war they were conducting, and they set off for the forest, for a nearby pond, in the direction of fields and meadows, silver poplars and brown earth.

In one of the parks, there was a post-German swimming pool. I went there with my grandfather, who swam slowly on his back, rising and falling like a vessel on the Dead Sea. After swimming, I would lie on a wooden bench and look straight at the sky. Delicate clouds with changing contours moved along it. Between the clouds rose a small hawk, tiny as a pinhead and looking at me carefully. Great leaves of burdock steamed. I felt my skin drying. My hands touched the grass; my palms got tangled in the bitter stems of grass, and for a moment they belonged more to the world of plants than to me. Beetles with hard black wings, and the small, eternally hurrying ants.

This park, in which the grass grew tall and some of the old trees were taller than the tenements on the main street, belonged to me. At least that's what I thought. No one else wanted it. The older generation kept looking at the flowers and trees growing in this city with disdainful tolerance. Only the gardens left behind over there, in the east, counted. But I knew only these poplars and ash trees, and I liked them more and more. I liked the taste of mint leaves; I liked the rough trunks of the few pines and the smooth, ash-gray trunks of the enormous beeches on which lovers carved their intertwined initials with a penknife. I did not become a nature lover. The world simply appealed to me. But in the eyes of the older people, and especially of the oldest, I became practically a traitor. It was inappropriate to fly into raptures here in this accidental city. Things that I took seriously were supposed to be treated with distance, aloofness, disdain. I had fallen in love with appearances. Leaves unfurled in spring; in summer they flaunted their emerald greens, the perfection of their fabric, its cut, and it was precisely then, in a moment of highest bloom, that they grew no more, stopped; and only the fall, and the cold dusk of an autumn day, awaited them, the tug of war with gusts of western winds, and, finally, the humiliating landing at the edge of a puddle, under the heel of someone's shoe, in a wastebasket, in death.

Things were different with Lvov leaves. They were eternal, eternally green and eternally alive, indestructible and perfect; they moved as lightly and gracefully as dolphin fins. Their only flaw was their absence, and even their nonexistence. But existence is not a characteristic of things; Kant noticed that a hundred existing thalers were in no way different from a hundred imagined thalers.

I liked these parts—the park, the swimming pool, and even the entirely black river, transformed years ago into an industrial sewer and reeking of chemicals, not water. Next to the park was a sports stadium. On Sunday there were masses of people, but on a weekday not a soul. One felt only the absence of a great crowd—not solitude, but the negation of the shouting and breathing (which amounts to the same thing) of thousands of people. Here, for the first time, I came to know the peculiar feeling that is connected to the contemplation of places set aside for enormous public spectacles but momentarily standing empty (today it is enough for me to enter any of the old French churches to feel a similar emptiness; similar, but not the same).

I liked these surroundings because I knew no others. I was interested in what was happening because I had no other experiences. I was born a month after the war ended. I knew nothing. Sometimes I think that the old people I looked at and also the middle-aged ones, who in my inexperienced eyes were the only ones subject to time, the unfortunates who had been incautious enough to get old, had behind them the most extraordinary experiences. They had survived the war, two wars, and actually three occupations—Soviet, German, and then Soviet again. There must have been the most varied people among them: those who rescued Jews and those who turned them in. Among them were traitors, heroes, and ordinary walk-ons; master tradesmen, masters of cunning, masters of prayers, goodness, or cruelty. Now they ran into each other on the same street and certainly knew a great deal about one another, but generally they did not pass this knowledge on to others. They had survived by accident or miracle, they survived by decree of Providence or by paying a terrible price. Each of them had his own vulgar or moving secret. The few remaining relics threw light on the fate of some of them, but in general this entire secret reality of memory—the reality of interrogations, searches, camps, escapes, and unbelievable coincidences—disintegrated without trace.

In their view, the fact that someone was born a month after the end of the war bordered on a joke. It would be like arriving at the Philharmonic ten minutes after the end of the concert, in time for nothing but to grab the umbrella left behind in the cloakroom. It was true that the war of the two great beasts continued. But no one was dying in the streets (though perhaps in prisons); there were no roundups, no stealing across the "green" border, no mass deportations to Germany or to Siberia.

From their vantage point the era of Action had ended and the epoch of the Imagination had begun (or perhaps this was only from my vantage point).

From their vantage point . . . As if I could know what they were thinking then. I should limit myself to what I saw, what I remember, what I want to remember. In the park I liked the absolute, as it seemed to me, reality of trees and shrubs and even of the crafty, obdurate grass. The park, pool, river, and empty stadium constituted a community inhabited by no one. Here a blustering flock of rooks took refuge, here discreet, yellow-beaked blackbirds lived, and here rested a gigantic boulder that no one could move; nothing happened here.

At one point everything began to change. I lived in a kind of bildungsroman. Every month I was passionately interested in something new, absorbed in increasingly frenetic interests, roads, and shortcuts leading to initiation. I became a scout, tourist, soccer fan; with my father's help I built a crystal-detector radio; I took photographs and collected minerals, postage stamps, postcards, maps, and books.

I do not recall how I became an altar boy. Apparently my parents had nothing to do with it; they were practicing Catholics, but without excessive zeal. In the battle of the two beasts the church played an exceptionally important role. Perhaps one could say that our great beast lived in the churches, took refuge in them, revitalized its forces there, nourished itself in them, rested and regenerated itself.

Well-known Father N. gave bold, angry sermons in which he did not condemn the new system but, like Savonarola, attacked his own society. "You are lazy, spiritless, cowardly," he said every Sunday from the pulpit. "You are sluggish, your faith is lukewarm, you betray Christ at every step." At the beginning it seemed to me that no one would want to hear his sermons, but I was wrong. Father N. was the most popular priest in town. He was handsome, with dark hair, a narrow face, and dark eyes in which flamed a sneering inspiration, fortified, it seems, by a tubercular fever. Everyone was afraid to go to his confessional booth. In contrast to the other priest-confessors, who listened to the intimacies of their kneeling penitents calmly and drowsily, Father N. fired aggressive questions. "Have you lied? Perjured yourself? Have you had impure thoughts?"

Who *didn't* have impure thoughts? Yet the lines next to his confessional were the longest. After confession the girls told one another what the priest had asked them, but the boys ran out of church and furiously kicked at chestnuts lying on the gravel path.

After a while, Father N. vanished and was replaced by Father O., bald and swollen-faced. In Father N. everything had been sharp, elongated, dark, and angry; in Father O., in contrast, everything was round, soft, white, shiny, and damp.

I became an altar boy. For the first time in my life I had access to a place that was closed to the majority of ordinary mortals: the sacristy. I rose early and ran to church (a large neo-Gothic structure of red brick). The sacristy was dusky, sleepy. Tall credenzas full of drawers rose against the walls. In the middle of the room stood an old oak table. The smell of wood mingled with the smell of holy water (of course, holy water smelled different from regular water). In the deep drawers of the credenzas rested the surplices and chasubles (smell of mothballs), folded like tablecloths. The true master of this space was the old sacristan, for whom the parish priest and a small herd of curates, not to even mention the altar boys, were dispensable, temporary, coming and going; and it was only he—so very bent that there was not much he could see beyond the stone tiles of the floor—who was here forever, to the very end, day and night.

I had to learn the Latin Mass (this was before Vatican II) in order to be able to respond to the priest standing at the altar.

In the sacristy, rays of sunlight as narrow as the sheaf of light from a film projector played over the credenzas and walls and touched the feet of Christ nailed to the cross, a bouquet of wilting gladiolas, the shiny cassock of the priest. The neo-Gothic window was an extremely stingy source of light. Dust motes trembled and traveled slowly in the corridors of sunlight.

The art of being an altar boy consisted of four basic elements: choreography (that is, the complicated sequence of movements and gestures, kneeling and rising from one's knees), recitation of the Latin rite of the Holy Mass, manipulating a battery of bells, and learning to use the censer.

The Mass was begun with an energetic tug on yet another bell that hung over the sacristy door. From the neo-Gothic depths emerged a grave priest, and right on his heels came two equally grave altar boys in white surplices thrown over regular clothes. All three had their eyes glued to the floor and they appeared not to notice the crowd present in church (if there was a crowd, because the morning Masses to which I, a beginner, was delegated, attracted mere handfuls of the faithful).

But in the sacristy there was a completely different atmosphere. The altar boys rolled around with laughter. Father O. distributed punches and tried for a while to control the situation, and then he himself began to laugh, indistinguishable then from the twelve-year-old boys. Someone climbed on a chair and pretended to be the Pope, blessing the city and the world. The two K. brothers, twins, whose round heads were covered with identical curls, fought almost without respite, as if they were trying to cut, wound, and destroy the similarity joining them. Father O. alternately took the side of one, then the other. Someone else whistled the latest hit ("Remember That Autumn . . ."), and two other boys danced cheek to cheek, pretending to be lovers. Someone else recited the Latin Mass, but backward, so that the sentences made no sense. A small heap of crazed altar boys thrashed around in the dusky half-light and over them rose the joyous face of Father O. Only the sacristan, silent and grim, never participated in these frenzied orgies.

The altar boys were nihilists, not at all interested in faith or metaphysics, Christ or Judas. Interested only in the efficient use of the censer and an assortment of bells, an impeccable choreography, and in the ability to assume the look of serious concentration the moment the retinue left the joyful sacristy. The same skills decided the hierarchy within the group of altar boys. Their leader was a thin boy older than I. Perhaps only he did not reveal his cynicism; his technical mastery as an altar boy was so advanced that he was practically ashamed of his fluency.

I left the sacristy relatively quickly (to tell the truth, I was never able to master one of the elements of the craft—operating the bells). Shortly thereafter, Father O. appeared in our apartment to demand that I return. Luckily my parents helped me out. I was grateful to them for this. Meanwhile, in keeping with the requirements of a bildungsroman, I initiated the next episode of the novel. I decided to become a scout. The censer was replaced by a penknife, compass, and whistle.

I had no idea then how different the two vocations were. An altar boy is one of the forms of an intermediary, someone who operates among people and in front of people, in relation to the public. A strong dose of acting is needed. An altar boy does not think about God, because he deals with a priest and with the group of people present in the church. Basically, the more mystically inclined the priest is, the more ingratiating and humorously good-natured the altar boy should be; negating extreme tensions is one of his responsibilities. Later, in meeting people who have achieved a certain worldly success, I often found out that they had been altar boys in childhood. Apparently this is good training for those who change into professional intermediaries.

A boy scout, on the other hand, vacillates between two completely different careers, that of a soldier and that of an adventurer. An adventurer acts alone, a soldier usually in the company of other soldiers; but at any rate, neither has anything in common with the ingratiating affability typical of intermediaries.

One of the delights of being an altar boy was undoubtedly being together with masses of people. Especially in winter, when the frosty cold turned the air into a burning gas that tore up the lungs ("What cold," the old people said contemptuously. "Real winters were *over there*"), the crowd really did become an animal: fur caps, steamy breath, liquid eyes and sweaty foreheads, beads of water on hair and beards; the crowd took on the aspect of a mustached monster, shook snow from its boots, grew pale then red, coughed, sneezed, and breathed in an even rhythm.

I often thought that something had to happen. The church, after all, was bursting its seams; it was filled with countless anthills of humanity, dutifully ingesting the sermons of Father N., and then of Father O. I thought that something was about to happen, that soon a war or revolution, uprising, triumphant march on Warsaw, Lvov, or Paris would begin. Loud church hymns resonated; the walls of the sanctuary shook. Then— nothing; nothing happened. The crowd broke into smaller particles, atoms, and headed home in the snowstorm for a holiday breakfast, awaited by helplessness, powerlessness, and loneliness. In homes, in apartments lived small families, seg- regated with the help of the cunning system of *principium individuationis*. Father, mother, two children (at our house). Too few to start a revolution. Snow covered the streets, an early dusk blurred the contours of tenements and trees, silence fell, rooks shook the snow from black wings. From a nearby train station the doleful lament of a locomotive, stopped by a lowered semaphore, reached our ears.

At Christmastime carols were sung in some of the homes. In many others was silence. One of my father's friends lost his wife and child in the Warsaw Uprising. He was a taciturn man. In former wars it was usually the men who died; in the last one it occasionally happened that soldiers mourned the deaths of their wives and children.

The adults of my childhood were very tired and apparently only pretended that they still believed in something. They attended church, prayed, and lived by force of habit; they were rescued by prewar models and previous conventions; even the patterns of old suits and titles and hierarchies that hadn't been used in years helped them. I had revolt in mind (I didn't know what kind exactly), but they and I, too, were subject to the pressures of a cruel and radical revolution diluted by months, weeks, days. The aim of this coup was the complete and ultimate making over of the human collective, also made up of types and forms constantly modified but appearing anew with each generation, as in Tarot cards: we will always find a Cheater, Globetrotter, Gadfly, Drunkard, Proprietor, Tenant, Seducer, Seduced, Pawnbroker, Priest, Artist, etc. Thus the social upheaval planned by the Communists assumed that there was something evil and sinful in this variety of types that has existed since time immemorial and the authorities strove relentlessly to produce only three types of man: Functionary, Worker, Policeman.

Some aspects of this program could be attractive. For example, the Proprietor type does tend to be revolting. The thought that he would disappear from the face of the earth must have been tempting (for Tenants, Readers, Artists). No one foresaw, however, that the biologically healthy Proprietor would manage just fine under the new system. Some Proprietors made a living with private stores and shops, while more ostentatious ones quickly transformed themselves into Functionaries and in a while began not only to give orders but also to delight in possessing, secretly or quite openly.

They wanted to change human nature, its animal-aleatoric, dual visage (the duality stemmed from the perception that everyone on one side belonged to a certain type, but on the other side could occasionally attain something of a higher order, a sphere of freedom and generosity, a region in which all the old typology suddenly lost its meaning, for a moment or even for always). And all this took place in my city, in my school, on my street, in my life, although for a long time I did not realize the seriousness of the situation; and then, considerably later, when I had a good sense of the arcana of this struggle and its stakes, I did not want to allow this conflict to entirely dominate my way of thinking about the world; there was something else, I was sure of it, even if I could not pinpoint what I meant every day.

Meanwhile I took up scouting. This happened after October 1956, which, like a caesura in a poem, divided my childhood into two separate phases. Communism became a bit more bearable, and scouts were allowed to prowl the forests with map and compass. I took advantage of these new freedoms and really did prowl the forests, with a map, compass, and Finnish scout knife. I began to understand, however, that I had gotten into the clutches of yet another enormous beast, and it was the kind that was not in the least ashamed of its uniformity; on the contrary, it flaunted it at every chance. The ideal soldier was respected more than the adventurer, who acts alone, tramping the wilds of Africa or writing a book uncommissioned by any publishing house.

The next mob I came to know was the public gathered at the soccer stadium, the same one I liked to look at when it was completely empty and silent, recuperated from the shouting and whistling. Two years later I was a fanatic fan of an incompetent, eternally minor-league soccer team. Its worth depended exclusively on its being a local club, representing our city in the complex hierarchy of European sports (and Europe never found out about my club).

The difference between a crowd that was going to a match—full of expectation and tension, in a state of holiday openness to the new unknown, the unforeseeable (because one thing is certain: soccer matches were the domain of freedom; one never knew the outcome ahead of time)—and a crowd returning from the stadium down Kujawska Street, heads down heavily, lazily, mournfully if we lost at home, heads up joyously, quickly, and combatively if there had been a victory. A tie inclined the crowd to assume an ironic stance, more or less philosophical; and to persons of a less intellectual temperament, a tie was an open door to an ill-boding, furious sneering and predictions that no longer would they be spending their Sundays at the stadium. After which, of course, in two weeks these very same embittered and cynical fans appeared at the next match and again awaited a miracle, that is, victory.

On the Monday following each "soccer Sunday," I had the pleasure of opening the local newspaper, still smelling of printer's ink, to the last page, where I found a review and report of important matches and also brief mention of the minor-league game, which I had witnessed.

I did not study the remaining newspaper columns. The usually massive skulls of Party leaders graced the first page along with headlines such as "The New Aggressive Plans of the NATO Pact" and "Continued Progress in Agriculture." On the second and third pages the headlines were a bit more modest. Here one spoke about the "Lack of Frozen Foods in Chorzów" and about the "Continuing Remodeling of Katowice Schools."

But the last page was beautiful. On Monday it was always graced by a photo of this or that goalie, grown one with the ball, floating in the air for an infinite second. The goalkeeper was taking a magnificent aerial journey; he could look down upon land and sea, cities and landscapes. Usually dressed in black, in gloves, he defied gravity, and his shoulders, inclined toward the ball and palms, radiated the devout zeal of medieval monks. He flew, floated, rose lightly, remained fixed over the surface of the playing field (over the green, the commentators would say), suspended horizontally, more pike than Homo sapiens, a being from another world.

Photojournalists must have been aware of the irresistible magic of these shots, because during the more popular matches—of course, not the minor-league duels of my desperate team—they jammed both sides of the goalposts and waited for the moment when the nervous, leaping, and skipping goalie (so restless that he reminded one of a patient from a neurological clinic) would throw himself at the ball and hang suspended over the earth for a moment. Flashbulbs popped, shutters clicked, and, thanks to all this, a photo of a goalkeeper-astronaut, leaving the pull of earth's gravity, could appear in the Monday papers.

This was astounding. A match lasting one and a half hours, made up of an unbelievable mass of tiny incidents, events, actions, shouts, and gestures, was represented on the final column of the newspaper by a photograph having something unreal in it. Movement was represented by immobility, tension by an instant of nirvana, din by silence.

How was one to present reality? I too took up photography; I had the cheapest camera, a Druh, an enlarger, and reactive paper indispensable to completing the long developing process, which began with pressing the shutter button and ended with a dry, shiny print.

I photographed blossoming cherry trees, sunsets, footbridges over streams, wooden village churches, the Baltic seashore (during summer vacations), fishnets, fences, snowcaps on low roofs, lighthouses and shadows, dark juicy shadows faithfully accompanying all objects. With the aid of a rather primitive time releaser, I also made self-portraits. I always came out looking a bit startled, unprepared, grimacing. I did not take pictures of members of my family, representatives of the older generation. Perhaps I felt one couldn't take their pictures, because they were part and parcel of an invisible city, existing only in their memory. In winter they were muffled in scarves and woolen or fur caps; in summer they were covered with memories.

I showed more feeling for objects than for people. I was drawn by steel constructions, the wrought-iron balustrades of nineteenth-century bridges, the Gothic roofs of hundreds of small cities, the rhythm of balconies and windows, ladders and stairs frying in a July sun. I was a late constructivist, an unconscious epigone of currents from the twenties. I kept wanting to admire things and their rhythms, as if I did not know that even things are tired, indifferent, and sad; objects, too, had survived the war, administered death, become declassed and degraded.

I liked the graininess of photography. The surfaces of photographed things and people were not composed of dense, solid areas; they were made up of nothing but points, grains; they were unreal, foggy; they testified to the fragility of the world. Between the black points, out of which things were woven, gleamed a white thread.

Everyone was waiting for something. Something was supposed to happen. After catechism lessons no one wanted to go home. Going home from school was also put off. I roamed the streets with a group of friends. Sometimes we hopped a tram and rode it to the other end of Gliwice, but we returned quickly because nothing caught our attention; the other end looked no different than our own. I still believed that there was someone who knew everything, who understood, someone who had figured out the meaning of things, war and peace, horror and unconcern. I dreamed about meeting my spiritual master.

Meanwhile, the majority of my teachers were liars—not

bald-faced, arrogant deceivers but, rather, hesitant people who let us know they had to lie and thus warned their pupils not to take them seriously. The same thing was to happen at the university, almost the same kind of apologetic lie.

Something had to happen. The sky is a screen upon which prophecies are projected. Dark clouds bring sadness, luminous clouds promise a little joy. Once, after catechism lessons, we stood next to the small parish rectory, the boys looking at the girls and the girls pretending not to notice. We stood there for a very long time, an infinitely long time. No one looked at a watch. Dusk fell; bats spilled out of the trees; the streetlights went on; moths made enormous, nervous circles in the air; a ruddy moon appeared. We spoke with lowered voices. Each of us had his destiny woven into his hair; it appeared in a smile, in silence. One of my pals was to die, as a student, during an ascent of the Dolomites. Others were to live.

We were joined by history, divided by fate. We spoke about anything, I don't remember what. The evening lasted a long time. Twilight has many hues; it begins with a light grayness, fog, mattedness, exhaustion, graphite. Then the world goes blind, and peevish night arrives. Somewhere far-off a dog barked. In the dark this average-sized town changed practically into a village. We kept talking, we were not in a hurry to get anywhere. It wasn't so much that the future was being revealed to us as much as the possibility and even necessity of the future. We felt uneasy, full of longing. This unusual evening was like a lens through which roamed the shadows of distant events, the indistinct silhouettes of people we were to come to know, love, lose, and regain.

Father P. looked out his window and jokingly urged us homeward. We did not want to go anywhere; for a moment we had no homes. We were peers; our fates touched, then diverged. We were supposed to return to our homes but we kept putting it off. We were together, night had fallen, it was May, nothing was happening; a plane flew overhead, rocking its green and red lights. The last bus drove past. The city was falling asleep.

I had experienced something new: one could be with others, in a group, in a small crowd, and remain oneself. One could feel acutely, movingly someone else's presence, and at the same time not lose oneself or that which was individual and ordinary.

I had the feeling, though, that these kinds of moments of friendly intimacy could not happen too often, that one could not will them. They happen infrequently, that is all one can say.

I was fifteen at the time. The evening was unending and in a way has never ended; it goes on even now, as I write these words. It lasted like a parenthesis, opened by the author but never closed, whether out of inattention or defiance. Various forecasts were recorded in the rustling of the evening, in the shadows and whistles of birds settling down to sleep. I am thinking not of concrete fortunes ("There is a journey and a brunette in your future"), only of a kind of lifting of the curtain, an unveiling of a new horizon.

We all must have felt the same thing then, we who had stood so long under the trees, not hurrying anywhere.

We had torn ourselves away from our parents—for a moment, because we were to return to them so many times—and we remained only in the tall chimney of the night, in the darkness, in silence.

School was something else. In our school, reminiscent of

army barracks, nothing could ever happen. The cleaning women washed the stairs, benches, and windows, heaving heavy buckets full of water from floor to floor or pushing them clumsily along the stone floor. In the school courtyard grew two enormous chestnut trees. Under one of them rose a mound of coke ready for winter. The minute the bell rang for recess, a large crowd of students rushed out of all the classes and in a mad hurry poured into the courtyard.

We still studied history, from Babylon to the October Revolution and back again. Our history teacher's nickname was Augustus. He was short and bald and wore glasses. He really did have the emotional instability of the late Roman emperors. Sometimes he was calm and self-possessed, and could explain the impact of the industrial revolution on nineteenth-century Europe with gusto. At other times he became completely incomprehensible and hysterical, and threw out into the hallway anyone who betrayed a second of inattention. He had his pets, whom he would flagrantly send to town to do his shopping. Without the least inhibition, he would hand his messenger money with instructions to buy him some coffee, raisins, sugar, or even vodka and then return to school with the articles.

His favorite subject was World War I. It might even seem that he himself had declared and won it. He would stand before the pink map of Europe and shout: "It was about the new division of a world already divided. Do you hear me? The new division of a world already divided!" He struck the pink map of Europe with his fist, and the map receded under his blows, the Rhine and Danube swayed lightly for a second, an earthquake shook the Carpathians, and new geysers spurted in Iceland.

Polish literature was taught by Professor M. He was very

tall. For unknown reasons he wore pants which seemed to be intended for an even taller man; at any rate his belt was always at the level of his chest. This took away some of his dignity. But dignity was one thing he had a lot of; he rarely laughed, and when he did, it was sneeringly at us, his pupils. He despised us and made pains to let us know constantly. His favorite authors were Maria Dabrowska and Stefan Zeromski. He liked to refer to the cooperative tradition, and of the philosophers still living, his greatest authority was Tadeusz Kotarbinski. He talked about his intellectual heroes, yet at the same time he let us know that these things were too difficult for us to understand. He spoke, it seemed, with half his mouth; he was always somewhat pained, haughty, absent, condescending.

Zeromski and Dabrowska were his "house" authors, who described the great family of Polish society. Professor M. did not accept, did not understand, and rejected such authors as Bruno Schulz and Witold Gombrowicz. One felt that for him everything should be if not collective then at least social, shared. In spite of this, his enthusiasm at the scene of the great fire in Kaliniec in *Days and Nights* was suspect, as if the greedy flames awakened in him some sort of repressed, dark, not at all collective, passion.

He was an embittered man, half caricature. For me he was at the same time one of the first figures representing—in a fractured and provincial way, it is true—a collective, civic ethos that was the raison d'être of practically the entire intelligentsia. Slowly I came to know the attractions of the civic world. Conversations, lasting long into the night. The piercing sense of community, intimacy, of possessing something elusive—that half-legendary country of Poland. For a long time I thought that one of the indispensable characteristics of the civic world is an inexpressible feeling of powerlessness. In the sixties and early seventies powerlessness seemed something obvious, tragic, accepted, and almost enjoyed. But I was wrong, because in the late seventies this changed and there appeared a greater and greater respect for the efficacy of action.

Another characteristic of the nightly meetings was the unexpressed conviction that we were innocent, innocent and maligned. The latter was true, the former was not. From a psychological standpoint, however, "to be maligned" is also an almost impossible emotional state.

An even more important ingredient of this philosophy was a thesis I knew well from the lessons of the grimacing Professor M.: that all is social, common, and collective.

I did not know how to formulate my opposition, I did not have the appropriate arguments at my disposal; but I did feel that not everything belonged to everybody. We are different and we also experience things which social groups will never know.

The civic world had its ethos, but it also had its aesthetics. In those days, it found its expression almost exclusively in conversation. I had the sense that grown-ups, whenever they began talking about civic matters, changed the tone of their voices, spoke much more kindly, as if with another voice, a communal, practically erotic, seductive voice. There wasn't anything one could do then, the civic world being in fact inactive, closed, boarded up; nothing was left but endless conversations. It is possible that the tradition of holiday moments, during which time stopped and families delighted in the presence of their loved ones and the absence of what was distant, suspicious, and terrifying, played a role here.

Professor M. announced to us one day that on the next

Tuesday there would be a reading given by a young poet and that therefore there would be no last class. We were glad, though we did not expect much from the poet. This type of morning meeting with authors took place at our school occasionally, and the stars were usually local graphomaniacs who spoke very seriously about their writing.

But this time it was Zbigniew Herbert who came to our school. Professor M. introduced him in his typical sweet-sour fashion. He said that there were two Herberts—one who lived in Poznan and the other who had come to our school—although one can't be altogether sure, because in modern poetry everything was possible. But Herbert did not need Professor M.'s help at all. He read fragments of *Barbarian in the Garden* and a few poems. He treated us like adults, which was flattering.

He was the first real poet I had listened to. He read, among other poems, the unusual but very simple "Biology Teacher." I understood then, or at least I felt vaguely, that social issues could be tied to nonsocial ones, that one could speak about something that belongs to the community in a way that goes beyond the limits of this category.

I moved between home and school. The older generation, however, left the house less and less frequently. I have not mentioned Aunt Wisia, my grandmother's sister. Aunt Wisia was a person full of idiosyncrasies. She was made up of practically nothing but. She distrusted beggars. She couldn't stand curds in her milk. She hated cats: she considered them false (what does *that* mean?) and believed they attacked people at night. Before the war she had worked at a Lvov bank or insurance company; after the war she was a retiree. She never married. She lived with her sister and her brother-in-law. She liked to play the role of aristocrat, a representative of the ancien régime. She had a rather weak, slightly hoarse voice, but she seemed to be proud of it because it fit the role she played in the family comedy rather well. When she wanted to discuss a subject that she considered unfit for children's ears, she spoke in French, and then her voice seemed even more fragile and hoarse.

She was the embodiment of fragility. Thin, impractical, she didn't know how to do anything, if one discounted her knowledge of French. She didn't really seem to like children, while we, the children, liked her because she was different from the remaining adults. From a child's vantage point, it might have seemed that she had a strong personality. She did not have a strong personality; she substituted eccentric behavior. She had probably read very few books. She would lock herself in her room (because somehow she always had her own room, even in the modest dwellings in Gliwice), and I think that here she occupied herself by endlessly examining her maidenly treasures, brought from Lvov, of course. Among them were patterned fans, delicate women's penknives inlaid with mother-of-pearl, postcards from Karlsbad and Abbazia, silver creamers, colored cigarette and mint-candy boxes, pocket watches which had stopped their march a half century ago, stale perfumes in cut-glass bottles, slender metal pencils that no longer wrote and fine notepads without the pads, elegant fingernail clippers and calendars from before World War I. She would lock herself up in her room, surrounded by old, melancholy objects, and smoke light menthol cigarettes with filter tips.

She probably looked into the mirror that stood on a beautiful—at least to me—commode with a marble surface, always streaked with pink powder. The room also smelled of powder, which formed chemical bonds with a variety of metals and substances.

In our family no one—except the children—took her seriously. She expressed no political opinions. That is, she most certainly hated the Communists, just as she hated cats and curds in her milk; but generally she was not aware of what was going on in politics, or who was tormenting us in a given decade, year, or month, and this was in no way a result of sclerosis but instead reflected a type of maidenly carefreeness, prolonged for an entire lifetime. She did not read newspapers. When during our Sunday evening meals, which were attended by the entire family, the latest moves by the disliked Party and disliked government were commented upon with no little malice, Aunt Wisia would merely toss out, *"La canaille, ils sont vraiment incorrigibles,"* and a moment later would hum one of her favorite melodies, a hit from fifty years earlier, long forgotten by the others. She liked mentioning balls she had attended in her youth and the brother of the famous General Jozef Haller who had once asked her to dance.

One of her favorite works was a poem about King Dagobert, who "put his pants on backwards." She recited this poem for us, the children, but it was clear that repeating it gave her enormous pleasure.

There was something dry in her, as if the consistency of pink powder were not alien to her essence. She gave little and received little. She snorted with displeasure if we brought her name-day presents. "What's this for?" she would say almost in a fury, and she was sincere. She put on no airs; deception was not her style. The things she saved in her treasury and played with every day like a large child were quite enough for her.

She gave us, the real children, presents though, by drawing bravely on her mysterious stores of treasures. She had enormous amounts of prewar copper coins—spanking new and wrapped in rolls just as at a genuine bank—in her drawers. She divided them into small portions and gave these away to her sister's five grandchildren in installments, as if she were paying us modest pensions. Sometimes she added a few silver coins, two- or five-zloty pieces of the Second Republic, coins which bore romantic sailboats and whose eagles wore small, graceful crowns, like elegant little hats.

She probably treated her life as a series of degradations. She did not get married, which, in her generation's view, was considered a catastrophe; she worked in a modest position in a bank or insurance company. In addition to this, that awful war erupted and she had to leave her own city. She was a little bit of a being from another world. She looked at all of us with slight condescension (which was returned to her with interest); she would have gone back to her Lvov apartment, and most gladly to a ball. She did not feel comfortable in this city, in this family, in her own old age. She was even more déclassé than others, although her declassification had to do with daydreams rather than reality. She never complained though; it would not have occurred to her. In her dry and laconic way she was proud. She had her own acrid sense of humor, enough of it at least to make her laugh, for others were not at all inclined to be amused by her jokes. She passed for a weird bird and certainly was one, except that the label is not very precise. Her weirdness was based more on a certain inscrutability, alienness, than on anything else (she was yet another guest in reality). She must also have been strange to herself; I knew her for several decades, and I know that she did not change at all during that time. All she had in her head were balls, women's small penknives, and nonwriting silver pencils.

Because she had never gotten married and never experienced births or miscarriages or marital spats, never raised children nor lost them when they grew up and set up their own homes, she was unused in a very strange way, as if she was still indulging youthful illusions, whose fulfillment she kept putting off until later, to the next month and year. She was lightheaded (her thoughts were light). Perhaps a little happy? An eternal teenager, sheltered by her family until death.

When she was very, very old she began to lose her memory, until she lost it altogether. Of course, then even she moved mentally to Lvov. She never left the house and would spend the long days in an armchair, never uttering a word; and only occasionally, when guests came—whom she could no longer recognize—did she recite Kazimierz Tetmajer's poem in her hoarse, dry, breaking voice:

> And when you will be my wife,
> Beloved and married,
> Then will a garden open for us
> A dazzling garden, full of dawn.
>
> Blossoming orchards will burst into fragrance,
> Grapevines will offer their luscious scent,
> And lovely roses, honeysuckle
> Will shower their kisses upon your hair.
>
> We will go silent, thoughtful
> Amid golden mists and beams,

We will promenade slowly through the streets
Between trees, quiet, alone.

Branches will bend our way
Narcissus will climb a silver trellis
And the white flowers of linden trees
Will drop gently upon our loving heads.

The guests, of whom I was one, would interrupt their conversations, somewhat embarrassed, and wait until she finished
declaiming before they resumed their train of thought. But
Auntie Wisia would not give up and, in a few minutes, like
a music box began reciting the same work, of which, it seems
to me, she liked best the line "And the white flowers of linden
trees / Will drop gently upon our loving heads." Of course her
hair was absolutely gray, and had been for a long time. It was
her hair that was white and not the linden flower. I think that
her entire soul took refuge in Tetmajer's poem—no, more:
she became the poem, she lived in the four stanzas as if they
were four rooms.

She died in 1980 at age ninety-nine, having outlived her
peers, two world wars, and all her daydreams.

My grandfather died ten years earlier at age ninety. Both
were victims neither of Nazism nor of Communism but of
time, that disheveled monster who left his watchmaker's cave
toward evening and looked for tardy pedestrians.

One of my many passions was cycling. I jumped on my
bike, depending on the weather, the caprices of early spring,
in March or April, and sped down the asphalt roadways en-

closing the city. I literally sped down the streets. I did not know how to ride slowly, I was always in a hurry, I used all my strength, all my energy. I rested only when I rode down an incline, when I did not have to pedal, when I was pulled by gravity. Then I could look at the fields and forests. I passed quick flashes of cherry or walnut trees growing right next to the road, green blots of winter wheat in the distance, and, even farther, the calm, majestic hills. Beyond them was only the horizon, but even it was not immobile; it dipped and rose, widened and narrowed, depending on me and my bicycle.

Sometimes it happened, however, that I stopped, breathless, at the peak of a midsize hill, and then the landscape stalled, the horizon stretched away in a sure and thick stroke, unless it was tattered by the fir tips of a distant forest. In the villages stood tiny old churches made of larch. Fear-stricken chickens, flattened and elongated in frantic escape, splashed away from the front wheel of my Czech bicycle. The houses and shutters were usually closed, but every once in a while from deep within, behind the mirrors of windows, I noted the faint silhouette of an old woman combing out her hair.

I rode my bike right over reality, over the main thoroughfares and over the side streets. I returned to the city, and there, too, reality waited for me. Summer. Chaos. Hundreds of apartments, thousands of windows, flowers in flowerpots on windowsills. On the roof, pigeons tired of the heat, turtledoves complained of the routine of life. A man, naked to the waist, if one did not count his scarlet suspenders, stands in a window and shaves. Someone else is beating a rug, and the echo of powerful detonations bounces off the walls of the tenements. In a sky pale with excess of light, black-and-blue storm clouds gather, almost indistinguishable from the backdrop. Our neighbor Pani Mazonska, leaning on a cane, stops, rests, and looks at the red fire truck that is returning from a blaze. The black river flows indifferently through the city. Linden trees blossom. A militiaman looks up and stares at a small plane that is swallowed up by a violet cloud. A storm approaches. A drunkard sleeps on a bench. A giant black cat sleeps in the courtyard. Perhaps they will meet in their sleep, on the shore of a mountain river. Chaos. Scorching heat. Luckily there is history and the battle of the two great beasts to give order to a slothful, porous reality.

But it is exactly this corner of the world that no system, no ordering principle, no textbook has reached that aroused my overpowering desire. This would happen at various times of the day, most often in the evening, when the red sun hid behind buildings of Prussian brick and long, unreal shadows greedily fell upon rooftops and the stone plates of sidewalks, onto balconies and gardens. Desire overcame all of me, moved into my skin, as if a shadow had stuck to me, the messenger of twilight. What did I desire? Everything. This was desire born of love and sex, philosophy and poetry, politics and metaphysics. Nothing could sate this gargantuan desire; my only comfort was that it seemed to stun itself, drink itself, and finally go out slowly, vanish, withdraw, warning in a whisper that it would return.

It seemed to me that what was real must be the opposite of convention and schema, it must be as fresh as early morning and as dense as ash leaves. That is why some aspects and manifestations of the new system seemed, at moments, altogether attractive.

I did not do anything really awful. My betrayals were measured and rather childish. Yet—usually to spite the rigor of the gestures of the older generation, of the unreconciled—my rebellion would boil down to my assuming, as an experiment, individual elements of the new faith and scaring my family, all the generations that were still living, with it triumphantly. They, on the other hand, members of the family clan, looked at me half ironically and half afraid, and, just in case, lowered their voices when they embarked on discussions of the political news of the day.

The crowning glory of these experiments was my signing up for the ZMS—the Socialist Youth Union—as a joke, and right afterward, also as a joke, announcing my candidacy for the position of the first secretary of the school branch, while my friends at school, also as a joke, voted me in (offered me their support, as the local newspaper would say). My career in the ZMS was short-lived and had no influence on my later choices; I was a little ashamed of this joke, and when I became a university student I said nothing of my "organizational affiliation."

I did not know at the time what I came to know much later: as a man, as a character, I am both weak and strong. My strength tends to be frail; it can betray me. I am capable of submitting to an outside pressure, conformity, the mood of the moment, someone else's enthusiasm, my own uncertainty; and, it is true, always after a time I am capable of shaking off the bad influence. But with all certainty, I do not belong to those phenomenally resistant, arrogantly sovereign natures. Perhaps I am strong, but my strength is welded to weakness, doubt, dislike of quick decisions. I belong to those who err.

Consequently I also have an appropriately affectionate attitude to becoming, maturing. Those who are genetically independent might certainly disdain the element of development, time, maturing, because at any moment, regardless of challenge, they are ready to show themselves to the world in all their perfection. Time for them is nothing more than the shutter click of a camera, an instant of unveiling their unchanging substance. For me, on the other hand, time—the time of maturing, redressing an error, arriving at a clear understanding of one thing or another—is something vital, indispensable. Maturing—in my case—is never ultimate and finished. I will always be ready to commit a new error, and then I will try to understand it and correct it. *Usque ad finem.*

It is dangerous to mention this kind of thing. Talking about one's own flaws is a highly risky literary venture, because we begin to try to exploit it for ourselves and brag about this or that weakness. Pascal knew this very well:

"Vanity is so deeply rooted in the human heart that . . ."

And perhaps I, too, who quote this . . .

And my reader . . .

And those who now search with the greatest outrage for the least trace of conformity in each biography . . .

Did I collect stamps? Yes, I collected stamps. I attended the meetings of the philatelist club. And there at the tables sat older men with wrinkled faces in clouds of tobacco smoke who negotiated with us, underage enthusiasts, cheating us unmercifully. Mr. Mazonski offered me a complete album of stamps, most of which were from before the war. Zebras and giraffes grazed on the stamps printed in Togo. The stamps from East Germany were reminiscent of miniature ads for tool factories: they depicted almost exclusively compasses, cogged wheels, and cylinders of internal-combustion engines. Flowers blos-

somed prettily on Swiss stamps. It seems, however, that they
did not do this disinterestedly, because over every flower were
the words Pro Helvetia. British stamps did not interest me
much, as their only decoration was the marble profile of the
queen scrutinizing the surface of the envelope. Small kingdoms, especially Monaco, belonged to the most serious pro-
ducers of stamps. The Olympic series issued on the occasion
of the Olympics in Melbourne has engraved itself on my
memory.

Someone will ask: But what about the winter? In the summer
the heat led to chaos, but what happened in winter?

In winter the horses pulling wagons of coal slipped dangerously on the ice-crusted paving stones, and I watched them
with pity and despair, for I knew that a horse that breaks a leg
must die.

I was enthusiastic about jazz. At first it was New Orleans
jazz, the easy, rocking, languid rhythm. This original jazz had
something innocently liberating about it: it was as if a firemen's
orchestra suddenly became inspired (as if the Holy Ghost descended upon it). Then I got to like modern jazz. This took
place in the early sixties, and the bebop and "cool jazz" periods
were not all that distant in time, especially if one takes into
consideration the usual time lag in a country behind the Iron
Curtain.

I was attracted by the principle of improvisation at the basis
of jazz. My first inspirations, which so overwhelmed me, co-
incided nicely with the lyrical exaltation of Charlie Parker,
Dizzy Gillespie, and even John Coltrane. Some of these improvisations bore all the trappings of the Great Adventure; they
swept away, or so I thought, so I felt, the entire soullessness
and pettiness of a conventional reality. After all, Polish liter-

ature was on intimate terms with improvisation. Wasn't the Great Improvisation the heart and core of *Forefathers' Eve, Part III*? Hadn't Adam Mickiewicz made himself famous as improviser extraordinaire?

At midnight I set my radio dial for the Voice of America, which transmitted John Conover's jazz programs in English, daily except weekends, if I remember correctly. Unfortunately, the radio had to be plugged in to the socket in the next room, occupied by my sister, who usually shut off the power after a few minutes for the simple reason that, insensitive as she was to the philosophy of improvisation, she wanted to sleep.

Original Western jazz records were extremely expensive. In my eyes unimaginably expensive. A record like this cost three hundred zlotys at the time, one half of my annual budget. I did, however, have a considerable number of silver coins from the time of the Second Republic, given to me by Auntie Wisia. I behaved like Judas, Judas squared. I sold my silver coins, minted in prewar Poland, coins with sailboats and eagles wearing crowns on their tiny heads.

Thanks to this transaction I was able to afford the purchase of two of the most original records, one with Charlie Parker and the other with the Dave Brubeck quartet (the latter was also made out of a transparent plastic). To me jazz was a paean to spontaneity, even to freedom. Meanwhile, the city in which I just so happened to live was full of conventions, endured by dint of convention. I rebelled against it and looked for support to jazz saxophone players, usually no longer living American Negroes.

Sooner or later I had to become acquainted with the paradox of records, most of all the paradox of a "set" jazz improvisation, recorded for all eternity. Nothing changed in Charlie Parker's rousing improvisation (I, too, referred to him by the familiar Charlie or Bird). It was always the same. Exactly the same a month, year, or hundredth or two hundredth listening later. I finally learned these improvisations by heart and they stopped being improvisations.

The records I spent a fortune acquiring bored me. The subtle law of compensation was in force: a Haydn sonata, composed centuries ago, continues to provide a great deal of freedom to the pianists interpreting it. Parker's improvisation, recorded relatively recently, does not allow for the least deviation.

I began to listen more frequently to classical music. The frenzied energy of Stravinsky's *Petrouchka* equaled the emotions of good jazz (I was not yet familiar with Gustav Mahler's Fifth Symphony and its stunning opening funereal-tawdry march). I did not know what music was, the spaces it concealed itself in, and in what relation it stood to the historical world. Later I became convinced that no one knew this, no one.

I read a lot. One day—I do not remember the date and I don't even know what I was reading at the time, whether it was Bruno Schulz or Marcel Proust—I made a discovery that changed everything. I discovered (please, do not laugh) that there exists a spiritual world described by great writers. I saw that in addition to the trivial, empirical reality there exists the domain of the imagination, which is basically the same palpable, visible, and fragrant world except that it is enriched by countless legions of spirits and shadows. I did not understand how these two regions were joined, how they connected, but I was certain that their simultaneous identity and distinctness was something as mysterious and real as the ontological status of the Holy Trinity.

I was stunned by this discovery. I became a neophyte. I

began to separate people into those who knew and those who did not. I was convinced that only a handful of the select *knew*. The great majority of residents in my city—because these were the only ones I could encounter—seemed to be cast into the darkest, most profound ignorance. For them a bicycle, a wicker basket, a pool of light on the wall, an oak table were items barely worth cataloging with sharp contours, just like human life, fitting between the year of one's birth and the year of one's death like an egg in a shotglass. They did not realize that human life and objects and trees vibrate with mysterious meanings which can be deciphered like cuneiform writing. There exists a meaning, hidden from day to day but accessible in moments of greatest attentiveness, in those moments when consciousness loves the world. Grasping this difficult meaning results in an experience of peculiar happiness; the loss of it leads to melancholy.

I quizzed my partners in conversation, I checked to see if they *knew*. I asked them innocent-sounding questions. What do you think, I asked, about Swann's love? And you, Madam, you lived in Drohobycz. Did Schulz get its atmosphere right? (This was a devious question, because Schulz's Drohobycz had nothing to do with the real city.) What do you think of Gombrowicz? Do you like Boleslaw Lesmian's poems? Why? Why not?

The exam usually exceeded the capabilities of those I assailed with questions. They answered carelessly, superficially; they excused themselves by saying they lacked time, were fatigued; they complained that Proust was excessively refined, that Gombrowicz was too weird, that Schulz never even told a story.

Practically everyone flunked the exam. I looked at them

with poorly concealed contempt. They did not know. They lived in a narrow, dreadful reality between office and home, between tram and restaurant, between marriage and funeral. Even among my peers I was able to find no more than two people with whom I could discuss Soutine's paintings and the aesthetic pitfalls of dodecaphony.

As a proselyte I must have committed a good many mistakes. I did not realize that a positive majority of people belonged to the domain of profound meaning not through their knowledge—because one doesn't encounter this too often—but through their lives, through their radiant living substance, and that is why it is dumb and absurd to accuse them of ignorance. Instead of asking and checking and tormenting them, I should have looked at them and understood them. I should have looked with tenderness and understood intelligently.

I am afraid that to many of my interlocutors I must have appeared to be an unpleasant and conceited upstart. I thought I was being a very ingenious and discreet examiner, but, now I am certain of it, the others had figured out my motives and moods without difficulty. Perhaps they did not know the answers to my questions, but they did see something of which I had no inkling: that I was ridiculous.

Thus began a lengthy period of imbalance between my inner life and the way I participated in collective life. My passions and interests were authentic, they engulfed me completely, but I did not know how to express them in my behavior, conversations, or even dress, not to mention writing, about which I merely daydreamed.

Later, in Cracow, I reached for a compromise solution. By then I was a young, beginning poet and had published a few poems. The solution consisted of spending a lot of time with other young poets. Their company rescued me for some time because they, too, were awkward and belonged to no other circles. If that's how things are, my friends seemed to say, then let's form our own circle. Being a young poet is one of the most difficult predicaments: one is still so unexpressed, inarticulate, yet one craves statement, expression, the materialization of vision so desperately.

But in a certain way the condition of the young poet, with all its desperate helplessness and even with the disdain shown to a young poet by everyone—older poets, lawyers, merchants, policemen, art critics, doctors, statesmen and their wives, daughters, and mistresses—more accurately mirrors the status of poetry than the considerably more dignified material status of older writers, praised and showered with awards, does. For if the instants of rapture, instants in which vision is born, belong to an entirely different order, to a dimension of time other than the drudging, everyday existence that fills the calendar, then the division has something dramatic and unfortunate about it, and the bewildered young poet is closer to the truth of his life than the august laureate.

The same split contributed to my seeing my city in a new perspective. All that went on in it and all that endured in it revealed itself to me in a different light: the priests and teachers and my peers existed, it turns out, in two different ways. The first, most real and passionate way, by taking part in everyday battles and conflicts whose stakes were their very survival and also the quality, the dignity of that survival. But they also existed in another way, for they led a life that was appropriate more to figures represented on a painter's canvas than to flesh-and-blood people, a completely luxurious existence whose single goal—if one can regard it as a goal at all—was looking, showing off, expressing oneself (just as one finds it in Manet's painting *Breakfast in the Workroom* in the Munich Neue Pinakothek, where the two painted men and one painted woman have only one care: to appear, shine, and show off their advantages).

That is how I saw them. Sometimes they were historical beings, completely absorbed in their assignments and worries of the day and month; and at other times, in brief moments of another vision, they became magnates, unconcerned with time, centuries, political systems, as if the very fact of their existence elicited a holiday, an unconditional affirmation of life, and caused their shabby postwar clothes to assume the luster of Titian silks.

The same streets, so extraordinarily common, created only so that the tram, car, and droshky could travel along them, became almost as beautiful as Venetian canals. I was stunned, awed. Sometimes during a school dance, the dancing pairs were woven into an endless rhythm that led no one knew where, as if the dance became a version of the Crusades, an unending, sublime march. So that now even I began to walk two cities, just like my grandfather's generation, for whom each corner could conceal the holy walls of Lvov. The windows hid other apartments, books opened a different reality, Sundays were gateways through which one could escape the monotony of rainy weeks.

For a long time I was helpless; I did not know what to do with those other experiences and with the joyful amazement that went with them. Not only did I not know how to express them yet, I was also tormented by the uncertainty and thought of whether they were a sign of illness or health. Nor was I certain what was more real, that which was ordinary and every-day, known and judged through common sense and civic discussion, or that which was lustrous and immobile, reflected in poems and canvases. I was sixteen, seventeen years old; at that age nothing seems obvious and normal, let alone the wild, exuberant experiences evoked by music or simply by wind and the world. I also slowly began to know the price one must pay for those short moments of omniscience: doubt, darkness, despair, just as if the uncommon flash of light, proper to the highest moments, deprived the most prosaic days, dragging themselves sluggishly along the bottom of a wide, sandy valley, of their electricity. There was always too little knowledge. Too little brilliant revelation. But doubts, those sparrows of the intelligence, were never lacking.

I sought answers; I wanted to understand. Did I sense even then that the answers and thoughts would never arrange themselves into a system? Who was I then? A young anarchist? A young aesthete? I did not disdain the simplest question, however: how to live so as not to hurt others, to help them, while at the same time never ceasing one's own searching, never ceasing to think. Who was I? Was I like the young black cat I saw a few days ago during a walk (here, near Paris)? The cat, very sure of himself and his strength, showed off in front of me, jumping and climbing all over a tree trunk. It seemed to me that he wanted to say: I am young and immortal, and you are middle-aged; look around and you will see the thick line of the horizon and a tired sun that is incapable of keeping itself up in the firmament. Was I like him? I was at the start of my journey; I had fantastical imaginings and hopes tied to the spiritual life and its might.

Meanwhile, the city was changing, evolving. Radicals died;

moderates lived on, furnished their apartments, took refuge in their furniture, raised children, and their children raised the next generation, which spoke Polish with a different accent, just as if the singsong language of the East had gotten mixed with the hard sounds of the Silesians. The goalie of our sluggish soccer team sat in the window (he lived above a pharmacy, on the second floor). A small pillow lay on the windowsill, and he leaned his elbows on it and observed life on the drowsy street. Once every twenty minutes a noisy red tram shot by. Occasionally passersby would greet our bored goalkeeper, and he had obviously been waiting for that. His face became animated, he smiled and returned the greetings. Unfortunately, he got fatter and fatter, and his elbows left deeper and deeper dents in the velvet pillow. His wife, the prettiest girl in the whole neighborhood, also began to gain weight right after the marriage. Now, as I write these words, both of them must be pretty fat.

Almost everyone who made himself a target of others by taking a visible position and serving the new authorities tried to unveil his life, as if he had wanted to say, "I could not do otherwise; do not be angry." The director of the gymnasium took walks with his unfortunate, retarded daughter, whose development had been arrested and who had the wrinkled face of a little monkey, red nose and eyes.

Those, on the other hand, not in possession of such glaring evidence of the gods' disgrace, at least drank vodka and were not ashamed of it at all. And this was accepted as a kind of satisfaction—whoever showed his weaknesses could count on the indulgence of his neighbors and fellow citizens. Everyone tried to ruin his life as quickly as possible, and if he was not successful he waited impatiently for old age and its diseases to strike. There certainly did exist, as well, absolute baseness,

servants of the secret police, professional informers, and hang-
men, but these had to act surreptitiously. I did not see them,
I could not remember them. No one knew very well what a
successful life, career, or happiness consisted of. Leave the
city? And go where, if it is the same all over? Get famous?
How, if the new authorities controlled everything?

Some representatives of the younger generation contemptuously dismissed the warnings of their elders, signed on with
the Party, bought themselves leather briefcases, hats, and
gloves, and pretended that they were setting off on professional
careers by becoming engineers, journalists, or historians. They
discussed this matter-of-factly and as dispassionately as if they
lived in Austria, Australia, or Asturia.

In the summer we drifted along the lazy, practically unmoving river, along which skated insects, industrious as Nor-
wegian skiers, intent on reaching the opposite shore. On both
sides of this unhurrying river grew a neglected park, weary of
the constant change of seasons. The long, soft branches of
alders, oaks, and beeches hung over the water. Some of them
touched the water, played with the river, drowned a little,
bobbed a little on the surface, until another stroke of the heavy
oar submerged them again. Don't memories act the same way
under the shower of typewriter keys?

I understood less at that time than I did a few years later,
in Cracow, when as a twenty-six- or twenty-seven-year-old
author I became something of a literary doctrinaire who
seemed to know what poetry, human fate, and the obligations
of the author were. I understood less and thus was wiser than
my older and glibber self, writing literary manifestos (even
though they may have had some intellectual significance) and
attacking recognized authors.

Who would not want to know the pleasure of understanding?

The moment when things and ideas become obedient, turn their faces to us like well-trained circus animals, as if pretending they have no more secrets, justly enjoys its fame. Creators of philosophical and ideological systems especially adore it. Shortly evening and night arrive, however; shadows grow, ideas lose their luster, are covered with dew, and it turns out that we know little, we understand little. But even in this there is the acrid, difficult satisfaction, the anxious ignorance, when the gray, dense fog fills the gaps between blots of steamships.

I am sitting at a table in a room on the sixth floor of a monstrous concrete apartment house in a Paris suburb. From the window of my room I see the distant roofs of Paris drying after a recent rain, church steeples and trees, construction cranes and television antennas. I am listening to Mozart's Violin Quintet, K. 516—more precisely, to its first section, bearing the classic Allegro label.

Yet this Allegro is not at all cheerful; there are two motifs bound together in it, one light, rococo, and the other sad, even grim. The one conventional, almost porcelain, the second tragic. Rococo and suffering. Rococo and death. In this music two cities converse with one another. Two cities dance with one another. Two cities, different, but destined for a difficult love affair, like men and women. Rococo and fear. The eternal existence of music and the dread of people transported to their death. The sated calm of museums and a child's crying. I listen to Mozart's violin quintet. Evening approaches once again. Again the sky conceals itself under a dusky lid.

OPEN ARCHIVES

Instructions for the Secret Police
Introduction

As a result of the radical political changes that have transpired in the Eastern European countries, police archives have been opened. "Opened" may be saying too much. Opened a crack, perhaps. These archives contain material so sensational that responsible politicians, in taking over Communism's thankless heritage, proceed extremely slowly and cautiously.

Instructional memos and booklets are also surfacing, along with lists of informers and secret-police collaborators. The public is not all that interested in them, for no one suspects that the in-house publications of the Department of Internal Affairs could have the least intellectual value. Some of them, however, are not without philosophical aspirations. For example, a memo marked "top secret" and bearing the title "Instructions for the Secret Police" has fallen into my hands. I have decided to reprint a few excerpts from it, even though it is quite evident that the cynicism of this confession of disbelief in man is unappealing to me.

My friend, who is working on the liquidation of the police archive, has not authorized me to give his name. Thus we are dealing with the anonymous author of a text and with an anonymous middleman-donor. I thank the latter. What the former is doing I know not. He is likely an older retired man who, following Voltaire's advice, tends a garden and expects nothing good to come of the democratic future.

These idiots forget what force is. Practically nothing but saints, moralists, ascetics come to your offices. I hope this does not overwhelm you. You ought to be thoroughly versed in theory; it is for this reason we are constantly organizing course work and training. I cannot believe that a single one of my subordinates would succumb to the charms of weakness. Trembling hands, lean faces, eyes with dark circles under them—what's attractive about all that?

You are well prepared, yet I fear that one who is less experienced, younger, and sensitive will experience a moment of uncertainty and will wonder: Perhaps this intellectual hunched over before me is right. Perhaps that exalted student reciting clichés about dignity and honor knows more about the world, about its mysterious structure, than we, the police, do.

Just in case, I shall remind you what reality is.

1. The essence of reality is force.

2. The universal delusion (so universal, in fact, that you will find it in the west, the south, the north, and the east) dictates that the world is steered and governed by so-called values, that is, weakness.

3. Why this is, I don't know. That's the riddle I will never understand. Why this brutal, ravenous, cruel world transforms

itself beyond recognition when it is ready to keel over and gives a speech—no, this I'll never fathom. Nor will you.

Why do only baseness, ruse, cunning, and brute force emerge in action, and why does everything, even a good up-bringing and talent, absolutely everything, serve just one purpose: to conquer the rival, opponent, foe; while in language, in a sentence, in practically every statement, one must endlessly, hand over fist, employ concepts such as the good, justice, beauty, gentleness, and tolerance. No, this I will never know, nor will you.

The world is debased, but it doesn't want word of this to spread throughout the cosmos. This is the most masterly conspiracy of silence that was ever organized. I emphasize, however: this is not our business. It is not our job to judge the composition of the world. We did not create it. We are, it is true, representatives of an ancient occupation, but, in this case, I repeat, we were presented with an accomplished fact. Evil was separated from the good, although not in the way moralists imagine: "evil" has been the scene of deeds, actions, and accomplishments, while so-called good made itself dangerously at home in the language.

And that is how things have remained. Have you ever heard a murderer say, "I am a wretched murderer. I want nothing but blood and suffering"? No, instead he requests an alteration in mores; he will want to assure the human race, or at least his own clan, of happiness. Have you ever heard a thief proclaim, "I steal because I worship money, beautiful homes, and plush couches"? Oh no; a thief will speak of love for his country, sacrifice, and boundless devotion. Have you ever heard a pastor say from the pulpit that he likes a warm featherbed and poppyseed noodles, juniper-flavored vodka, and smoked sausage? Of course not. In church you will hear a zealous sermon about the Passion of Christ.

Perhaps only seducers have enough honesty to brag about their techniques. On this point humankind is less demanding. I hold it against Mozart that his Don Giovanni does not commit the crimes we are forbidden to confess, but this is merely an academic issue now—as you know, women's organizations have demanded the verb "seduce" be removed from the Academy's dictionary.

Have any of you ever met a poet who would admit to liking fat stipends, flattering reviews, and being the emptiest creature in the world? To the degree that he could not survive a week without compliments and praise? Oh no; a poet will tell you that he sings about beauty and pain. And if he is clever, he will also add that he fights for justice and defends the interests of the poor and oppressed.

Reality, therefore, is "evil," while good inhabits rhetoric. For that which leaves the lips—regardless of whether they belong to king or dissident, monk or poet, journalist or soldier (generals, too, do not have the habit of shouting "Kill!"; instead they declaim stanzas about honor)—we call rhetoric.

You will come across it everywhere. Primarily in your studies. You will find it in newspaper columns and in books.

Imagine a creature, similar to a human, that would have one muscular arm and, instead of the other, a white downy wing. This is our world. When it comes to acting, it doesn't think for too long, it strikes. When it is supposed to give a speech, however, it uses a refined syntax and lies beautifully. (One should modify Aristotle's definition: man is a feathered being that lies.) The white downy wing we call rhetoric.

As I have said, everybody uses it. But it is used most willingly by politicians and literati (because speeches for heads of state are usually written by writers). The difference between them is not as great as it seems to writers, and by that I mean not the degree of falseness but its breadth and application. The premier of a country that conquers another country will emphasize the benefits of civilization which the partition will bring to the smaller neighbor. While the poet, who sings the praises of a sunset at a moment when, let us say, twelve thousand people are suffering, acts on an appropriately more modest scale.

Even a wise man as penetrating as Schopenhauer—beware: you do not have to bother reading his work, it's not for you; it's enough that I ruin my eyesight in the library—even so, I repeat, a penetrating philosopher like Schopenhauer, someone who with a rare ingenuity examined and described the cunning of force, got cold feet and began praising—what? You would never guess—music, poetry, art in general, that is, rhetoric.

This is really strange. I remember well the moment when, lost in reading *The World As Will and Imagination*, I reached the chapters which turn into a hymn in praise of art. It was late afternoon, snow was falling, covering the roofs of apartment buildings and cars. There was complete silence; only the clocks were ticking, and the pages of the old book rustled as they turned. I felt as if I had lost a friend. Or worse yet: as if my closest friend had stuck a knife in my back.

Afterward I thought that perhaps there were two Schopenhauer brothers who, as a joke, gave their work to be bound by the same bookbinder. Two brothers—one a hackneyed dreamer and glorifier of deception, like the hundreds one meets in history-of-philosophy textbooks; the other a brilliant, cynical

thinker, someone who is able to unveil and decode the meaning of everyday hypocrisy, everyday comedy, spectacles we can
enjoy to our heart's content everywhere, in our studies, on the
streets, in our homes, and even in our mirrors.

Brilliant Schopenhauer voiced the ultimate truth about the
nature of the world as a circus full of cruelty. Immediately,
however, his brother, cheater, hypocrite, showed up, and
again we were thrust under the governance of beauty. Music
. . . Ideas . . . Rapture . . . Disinterestedness . . .

You must reconcile yourselves to this: there exists a secret
rule which does not allow knowledge about reality to spread
and last. Whenever someone extremely clear-sighted appears
—Schopenhauer I—at his side appears the cunning censor—
Schopenhauer II—who says, Well, yes, but Beauty . . . Sunsets . . . Music . . . Drama . . .

Machiavelli tried once, and to this day the stomachs of
universities have not digested him.

Remember: one is allowed a great deal. One is allowed to
compete for prizes, distinctions, honors, and money; one can
flatter the mighty. But when one has all the trophies in hand,
then one should get up on the tribune and say: Humanity . . .
Virtue . . . Good . . .

Our world is revolting. Hideous. It is made up only of greed,
cruelty, and ambition, and the only thing that beautifies it is
lying. Even the children are infected with this universal deceit.
Even dogs. The revolution not only did not help the situation
(we are speaking frankly, man to man) but made it even more
unbearable. I am not going to talk about politics, however.
What do we care about politics, strategy, ideology. We look
at the illnesses of the world up close; we do not need the
intervention of golden-tongued orators. Our profession does

not incline us toward effusiveness. The internal report, a brief note, a few pages of instructions—no more is needed. Writing forces one to beautify, decorate. Be laconic. Use the telephone; do not trust your pen or typewriter.

Always Nero . . . Always emotion and the flute and mawkishness. Comedians. They can't stand the truth. There is enough hardiness in them for only the first volume. In the second volume they always offer you the inevitable medicine, whether it is God or beauty or democracy. Thanks but no thanks. And I urge you to say no thanks as well. We will stay in the first chapter. Perhaps this is the only profession in which hypocrisy plays a minimal role. That is why I think with sympathy about people like Joseph Fouché, who changed political regimes without batting an eye. Why even blink if political systems mask the same disease, the same madness, the same force with such difficulty?

"I desire, demand, want. I have to have this. I have to be famous." That's how they think. Yet they know well that in making their dreams public they would be met with an explosion of scornful laughter. So they think up circuitous routes. What they will not do to attain what they want. One will cure lepers, the other will journey to the North Pole, the third will found a new church. Unbridled ambition will push them to do anything. They are ready to share the fate of beggars, shiver from the cold in the wilds of the Arctic. They are close to dying of starvation. For twenty years they are capable of working in concealment in order to later reappear triumphantly and, with a humble, deceitful grimace (which journalists will call the radiance of otherworldly wisdom), accept appropriate praises and awards. Yet their smile means only one thing: I won!

How many of them perish along the way! They contract leprosy, fall into alpine chasms, die of hunger, place their heads on the chopping block, vanish in psychiatric hospitals. Good for them. I will be the last to pity them. They are victims of hubris. Instead of being content with an ordinary, modest life and decent anonymity, they dream about standing at the head of humanity. Think about it. If they weren't breaking their necks on their risky trails, we would have even more leaders of humanity. It would be unbearable, really unbearable.

But later, when they stand at the top, they give their long and noble speeches. For this reason, the distinction between people of action and philosophers ceases to exist; both are heavy-handed with the platitudes.

I feel alone. From the minute I lost my last friend (Schopenhauer), I became a lonely man. But not an embittered man. First, I have you and I believe that in one of you I will find my intelligent successor. Second, I have to say that the spectacle which is playing itself out before our very eyes is as horrifying as it is comical. I look at this anthill, at the ambitious and hardworking ants climbing up the steep sides! Every second, one of the ants falls and disappears under the sole of an indifferent passerby. For a moment there is peace; the other ants gather, and an ant in a white chasuble stands over the grave and in a mournful homily praises the deceased ant. He talks about his virtues, about the unblemished life of the deceased, about the example he set for posterity. He consoles the ant-widow and for embellishment adds praise of the long-lived marriage of the ant-victim and ant-widow. The ant-mourners listen and sadly twitch their antennae.

Yet it is enough to look into our archives, fellows, to conclude that all this is untrue. The deceased ant was a drunk, coward, and careerist, which we skillfully exploited by blackmailing him for twelve years and gleaning from him copious information about the other ants, the very same ones who now sadly twitch their antennae. And, of course, the married life of both ants was far from perfect (so we took advantage of that, too). We even know a few things about the ant in white chasuble who should, on principle, be above suspicion, and at the appropriate moment we will make good use of that knowledge as well.

I think that even you will learn to delight in this spectacle in time. We are anonymous workers; the pleasure of celebrity, television interviews, and photos on the covers of illustrated weeklies is not for us. You should know, however, that these are trifling and ephemeral pleasures unworthy of intelligent people. Yes, trifling and ephemeral. Remember that the faces on the first pages of weeklies will be forgotten immediately. One face will obliterate another, one nose will replace another, lips will cover lips, teeth teeth, eye eye, name name. To look, to stare—how much more this is. To look and only look, never making any use of it, never taking up writing or painting, because here the dangerous temptations begin, here rhetoric waits in ambush. No, I have already said that with writing one must limit oneself to notes, reports, instructions.

We are writing only the first chapter. Pure description. Pure contemplation. No conclusions, recommendations, reflections on how to find salvation. Only looking. And, of course, doing what we are supposed to do. I probably don't have to remind you that these are very elementary and easy things.

Remember that your clients, all those impoverished moralists, melancholy conspirators, unsuccessful dissidents, know the world a lot less than we do. Oh yes, and they have their lectures and training, but, I assure you, one does not speak honestly there. There one declaims and declines: freedom, justice, democracy. They will throw these harmless metaphors in your face; they will add dignity and truth, never understanding that the latter is a resident in our quiet offices.

I trust that you are educated and bright, but that does not allay my fear that you will ask yourself the question, perhaps there is something to those hopeless incantations, maybe that nun knows something we don't, maybe that high school student with fiery eyes has solved the riddle of the universe.

Do not forget that your guests are basically candidates for the leaders of humanity in a larval stage. They are those monsters of ambition, tyrants *in spe*, dictators in diapers that I mentioned earlier; for the time being, they are weak and defenseless, and that is why they are attempting to enchant you with the siren voice of beauty (for what is defenselessness if not a cunning ruse?), a voice which will undergo a mutation and become like those shouts and whistles and seductive arias that you know intimately as the sneering satanic expression of omnipotence.

Please be careful. Be cynical. Only in this way can we— and only we—rescue the world from the next cataclysm. For you know that these dopes would gladly, immediately cook up the next revolution, the next paradise, a new calamity. Be ruthless. No illusions.

BETRAYAL

WHY DID I do that? Why did I do what? Why was I who I was? And who was I? I am already beginning to regret that I agreed to grant you this interview. For years I refused; you must have asked me at a weak moment or in a moment of anxiety. To sate a stranger's curiosity with one's own suffering—you will admit that there is a disproportion here between the appetite and the nourishment.

How did that world look? The one you were too late to get to know? The same as this one. Completely different.

I don't know where we should begin. I assume you have read a lot: memoirs, analyses, archival materials, historians' treatises.

It wasn't all that long ago. No one is capable of writing about that short epoch, no one. You see, some of the names, cold today, half forgotten, glowed then like hot electrical wires. Especially those that began with the letter "B." It is not enough to say that these names (one rarely said them and then only cautiously, looking around) elicited nothing but fear. Mainly fear, of course, but also a certain fascination because they radiated an unusual energy. Comparing them to high-voltage wires would not be an exaggeration. One had the feeling that gods moved among us. Evil gods, it is true, but supernatural beings nonetheless. Other beings. Newcomers from another planet. Today these people are lifeless, even if they are still alive.

Did I get my knowledge of Communism at home? Oh yes, but was that knowledge? Take a look: my father, my aunts, my friends at school. Behind each one, parents, uncles, as in a gigantic family portrait. The aunts of my classmates. The dense forest of cousins, uncles, godfathers, in-laws, first cousins and their fiancés. Forests of male cousins. Gardens of female cousins. On Sunday everyone met over tea and plain cookies. And my aunts whispered, in an accusing way, that someone had been beaten or killed, someone's house and land had been confiscated, someone had shot himself in despair. They saw only single facts; they were unable to join them into a system. There, on the other side, was the great mental effort, modern Thomism, with its ambition of encompassing all being. And here my cousins leaned over lampshades blackened with age, their heads ringed with the deceptive halos of apparent holiness, lamenting, and sometimes half happy, when misfortune struck a disliked neighbor. Oh, then Communism was still showing its better side. But right after that it returned to its usual place, the bench of the accused. And one could have foreseen that it would be a new Jewish plot. Some laughed, someone else said a gloomy nothing, children shouted, the dog barked, the fire truck drove down the street. The generation leaving for the past drank tea. Meaning, order, and verve were elsewhere.

Remarkable energies. This cannot be reconstructed. Do you

know what predicament the historians find themselves in? Please imagine a large holiday display of fireworks. Cascades of fire in the sky, windmills, plumes, unreal chrysanthemums blooming at night, enormous and frail structures disintegrating into nothing, sudden falls and even faster, breathtaking, vertical flights of fire, as if the illuminated fingers of giants were emerging from behind the edges of invisible clouds. Even someone who does not like fireworks, who despises them, who prefers the most humble little rainbow over the most sophisticated fireworks, would not be able to walk under a purple sky with indifference.

Good. Now try to imagine that the next day the weather changes; there is an annoying, cold rain. Nothing is left of the fireworks if you don't count the sodden cardboard shells and crooked sticks—which functioned as mysterious launching pads the night before—pounded into the meadow. Someone is coming through the meadow carrying a black umbrella, and, with a condescending smile, he looks at the scraps of yesterday's orgy. This is a historian. He sees the installations, the theater of events, the same sky, the same meadow, maybe even the same people. The only thing he does not see is the electrical current, because it is invisible. And reality, my dear sir, is a combination of immobile things, that is, the meadow, sticks, cardboard shells, and energy, electricity.

I do not mean by this that Stalinism was a splendid firework. Oh no, you won't catch me saying that. No. Unless we imagine a display of fireworks in hell. Can you see it? Tribunes erected for Lucifer and his subordinates, crowds of the condemned in gray overalls. And then rockets on the low sky of hell, the hiss of violet tentacles. And boys who take advantage of the situation by selling ice cream and pretzels. No, Stalinism had nothing in common with fireworks. I needed the comparison only to show you what energy is and how difficult it is to reconstruct when it is gone.

The world of that epoch was saturated with energy. The thrill of fear, hatred, but also of ambition, envy, hope for a career. There was a lot of horror and a little pluck. It had its hierarchies. It seemed that they would last long, maybe even very long, that they would stay that way forever. Looking at a bygone era opens a completely artificial perspective; there is no thought more unnatural than a thought about destruction, about the collapse of that which actually reigns (even if it is hated!).

A historian walks into a mortuary and imagines balls, parties, carnivals. He asks the gravedigger how it was, how the princess looked, did the president stutter. Epochs die more than people, nothing remains of them. An epoch is like a blush. When it disappears, everything disappears. I have already said that some names were high voltage. Mainly fear, I agree. Except that fear, you see, does not like to show itself naked. It always pretends to be something else, like ambition, fanaticism, loyalty. Energy is everywhere, it spares no one. Ah, these so-called diaries make me laugh; intelligent and independent observers pretend to have written them then, at the moment. I wonder why these documents written on someone's knee appear only twenty-five years after the fact. A quarter of a century later.

And do you think there was a choice? That there was opposition? That there was one government theater and another, independent one? One literary monthly for socialist realists and another for independent spirits? That there were two countries, one disgraced and another decent? Two capitals? Two kings? Two languages? Two philosophies? Oh no. Do you know how it was? Those actors who had the luck to get into the theater and were talented gave everything they had, whether they were playing in some sort of propaganda play, written in Moscow, or in a play by the Romantic poet Juliusz Slowacki. They were overcome by the same energy that drove all the wheels and gears then. They wanted to be splendid actors; you don't really think that they would sabotage the theater by playing badly in A *Midsummer Night's Dream* just to get back at the regime, do you? There was a wild desire to have a career—or simply to survive. Please make a distinction between these two things.

Do you see young actors who said to themselves, "No, I will not support the Communists and their inhumane program; I will remain in the shadows, I will be a nurse, I will be an assistant driver"? Do you see them? Because I don't see them. Only those to whom God gave no talent or strength sat in the theater, in the auditorium, in the last row and looked at their talented counterparts with scorn and envy. There was ten times more envy than scorn, I can assure you. The best were on stage. It was the best who betrayed. The best recited Soviet poems. The pale faces of jealous mediocrities in the last row glimmered.

Let us take someone from that period who published a poem about Stalin—do you think that that someone anticipated your condemnation today, the outrage of a later witness? I can assure you that what he was most interested in was the opinion of those who knew something about poetry—was the poem good, was there some artistic force in it? Sure, a few people condemned those works even at the time. But an author of a poem would not have met them; he moved in different circles. Yes, he was obedient, but at the same time he wanted to write the best poem. Young, ambitious people appeared in the capital and intended to make the best use of their talents. As always.

A historian sees people from a given period as if they were mannequins steered by the spirit of history. Instead, we had headaches or were disappointed in love, or we didn't have enough money, or we were monstrously jealous of a friend, or we dreamed of a better apartment. Now one hears of captive minds, about the betrayal of humanist ideals. And toothaches? Sexual drive? Hunger? Or the desire to be best in the class, in one's generation, in a poetry group? All this was mixed, complicated. Even the so-called literary executioners, the Party trainers, knew a little about poetry. This was a mixed, not pure, substance. Coercion entered the chemical reaction along with completely spontaneous ambition.

There were too many—I return once more to this—poems about Stalin. Too many. Jot this down. One had to select. Not everyone could get into the columns of newspapers. Do you think that selling your soul was easy? It was a flea market; many were eager to do it, not everyone succeeded. There were a lot more candidates than there were places. As always. Why should it have been different? There was one world, one life. You awoke not in Stalinism, in scornful times; no, you awoke in bedclothes, in the body you knew to tears, full of needs and caprices. You awoke next to a woman you loved or next to a girl who was with you only because the other had dumped you. You were short of money. You were published and your family was proud of you. Your anti-Communist aunties were happy that their nephew wasn't just another face. Please, print him, maybe he'll be somebody when he grows up. It would be difficult to expect you to be outraged.

You ask, did I know about the torture, about people imprisoned without cause? You always ask that. You're right to do it. I knew and didn't know at the same time. You see, not long ago I read an article by one of your contemporaries, perhaps a little older than you; that author wrote that totalitarianism was death. Bitter laughter. Please note: laughter full of bitterness. What can one say so many years later when what you so learnedly call totalitarianism is gone or is at least so weakened that it is unrecognizable. Death was somewhere else. Of course, I had some idea that they were torturing, tormenting people; someone would suddenly disappear, a casual acquaintance; people whispered that he might not return, but those were only whispers and not knowledge. Some soldiers and officers served in very special units, and in return they were fed in very special cafeterias. I had some idea. And, of course, there was death; there destruction lay in wait. But I took this from the side of life. And even those soldiers probably thought more frequently about the cafeterias than about the torture.

Totalitarianism, to use your university term, is life, energy, ambition, awards, hierarchies, passions, lightning-swift advances, Napoleonic careers, enormous possibilities for young people from small towns. At the price of death. One is not allowed to talk about this. It is life severed from death. For you, anemic beings with melancholy inclinations, this system is death. But this is simply not true. Take the countless congresses, conventions, councils which took place every day without respite. Did death reign there? No, ambition—life's passion. Oh, it was a vital world.

I was certainly obsessed with ideas. Only in youth does one treat philosophy more seriously; only then does one search for an ultimate solution, a clear answer. That is why their philosophy was created almost especially for young people. Humanity in general lives without a program, an idea that now appeals to me; but then it infuriated and offended me. Even more than by ideas I was impassioned by reality. How can I express this—the world existed then. Are you able to imagine it? Do you know that the leaves in the trees rustled the same way they do now? Do you understand that the old women walking slowly down the street pulling their grocery carts behind them were beautiful girls then? You have probably spent a good many hours in the reading room of the university library studying back issues of newspapers and copying trifles and lies out of them. The fragile paper of old newspapers. You mention damagers, destroyers of culture. But we were boys. Boys ambitious as always. And perhaps you think what—that the wind was Stalinist, the water in the rivers in the summer was Stalinist, the fragrance of heather was Stalinist? Did you know that the world existed in the same royal fashion as it exists today and that what was spoiled in it was like a small worm in a large apple? Do you think, sir, that kisses were Stalinist? That the skin of girls was Stalinist?

Oh, for example, I remember, we were riding to some village in an open truck. Why? I don't know, I have forgotten. Perhaps to a meeting on collectivization. Yes. But it was June and everything was simply bursting with joy. The poplars standing at the roadside were full, full of leaves, branches, light, sap, shadow; and two steps away from me stood the girl I loved. There was a warm wind, the smell of hay in the air, a small cloud in the sky, dark junipers, meadows cut with streams, roofs of distant houses shining in the sun, fast swallows flying above us. When the truck drove through the forest, it suddenly grew cold and this coolness concealed fear, as if something had ended too soon. It was enough, however, to drive back out into the open to feel intensely happy again. We returned in the evening, slowly, and then I felt, with tremendous clarity, what twilight was. Gradually the light withdrew and there was something so gentle in that dying of the light that took hours; it seemed that entire years were passing before darkness fell, and there were so many fragrances in the air, the comic flight of bats; and voices sounded different, as if something were shifting, as if the hard covers of the world were opening, retreating. There was less and less light but more and more space, and where the houses or trees once stood there were only echoes now, dark traces, the outlines of things. She had on a green blouse, and desire was everywhere.

More took place than you are capable of understanding. It was a sensual world, and in us were senses and longing. The shortsighted, those hopeless scientists in thick glasses, judge us. The intellect is judging the senses. What is memory? That just world of your memory is inhuman. You are not allowed to make a mistake because then you arrive, the next generation, you sad researchers of bygone events.

It is true that the meeting which had been the formal reason for the June excursion was nothing for me to brag about. I know this. Those people were hurt, they were being threatened with imprisonment; then, I didn't give it a thought; today, I do, often. I am talking about something else. The world is something more than just a good or a bad deed. Only a fragment of reality is subject to ethical evaluation. Take a look at that day which has stayed in me, in my flesh, in my deepest memory. Life cannot be judged—what am I saying—even a single day cannot be judged; it is too full. Perhaps God is able to judge. One can condemn deeds but not dates. Can my love for my friends or my admiration for the majesty of the world be taken away from me only because the purpose of the trip was vile? There is no net with which to capture that day. There isn't one. What you don't understand is reality.

We do not always know how to express this, but only this is important. Put your arm on the wooden armrest of your chair, touch a cold glass. There is little to say. That which is splendid and that which is cruel can't get written. It's in us, but not in our words. Suffering is there for us to experience; it does not submit to study. There is more memory than remembrances. We have no control over the past. There are as many secrets in it as in the future. Tall poplars grew along the road, but not for me. I only saw them and admired them from a distance. The swallows were indifferent. The moon was not Stalinist.

I am guilty, yes. But I do not know the most important things. I do not know if I am a good or a bad person. You should ask my many colleagues about this; I am sure they have a definite opinion on the subject. Similarly, I have an opinion about each one of them. But I know least about myself. Can one live with the awareness that one is an evil man? Am I vainer than others, any more starved for distinctions, money, praise, prizes? I wanted to live then; I did not know that this was a period inhospitable to such an excessive ambition. Perhaps I wanted to be higher than others. This is not nice, but in other societies people like this are not censured; on the contrary, they are decorated with the Legion of Honor.

I do not know if I behaved too greedily. Was I more rapacious than others? I don't know if I was repugnant in fulfilling my desires. Whether I was a greater coward than others. Some people eat prettily, others eat in an ugly way; there is nothing one can do about that. What is more mundane than satisfying one's needs? Even in decent countries, meeting one's needs is infinitely mundane. In a tyrannical country, it changes into something revolting.

I lived with my parents in Cracow. The windows of our apartment looked out onto Planty, the park that surrounds the old town. On the walls of the buildings one could still see scraps of prewar ads and signs. The streets had already been conquered by the new system, but lilac bushes growing in yards maintained their prewar dignity and every spring—ignoring the severe exhortations to frugality—blossomed luxuriantly and arrogantly, their intoxicating fragrance wafting throughout the entire city as if it were a call to counterrevolution. One year the winter was so harsh that quiet sleighs appeared downtown. Steam rose from the horses. In our house we heated only one room. I was twenty years old, I was reading Rilke, and while I was reading the first elegy, my father was washing himself behind a thin screen, trying to reach his back in a Promethean effort to overcome the imperfection of human anatomy. And I was reading, "Beauty is only the beginning of horror." Snow fell. Sleigh bells moved from place to place quickly, as if the sleighs were nonmaterial, for they gave off no other sound. One could imagine surpliced altar boys scattered all over the city. The horses moved in great puffs of breath, as if they were at the bottom of a sea. My brother was learning to play the harmonica. The hard, frozen strokes of church bells encouraged people to go on. Peasants clamped into thick sheepskin jackets, which gave off an acrid, animal scent when the thaw came, sold firewood. They shouted in hoarse voices that spoke to closed windows, shut gates, and a city lost in timid immobility. The black branches of chestnut

trees bent under the enormous clumps of frozen snow. Sometimes the breeze would liberate one of the trees from its white
burden, and its boughs returned with relief to a normal, carefree existence, as if their freedom and youth had suddenly
been restored to them. Rooks no one liked stepped carefully
on beaten paths, rocking from side to side like a squire walking
through a meadow. Over the rooftops the sun grew larger.
Black strings of smoke climbed tentatively into the pale sky. I
understood that beauty was something real, that it touched
objects and people.

In the spring the city expanded, grew, adding sounds and
smells. Knife sharpeners wandered from yard to yard, plumes
of sparks shot out from under their fingers, and the high piercing ringing of metal rose in a sharp arc over the buildings.
Windows were wide open, damp air entered the houses mixed
with the gentle singing of birds. First the blackbirds chirped
angrily, as if to assure themselves that spring was close by, and
then, in March, they sang rapturously, endlessly, like black
women singing the blues, their recordings worth their weight
in gold. I took longer and longer walks, greedily searching for
new signs of spring. Alders stood in melting snow like ther-
mometers immersed in an ice-cold river. Church towers vanished in a distant cloud that stopped over the marketplace.
Each day the hills revealed a different line of horizon, delicate
and blue like Chinese porcelain. Enormous flocks of starlings
with iridescent wings descended upon empty fields, excited by
their return to a familiar place.

Crowds now walked the streets, children jumped across puddles. Suddenly everything became easier and closer; fragrances
ran together. Open churches hungrily sucked in great gusts of
warm air, while the stuffy smell of church candles escaped

into the street, as if the old saints, shut up within basilica walls for centuries and tended jealously and watchfully, also wanted to have a taste of March weather. The windows of offices, committees, and seminaries opened; for a moment spring was more important than the political system. The pale faces of seminarians and Party activists turned in the direction of the victorious sun. Forsythias flamed with the yellow fire of weekly praise. The first sprouts of spring greens appeared in the market—irrefutable proof of the existence of life on Earth.

I understood that the world was dual, divided, at once splendid and mundane, heavy and winged, heroic and cowardly. Beauty lives in it, but it has never moved there permanently, once and for all; beauty merely has its pied-à-terre there, like a millionaire living in the country who visits the city rarely, only to attend an opera premiere or a new exhibit of paintings, and who is quite satisfied with an elegant apartment in a building right across from the theater. I also saw the same split in me. One day I would be capable of grasping what is practically invisible, marked only with a light, nonchalant line. On other days I became a blind man; I neither saw nor understood a thing, I was insensitive to the call of reality, I moved light-years away from that sphere.

I understood that rapture was linked in some mysterious way to existence, and that the most common sounds—water running from a tap, someone's steps on the street at twilight, the quiet conversation of two old men reminiscing about the epoch before the two world wars—at this moment seemed just to play a modest supporting role to the calendar, as memory props, that all this was beautiful because it existed and because it was listened to without any hidden intentions, innocently. Someone who is really a poet can accept each sound, each image, each situation, each joy and pain; to accept means to recognize their audacious onetime presence, the presence of our brothers in existence, whether it speaks to us from a spoon that falls to the floor or from the gleaming wing of a titmouse.

I felt that this would constitute my courage, quite different from that of a soldier, judge, or politician; my courage would depend on my greeting these various voices with total simplicity, with complete attention, justly and precisely. I never thought that poetry could be something pathetic, murky, exalted. And here my defeat was greatest, for I rejected the quiet, fundamental courage whose meaning I recognized during my long walks on the outskirts of the city. That one day I began writing odes in praise of a tyrant meant that I had betrayed not just my nation, my family, and myself but also the nature of this work, this way of thinking which I myself chose.

We know well that not everyone has to be a poet. But there is this ancient truth: if a defenseless cell of reality is revealed to someone in an instant of painful illumination, then that person, chosen by fate and condemned by fate, cannot miss his calling. He notices the divine traces in the world, and that discovery marks him forever. Oh yes, he can wander for entire months or even years in various cities or countries hearing nothing, seeing nothing, as long as he doesn't give up the possibility of being healed. There is no more talk about freedom or searching in his life. Searching can pertain to only one thing: the return to the bountiful place, to a fullness of vision. This is a poet's basic loyalty. Its counterpart can be found in every other profession and calling.

I spoke about spring. The days got longer and longer. The first heat waves came as a complete surprise. No one remembers what the insistent warmth of an April day is like until it comes again, until the swollen stalks of flowers choke on their excess juices. Lemonade vendors wiped their sweaty brows; flies rose from the dead after the winter's passion; the park smelled of weeds and nettles, and their scent ended up on girls' lips and on the skin of my palms. Even shadows warmed up. Traces of winter vanished faster than wartime destruction. Like spacious train stations, baroque churches welcomed each passerby; the balance of energy shifted; churches changed into warehouses of coolness, and the wood of confessionals creaked as if the sins surrendered by generations of men and women and absorbed by its grain were trying to get out.

What is betrayal? Have you noticed, my dear sir, that as early as May or June we are already accustomed to the light of summer, to a broad sky, to air that is soft and filled with the light cotton flowers of poplars?

Do you understand the meaning of the phrase that we always use in reference to others when we say, "He is a broken man"? Usually we say that about others, but I think this about myself. I have never been able to come out from under it, that is, I have never been able to write anything on the scale of that vocation, on the scale of that revelation.

I walked the streets of Cracow stunned by the presence of walls, houses, and wooden gates, which concealed gardens and orchards; the melting snow uncovered the harsh surface of things, the infinitely complex skin of the world, and it seemed to me that scales fell away from my eyes, that I was seeing everything for the first time. It is enough to look carefully to see beauty. The black boughs of chestnut trees plastered with large, damp buds. A seventeen-year-old carpenter's apprentice—his hair full of wood dust—sits on the curb and eats a thick slice of bread.

What did I accomplish? A few articles. Maybe four decent poems, written later. Translations of English poets. A book about the poetry and life of Keats. One novel—so-so. A bad marriage. In later years, a few signatures on dissident manifestos. An interview for *Le Monde*. That's all that was left of that revelation. For an instant I was the owner of the world; I possessed the inaccessible gardens and the underground corridors. I was afraid that if I really wanted them to, the towers of the cathedral would come crashing to the ground. If only I had said the word. When I shut my eyes, darkness covered the earth. And then nothing. Nothing.

Pardon me, what did you say? I don't understand. Would you be kind enough to repeat what you said? What? You are trying to cheer me up? Amazing. You dare to cheer me up? You think that the books published after 1956 were very important? Important! Customs agents at the border and police officers at intersections are important. My poems. You say they meant a lot to you. Especially some of them. You say that I rehabilitated myself through my later actions, that I proved my devotion and courage. I redeemed the mistakes of my youth and I deserve Christian forgiveness.

This is comical. After all, you came to torment me, to get my admission of guilt. Please, here it is, you've got it. You have been sent here, unwittingly perhaps, by public opinion; by anonymous readers, engineers, attorneys, teachers; by recognized provincial geniuses; by students of Polish, German, and Romance literatures. Public opinion, greedy for revenge, sent you to me, as did decent intellectuals who, thanks to their blissful anonymity, can level their anger at me because their universal cowardice left no traces. The fact that they voted for years for the hated ruler and signed every appeal stuck under their noses, whether or not it demanded war, peace, or an execution; ratified every declaration, every invective; appeared at every Party meeting, condemning whomever they were told to condemn, the London government or the government of Australia, the Trotskyites or the Jews, the inhabitants of Mars or of Paris; approved of everything that happened in their town and country, with their worried silence under cover of virtuous pettiness, does not seem to count now; they have forgotten it. They demand to settle accounts only with me. They themselves were careful, signed their names illegibly, and quickly returned to cozy apartments; they were caught doing nothing wrong; and they have happily forgotten about their thoughts and shrugs. And you, a messenger from that gray and dishonest human mass, having accomplished what you had set out to do from the beginning, that is, my confession, begin to cheer me up.

You talk about my freedom, about the freedom of every man. You say that I was able to extricate myself from the trap. What can you possibly know about my freedom? What can you possibly know about the traps that lay in wait for me? You want to take away even my betrayal. You want to take away my defeat, take it from me and put it in your museum of civic virtues. Why, I told you a moment ago that there is no freedom from the moment you notice the internal image of the world. This is the source of the misunderstanding. You are still convinced that my betrayal took place in the external world, in a May Day parade, at a Party meeting, or in an article printed by a newspaper in the capital. This is untrue. But it all happened differently, quietly, furtively—I don't know—perhaps during a walk along the Vistula, or in my room, in a moment of doubt, in a moment when I rejected what I saw, when I replaced tiny distinct things having sharp outlines with large amounts, gigantic lenses, vague and triumphant formulas, the names of people I had never met and who later turned out to be criminals. I rejected the simplest things to take the side of tumult, force, lies.

How can I say this differently? I think that my youthful experiences taught me a lesson: I was supposed to have been a magnifying glass for seemingly insignificant observations; I was supposed to have magnified what was quiet, in order for it to attain its due measure. That which is most essential in us and in objects is not immediately apparent. Because of a certain type of commercial ontological injustice in the everyday perception, the qualities that stand out are those that have to do with the actual business transaction, with the use we make of ourselves and things. I was supposed to remedy this injustice and return meaning to the hidden, royal qualities.

This is what I was called to do. In this way I was supposed to make myself and my contemporaries aware that we live in a real reality, full of juices, colors, and meaning; and if it seems gray to us and common as a dollar bill too long in circulation, then the fault is ours, on the side of our weariness, our inattention, our grayness.

Meanwhile, everything went differently. Do you know what I turned into! I turned into a vile, diminishing glass. Instead of beginning with the truth being damaged by trivial everydayness, instead of helping it, honoring it, I inverted the order of things and turned to powers, to well-known and generally applauded slogans, and I diminished them so that they could fit into a poem. In addition, these powers turned out to be false. Do you understand? False. Even if they had been more decent than they were, even if they could have been defended,

I was a traitor nevertheless, at least in my own eyes; not of you or that which you call society but of my own solitude.

Do you know who I could have been? Do you know with what clarity I saw things and people, flowers emerging from sealed buds, the velvet power of death, the wild force of conflicts embedded in every life? I was not created to be the author of an idyll; my revelation spoke to me also about destruction, about death. I looked calmly at people and trees because their existence was circled with the clear contour of nothingness, and each of the blackbirds I admired sang about destruction, joyously, without regret. Do you know what I could have done, do you have any idea about the taste of works I did not write? If I had stayed there, in that small town, if I had known then that I needed nothing more except to quietly walk the same streets and look always at the same people as they age, look at their goodness and baseness and at night write down what I saw, what I understood . . . If only I had known this. You don't even know what you can forgive me for. We don't understand one another. You forgive me my unconscious sin, my mistake, my citizen's transgression. Which I do regret, that is true. But you have never noticed the real betrayal, my betrayal of the world, not its citizens. Is vanity speaking through me? Why, here I am, an old and mediocre writer, but I could have been a Petrarch. I saw the fire. I feel sorry not just for myself but for the world, which lost a song. I feel sorry for the world.

I feel sorry for you: you didn't recognize my vision. You are poorer for my nonexistent work. And that is why you are not in a state to appreciate the dimensions of my betrayal. Only —and this is impossible—if my works had come into being and not come into being at the same time, if they had been accessible and nonexistent, if you could compare what I wrote with what I did not get done, only then would you have some notion of my betrayal. I saw a town, a medieval town with narrow streets and many churches, slowly conquered by invaders. The city was under siege, but in such a way that the conquerors had long been within the city walls; the battles took place in apartments, in stairwells. Nuns in brown habits walked down the tree-lined lanes of Planty Park and met with groups of young agitators whose opinion was to destroy the old world. But there was so much of the old world in town! Almost everything was old: walls, trees, chapels, people. The old bishop in the cathedral.

This was one siege; the other assailant was the seasons, snow, wind, darkness, rain, time. Hungry stars appeared at night in the heavens. I walked to the cemetery and saw old women in black crying over every dead person, joining every funeral procession. A priest walked behind the coffin. Priests gave the impression of being satisfied persons, the cheerful functionaries of a large insurance company. One neighborhood was empty and ruined: the one in which Jews had lived. The rain rinsed the Hebrew signs from the walls of the synagogue. Feral cats and dogs wandered all over Kazimierz; there were no Jews. A willow with thin leaves cried every spring. In July orphaned houses were heated and lazy, just like the apartment houses downtown. No one remembered the Jews; even their houses were indifferent. New threats came, new posters spoke from kiosks, glue served any ruler who came along.

I saw fire. I saw how death encircled my city. There were order and peace in some of the apartments; the wall clocks did not hurry at all, the pendulums dozed. Chocolates lay in silver baskets. Rugs lay on the floor like bandages. But in other rooms lived refugees from Warsaw. Elsewhere in a crowded apartment one could find the family of a prince, which not too long ago had ruled over a thousand hectares of land. Now the wardrobe of ash had to substitute for the old palace, and the suitcases piled on top of it brought back memories of travels to Biarritz.

The caretakers followed every step of the prince and princess and their children. Honorable attorneys with powdered faces left for work in the morning. I knew that it would be impossible to save anyone. At night an owl read the names of the condemned, indistinctly, leaving hope in the hearts of the remaining victims. More and more inhabitants of the city crossed the threshold of the palace that served as Party headquarters. Altar boys smoked cigarettes while waiting for the priest. Avalanches of snow fell from the rooftops.

Sometimes I sat on a bench and watched the crowds moving before me, flowing like swollen creeks in spring. Women in flowered scarves carried loaves of bread. Young men walked with a military gait and middle-aged men marched just as energetically; these were soldiers dressed in civilian clothes, soldiers from various armies who had thrown jackets and coats over their shoulders but who could not change their gait, could not give up the pleasure of marching. Secret armies walked the streets, easy to detect. Other men walked a more feline step, looking around curiously; in them one felt a masquerade—these were secret-police functionaries whose job it was to track down the secret army. Among the soldiers and police were also priests in ordinary civilian garments. Women in colored dresses desperately tried to maintain at least some of the elements of Parisian fashion—a ribbon, a hat, or, if nothing else, a triumphant, victorious smile. Only the bent-over old people did not pretend anymore; they breathed greedily, drawing April air into their lungs.

Do you see that town in the spring, ordinary and quiet from all appearances, a city not only burned by envy and suspicion, not only destroyed by the passage of time, like all the cities of the world, but—as if this were not enough—also consumed by a furious though concealed civil war? Do you see the old noblemen with ruddy faces? And right next to them village boys with unformed features, soft noses, and hard chins, who are the proponents of the new philosophy, servants of utopia, cunning Bolshevik commissars. Do you see the aristocrats who walk about the cramped rooms of their delegated apartments —they who not long ago walked the broad fields of the Ukraine? And the hawk of time circling overhead? The two destructions. That was my subject. I knew each street intimately. My aunts took me to their friends' homes, thanks to which I got to know the apartments of the usurped princes and the modest dukes from the provinces—people who returned from Siberia and could never shake anyone's hand properly, because they had frostbitten fingers—and refugees from the Warsaw Uprising, fugitives from Lvov or Wilno, a few survivors of Auschwitz. I looked at them with tenderness—I saw in them the heroes of my future books. And those books don't exist; the fire sputtered, and only the smoke wrote the letters of my poems and stories in the sky.

This is my betrayal. Silence. I did not talk about what only I could explain. And don't think that anyone else living in those years in the same town could have done it for me. No one saw the same city, the same cruel war; no one heard the same birds; no one tried to taste the same handful of snow. No one passed by the gate of the prison on Montelupie Street at the same moment when I was there and saw the families of prisoners waiting patiently in the heat to see a father or brother. No one saw the same laughing priests playing soccer on the field in Debniki under a dark cloud full of hail.

You forgive me. Thanks a lot. It is easy to fall afoul of someone like you, and it is just as easy to receive absolution. But I do not accept it. Oh yes, one can erase guilt with declarations, by being in the opposition, with angry works aimed at yesterday's protectors. You know, of course, that I did all that, many times, risking a little but not all that much. And it is good this way; this is the most appropriate way to consume a mistake. After all, fertilizer is made of shit. No, I can't cancel the entire second half of my life, what would I have left then?

A person loses his fortune just once. That strange transformation happens only once: when the proud blue magnifying glass with which one can set a haystack on fire or read the writing on a postage stamp a century old becomes a servile diminishing glass.

It seems that I am boring you, young man. Oh, I see that you are taking a photocopy of some sort of text out of your briefcase. A copy of my article? Yes, an article written by me in which year? In 1951. Do I remember what the text was about? Just a minute, wait, let me think back. Oh yes, I remember. It was a hideous thing. In it I turn against bourgeois culture and suggest—no, I shout, scream hysterically—that T. S. Eliot is really an agent of American intelligence.

Please listen carefully. And jot it all down. That's how it was. In 1951 I worked for this . . . magazine. I left Cracow and lived in Warsaw. Listen carefully. New instructions came. The class struggle in literature was supposed to be intensified. Our magazine was accused of being lax in condemning the "kulaks of literature." The editor in chief called me into his office. Each of us was afraid of the other. I feared him because I knew that he had close ties with the police, and he assumed I had friends there. (He was wrong.) I went in and sat down in the chair across from the desk. He said: "There are new directives, we have to accelerate the struggle. You will write an article and savage K." You know K., the famous poet. At that time K. was a sickly old man. I had seen him a few times at literary meetings. I admired some of his poems, and I liked his beautiful, tormented face.

I asked the editor if K.'s name was mentioned in the instructions, or whether he had taken it upon himself to choose the victim. (I did not use those words.) "No," he said, "these things were not said." He repeated: "Write about K.'s deviant work; treat this as a Party assignment."

And then I answered in a poker tone—as if I knew about something that had not yet reached his ears.

"I will write a scathing attack," I said, "scathing. But it will be better for us both if it is not an attack on K."

He was silent for a long time. He was silent as if he were a tragic hero. He weighed his choices like Corneille's Cid. His forehead became a screen for thoughts and worries. He did not have a high forehead, but please remember that the hirsute foreheads of dogs and cats furrow in the same way. Whoever has a scrap of forehead announces his worries this way. He thought. The future was uncertain. The leaders were changing and at certain moments forgot about their subordinates. Then again, sometimes it turned out that people who looked defenseless and doomed had powerful protectors who looked after them very effectively, spurred by their own interests or simply out of a high-minded caprice. He was silent. The rain beat rhythmically on the windowsill like verses recited by a Greek chorus.

Finally he said, "You may leave; tomorrow I'd like to have that text."

I understood that K. would be able to survive this assault. I wrote a rabid article attacking T. S. Eliot.

As you can figure out, T. S. Eliot never found out that a certain fledgling Polish poet viciously attacked him. K., however, lived for another fifteen years and died a universally respected writer.

You see, articles like that could kill if they struck old, sickly people or people who were simply weak and sensitive, morally isolated. But I know that you appreciate only humanistic values; you despise my article because in it I destroy the ideals of Western culture. I despise that text, too; yet it conceals one of the most heroic acts of my life (which doesn't mean much). Compared to my boss's moment of silence, my signing a few dissident manifestos loses all significance.

You reason in absolute categories. But at that time people lived differently: making constant choices, in relations, in comparisons. One lived between possibilities. The choices were not too great, but that's another issue. As you see, I could choose between murder and baseness. Between abstract vilification aimed at ideas—but with the knowledge that some fifteen-year-old boy, sensitive as I was at his age, might read that article and would really think that the poets in the West were spies—and a concrete murder. A modest choice, it is true. And you don't have to believe me—the alternative I dismissed does not exist, there is no trace of evidence that I wanted to save K.'s life. And he never found out that I saved his life, so to speak. A few years later I went up to him, introduced myself, and wanted to express my admiration for his work, but he would not shake my hand. He did not shake hands with Stalinists.

On another occasion—please do not write this down—I will tell you something that did not happen, that did not exist. There was a very important meeting taking place during the course of which those present were to determine the tasks of literature in the coming years. Surely you understand: the production of wheat and cement was planned, and so one also had to anticipate the development of literary forms. The big shots came to this one: the economists of poetry, the designers of prose, the architects of the essay. I was invited, but, of course, I did not figure in the carefully chosen list of speakers. I say this, to remind you of the historical proportions. In this elite group I counted only as a young, beginning poet; I could not appear out of nowhere to speak before the moral leaders of the nation.

The meeting was convened. The Party, production, man, the future, decadence. I sat in one of the front rows among unfamiliar delegates from the provinces; they were so frightened they dared not swallow. I was thinking about other things, but occasional fragments of speeches, individual words, invective, and especially names reached my ears. I remember now that I had on a new suit and I tried to sit so I wouldn't crease my pants. The sun was shining at an angle; it must have been winter.

Here, in this world, in these surroundings, there were practically no sensations—fragrances, images, impressions; there was no wind, temperature; not a branch moved; the roofs did not shine in the sun; flakes of soot did not whirl dangerously, like black hosts, about the heads of passersby; flowers stood in vases like hostages, tulips with smooth skin and slender stems. After the period of Cracow walks and moments, when my skin opened entirely to warm breezes and the fragrance of distant jasmine, I felt as if I had been transplanted into another geometry in Warsaw. The wide streets, parks in which young trees had just been planted; the conference halls, glasses of water on the tables, white sheets of paper, whispers, anxious smiles, eyeglasses like screens protecting wearers from an excess of light; finally, numbers—numbers and statistics concealing objects were suddenly appearing everywhere—ideas, slogans.

And suddenly something happened. Yes, in such a great hall, in me, not at the conference. Nothing could happen there. You have no idea of the precision with which these kinds of gatherings were prepared. You know what happened? I remembered a few lines from a Boleslaw Lesmian poem. Do you recall:

> At dusk your faded leaf turns rosy . . .
> A wagon clatters outside the window.
> Perhaps it is a dream, my dream
> Driving off into an evil darkness—

A voice in me recited these four lines. And I immediately regained my sight. And sense of humor. I burst out laughing, drawing to myself the suspicious glances of the entire gathering. The contrast between the inflated paper someone was laboriously reading from index cards and those light, fleeting words (A wagon clatters outside the window. / Perhaps it is a dream, my dream / Driving off into an evil darkness) was unbearable. The thought flitted through my mind that poetry cannot be the property of a nation, because that is how it is then taken over by the state. Poetry belongs to no one. "At dusk your faded leaf turns rosy . . ." and right next to it the police consider the tasks standing before literature in the transitional period. I laughed, knowing well that I was burying my chances for a career; from that moment on I was known as the "one who did not honor the solemnity of a Party conference." I laughed desperately because I suddenly realized with an enormous, emphatic, and stark clarity that I would never really belong to this solemn congregation, that—I don't know if you will understand this—in a certain sense my betrayal had never existed, because I had not immersed myself in this obedient, silent mass. I was different, completely different; even if I had tried harder, I would never have attained the virtues demanded by my employers. I was lost once and for all; moments of illumination are cunning, they cut us off from our brothers and sisters. Even then, in Cracow, when I was following the armies and the police, walking the streets, and watching the war survivors, I felt as if I were leaving them, that our relations were not as they should be, because I was looking *at* them. And that looking was fatal; he who once begins to look, instead of identifying with, half worrying with, half experiencing with, half working with, will never be an accepted or tolerated participant in the great herd.

So I laughed, trying ungracefully to conceal my amusement, as if I had only sneezed or had a coughing fit; I applied a hankie to my lips and cheeks; I laughed like a dead man, desperately, hellishly, because I understood that all was for naught, I could not even be a decent traitor, I had lost one set of friends and would never gain another. The only thing I knew how to do was betray myself; in this I was without peer. And it's happening again; my conversation with you can only confirm my thesis.

I giggled, shook with laughter—quick, nervous laughter. And nothing happened, nothing changed. And later? You're right, later I returned to my senses. You are right, I began to function normally, like others. Nothing had happened; yes, I agree with you completely; I returned to my daily routine.

A hall full of wolves. Had that been a dream? And in that crowd someone who at least for a moment was true to his vision. Don't you agree that poetry is a weak weapon? And don't you think that it is cruel to demand superhuman resilience from a poet, to surround him with a pack of wolves?

Is it possible that that reality has transformed itself over the years into a nightmare? How did that happen? Instead of blood pulsing in its veins, instead of animal warmth, instead of love—a nightmare. The faces have changed into wolf snouts, the faces of my generation have changed into my own face, into wolf hair growing on the palms of these people. This is unjust. The wolf smell on my hands. It is unfair to forget about all the distinctions, about the fact that many people then were guided by noble intentions.

And you dare say that I was a Stalinist! How can one demand that a defenseless boy oppose the entire epoch? Do you think, perhaps, that I did not have an immortal soul? That I was an idiot who did not know Lesmian? Who had not read and had not thought about Rilke? My dear sir, people who were much older than I, men whom I considered experienced intellectuals, who were authorities for me, accepted the new faith. They did not share their doubts with me. If they shared anything at all, it was enthusiasm. Do you have any idea at all about how frail poetry can be? Is poetry surrounded by thick walls and towers to defend itself? What does it have that is made of marble, steel, lead?

And on the other side—they, their might, their palaces,

their tanks, their talismans. The crowds open gently before them. It seemed that only they commanded the sun to rise from under the mists in the morning, and in the evening they asked it to be so kind as to sink again into an ocean of darkness. They, giants. Untouchables. Do you know how difficult it was getting permission to talk to one of them? They rarely showed themselves, and crossed public squares with a rapid, energetic step; the bayonets of honor guards flashed for them, cannons boomed. Zeus the Thundermaker appeared, kindly greeted his gathered subordinates, and again disappeared into the clouds. He got on and off planes, and vanished into the depths of a palace. Wasn't poetry actually on his side? Why was the theater reformed in the twentieth century if not for them, and whom did the new music serve? Why were film and the news chronicle invented? Everything was for them, for the evil, capricious gods. And what happened to them? They turned into powerless old men walking with canes, into old geezers, retirees, idiots. And the few sentences written on the sly by an independent philosopher—because there were these—now have greater force than those tanks and bayonets; and even to someone very young it could seem that this wise man ruled the world even then, this oppressed philosopher, who survived owing only to a miracle. The good and evil dream swallowed us all.

Now it seems impossible to believe in an absurdity, in impossible forecasts. My mind rebels at the thought now. No, I could not believe in absurd things, in a black sun, in hot ice, in singing crows, in devout snakes.

Who was I? An immortal soul stuffed into a cramped body, a cramped epoch. Every rare moment of light liberated joy and courage in me, as if the air of freedom had torn into me with a wild, overwhelming energy. I looked with amazement at myself, at the calendar; I listened to my voice in astonishment.

Life is betrayal. Each person who has an immortal soul and has accepted life is a traitor. There is no form of life which could satisfy the postulates of immortality. There isn't any. To live means to betray what is most valuable in ourselves. Love betrays love because it has to be worse than daydreams, than fantasies of love. Heroes are empty and geniuses lazy. Rulers—even the best of them—turn into monsters. Priests are full of arrogance. Even murderers look for applause. Friedrich Hebbel had this to say about suicides: he who can shoot himself will not hang himself. Merchants cheat on the scales, and wise men in their arguments. Poets are sunk in despair even though they proclaim joy. And do you know the hierarchy obligating beggars? Beautiful women paint their faces. Pastors torment their own children. Bankers steal gold. To live is to betray, to be below value, below expectations.

How much patience it takes to bear the slow duration of life. The small eternities in which we bathe like sparrows in puddles do not add up. Someone drinks cocoa from a porcelain cup, and two hundred yards away an innocent man perishes. And the comicality of dates. Each day wants to have its own number. So many roles to play. Someone has to be the sergeant, someone the butcher. Why exactly do you hate me? The world is dual, always torn. Vile, even there in the most peaceful countries. Don't you know who the terror of everyone's lives was then? To the degree that compared with him I was a boy scout who got lost in the woods on a Sunday outing. That epoch exists only in reports, in comparisons. If you don't grasp that, you will understand nothing. Nothing at all. You must put me next to . . . that man. Coins from

Roman times were not alone in the world; greedy fingers grabbed and turned them over. Clasps from the neolithic were not alone.

There is no guarantee. Do you think that one could eliminate the very possibility of betrayal? Regulate, determine, foresee everything that will happen? One can deny oneself everywhere, even in the most civilized society. There are no guarantees. One can hurt oneself and others everywhere. If you suspect that some political system will save your soul, that it will give you a lifetime guarantee of infallibility—if you believe this, then you are repeating my mistake from bygone days, except that now it has a different costume: you believe too much in systems.

You will make mistakes; please get ready. Different mistakes than I made, certainly—perhaps more to the right; we cannot know yet. You appear a little too certain of yourself. I am allowed to diminish my attainments and I am allowed to push away your forgiving palm, but you should have a careful look at my books, which I disdain. I am allowed to laugh at myself, to make public the tragically unsuccessful account of my life. I do this from within, I burn myself up with the flame of maximum expectations. That is my affair. But I realize that my life seen from the outside is not a total failure. Yes, there was that period, but even then I was not just a common cheat; at that time my hope was the hope of the best European minds. And later—please tell me who more than I and my friends brought about the ultimate unmasking of the sinner, attacked the belief in nothingness, the illusion of perfection. So a little more respect is in order, young man. And historical imagination; a knowledge of the facts—even a perfect knowledge— is not enough.

In summer the leaves of chestnuts became enormous, and the gardens—lush as jungles and hidden by tenement walls —suffocated from lack of air. All the windows were open; someone sang an aria from *Carmen*, a dog barked lazily somewhere, people clinked knives and forks on their plates. After dinner the city dozed for a moment, life was sleepy and warm, wasps hovered over tables, cats stretched. Only a warm rain woke me from my drowsiness. I ran out into the street and felt the fresh smell of osiers, as if the rain had sprinkled river meadows whose chemistry I knew from vacations. I ran out into the street because I was afraid that I would lose, once and for all, something incredibly important: the damp, tropical afternoon, flowing through downtown Cracow from east to west like a slow-moving, stray zeppelin. Drops of rain spattered onto thirsty leaves; they struck the thick roofs of foliage and joined with particles of dust, as if they were ashamed of their unblemished cleanliness.

Oh, I see another clipping emerging from your capacious bag. How meticulously you have orchestrated this, my dear sir. What article is that? Whom am I attacking there, Homer himself? No. That is something else. I was afraid of that. I believed you would not find that text. I myself destroyed the same volume in the National Library. And in the Jagiellonian library. It seemed to me that not a trace existed, at least in the more important libraries. No, I have no explanation. Yes, that man committed suicide. A violent campaign was unleashed against him. How should I know? He stepped on the toes of one of the gods. I did not know him; it just turned out that I never had the chance to meet him. I said already that one had to choose constantly; sometimes the compromises were extraordinarily painful. All together there were about eleven or twelve articles written against him; all repugnant, ruthless. I once thought that I was one-eleventh or one-twelfth of a murderer. His wife left him at about the same time—he had very serious personal problems. Can one ever know why someone commits suicide? If there is some mystery in the world, then it has to do with that question. Did I think about his final hours? Please, let's not exaggerate; that would be crude sentimentality. And many years too late. At night it is so quiet. All the night animals are discreet. Owls, moths, bats—those are your witnesses. No one else saw it. Why did I do that? I repeat, I didn't know him. One had to sacrifice one for the other.

What? That was your father? How so? Why, you have a different last name. Your mother's maiden name. So that was your father. I could not have known. How could I have known? Those were difficult times. To save one person was already a great deal. I do not remember. You should go now. Please don't forget your briefcase. Please go now. No, the door is on the left. The elevator is out of order.

A Small Nation Writes
a Letter to God

Most Venerable Lord:

We are writing to You in the following matter. We are writing to You clumsily because those who could compose a really beautiful letter, poem, or article cannot do so, because they are no longer alive. They died in tragic circumstances, weakened and silenced, even though You had created them to speak. There are, however, those who are alive but won't say a word. Why? Some are afraid, very afraid. Their calves and knees, palms and thoughts tremble. Some were unable to get the appropriate education or, in the face of enormous difficulties or in fear of the deceit that could creep into their words, decided to strangle the voice of their vocation and occupy themselves with something else, one of many noble but mute activities. And that is how some have become cobblers, others assemble model airplanes, and still others take care of the books for a fur or milk cooperative. Someone else is a taxi driver, another sells tickets at a theater, yet another becomes a gardener. Many left for abroad (oh, how lucky we still have an abroad).

It all began with the trains. Ah, why were the steam engine, locomotives, and railroads ever invented? Why? Were they necessary? Weren't horse-drawn coaches enough? Couldn't people walk, spending the night in haystacks, drinking water from springs? Isn't the horse a perfect, strong, and patient creature? Our painters liked to portray horses in motion or resting. The first railway lines could have appeared idyllic; small stations, gaslights, stationmaster in a freshly pressed uniform, mustached cashiers, portraits of drowsy czars. But there were also many observant witnesses. Turner's famous painting depicting a speeding train conceals both rapture and terror. No one could have foreseen the most important thing. At that time, no one could have guessed the purpose to which trains would be put, or what their chief, though still hidden, fate would be. Trains serve to deport small nations. It is difficult to transport nations in coaches. An entire nation could not have fit into the cart which transported Marie Antoinette to the guillotine. Kibitkas could hold only a handful of frostbitten philomaths. But trains! Freight cars or cattle cars are excellent for deporting enormous masses of people.

And that is indeed what happened. The steam engine revealed all its secret qualities relatively recently. It is possible that we are not a very small nation. But one could reverse that definition: the nation that fits into a freight car is small and weak. It suffocates for lack of air. We will spare You the details. Tears, howls, hatred, fights, and, sometimes, a frail gesture of compassion. Life in a freight car should not be described.

Did these journeys last long? Oh yes, long, because the trains plied enormous distances. Sometimes they waited in front of semaphores, allowing military transports to go first. Animal screams broke the silence. But we promised You no details. We clamp our lips shut and we dull the nib.

Sometimes the journey lasted a week. Or more. The people were jammed in. Crushed. Bone on bone, shoulder to shoulder, in an unwanted embrace. Well, one could think, this was the dream come true of many a nationalist: the nation in a concentrated form, dense, endowed with one will, body on body, skull to skull, the end of capricious individualism.

It is indescribable. Perhaps You saw what was taking place. Perhaps in the bright sun of an August afternoon You noticed the red roofs moving slowly along the length of the train. Perhaps You caught the scrap of a stifled moan. Perhaps You noticed a naked shoulder protruding from the car. If the wavy, heated air did not hide the train from Your eyes. Light, translucent mists gathered over the fields, harvesters ate their dinners under a broad linden tree growing in the fencerow. It was so hot that hawks fell asleep in flight. And only a brown train patiently cut a shallow furrow through the heat. Rivers steamed. Creeks stopped in their tracks. Sap melted like a lump of snow. There was no mercy anywhere. Sometimes someone brought a little water to the station. What was this ill-formed, lazy train when compared to the beauty of a rustling wood? Thirsty snakes drank from puddles. Hurriedly buttoning their uniforms, sleepy stationmasters ran onto the platforms of small stations.

Perhaps You saw the rust-colored train, dragging itself along with the other, more important, privileged transports. In that train was our nation.

Silence for miles around. It doesn't matter whether it was August or January, the silence of frost or heat. Perhaps there was snow. A fox runs on a frozen pond. And that same train is still en route. Perhaps You saw it, although dusk comes early in the winter, and sometimes the wind causes snow flurries and then you can't see anything.

There is no season of the year that is right for people locked in freight cars. And there is no philosopher who could remain a philosopher in a freight car. Doctors stop being doctors, engineers forget they were once engineers. Midwives are no longer midwives. Carpenters change into former carpenters. Doormen stop being doormen. Informers no longer inform. Children stop being children.

Then, finally, everyone disembarks. This word, *disembark*, is inappropriate, for it harks back to a time when people took trains to May Day picnics. It is always some season of the year, and the survivors of the journey look around. They cannot look for too long, because on the ramp are soldiers of the great nation standing astride, and they gladly shoot or at least push the former philosophers and carpenters with their rifle butts.

Where are we? No one knows. Even You seem to have no idea where the train has stopped. What do names mean to You? Foxes and hares run everywhere, and everywhere there are spiders and nettles.

But You do probably know what happens next. Surely, You have read about it. So many books have appeared on the subject. Some enter rooms they never leave. Others stay in the frozen forest and build tent cities, like adult scouts.

After a few or a few dozen years some of them return. They are wearing denim clothes. They look carefully in all directions. Asked about what they went through, what happened to them, they do not reply. They hold their tongues, stubbornly looking up somewhere in the sky, as if they saw in it some other, crooked star. They hold their tongues. Sometimes one of them says, "It was cold." They pick up the bread crusts and hide them under the mattress. They stroll around their native city. They walk its familiar streets. Sometimes they end up in other cities. Luckily all cities are a little similar, especially if one compares them to the steppe, to the forest, and to the slow, stifling train. So that sometimes they do not realize that they have returned to a place different from the one from which they were taken, or they attach less importance to the place than we presume.

With what tenderness they look at the unassuming building of the municipal theater! How hungrily they look at an old poplar growing near the railway depot. They enter a library, ask if they can get a card again, and stroke the spines of books on the shelves. They lie on the grass and look at the clouds. They sit on the banks of the river and watch the whirlpools spin on the surface of the water, like the braids of drowned girls. In the evenings they sit in an armchair and say nothing. They eat slowly, attentively, taking a long time, as if it were not supper but the text of a medieval philosophical tract. They are lost in thought, like statues. In their presence one cannot throw out stale bread, mildewed jam, even a small carrot. They collect refuse, jars, and packaging; they are ready in an instant for a new war, a new deportation. Ah, they are not alive. Looking is all that they know how to do. They see better than others, more clearly. When the sun sets, they approach the enormous pools of shadow lying quietly on the asphalt and look at them as if they were unmoving, nice animals.

At the seaside they do not undress at all and they do not run into the water. They stay on the sand, at the edges of the beach, in their heavy, warm clothes, in their wool coats, and, as always, they look, they look greedily. Children make fun of them. They are always cold, and they always bundle themselves up in their coats or plaid blankets, even in July or August.

Even the sea is too small for them. They are not alive. Music does not interest them. They become a burden to their families. Someone who has come back is a real misfortune for an upright, hardworking family. What can we say about family if the ocean feels uneasy in the glare of that pitiful look. Even the linden trees and chestnuts seem to be embarrassed by their green, fragrant fullness.

Write your memoirs, their intelligent friends advise them. But how is one to write a memoir if it is impossible to describe? If you pushed someone away from a meal and because of that survived the winter, can you say that? Can you remember it? They deported our nation, and the look returned.

But it could also happen that those who return—if they are still young and strong enough—feel terrific, great. They are energetic. They sing, hum joyful songs brought back from exile. Except that they sing in a foreign tongue. As You see, all are dead, even those who could complain superficially about an excess of vitality.

You want to know in what language they sing those lively songs? Ah yes, we always suspected that You were not informed about everything. Surrounded by flatterers. They don't tell You about the cruel things. The reports You get are false. The statistics unreal. The evaluations tendentious. But, of course, You can imagine what language those songs are sung in.

What is it we are asking for? Allow us to endure. Allow us to keep our language and our songs. Allow us to live along the banks of our rivers, on the hills which You have given us, in our small towns, under trees which You planted on our land. Allow us to listen to whispering grasses and leaves in the evening.

Allow us not to be too pious. Our piety must irritate You,

and the ostentation of our prayers, the arrogance of our enormous pilgrimages, which move along the country like mobile forests. You are probably wondering why we consider ourselves the chosen nation, the best, the most experienced. It probably hurts You that we sneer at other nations, convinced that no one has suffered as much as we, and so long, and with such dignity, without any hope. The arrogance which grows out of misfortune can exceed even the conceit of a nouveau riche. Lamentation can change into triumphant song. The shoes of a poor man sometimes shine more brightly in the sun than the slippers of a princess. Oh, allow us to maintain modesty and measure in suffering. O Great Ironist, You, who next to majestic eagles created cheery and good-natured sparrows as well, allow us to laugh at ourselves; do not take away our sober gaze, our realistic judgment. That which is small becomes large. But greatness remains itself, unthreatened. Defeat is the inspiration of poets, and common men too can be cheered by the memory of past moments, battles, or even cool evenings by the fire, when in serene silence it seemed that reticent, male friendship appeared. Fair weather. At night, rain falls and one hears the curses of thunder. In the morning only puddles mark the storm's trail.

Someone is a taxi driver, someone else sells theater tickets, and yet someone else becomes a gardener. Many have left to go abroad. Some are afraid, others are brave, as bold as Athenian warriors, or like David. In the evening at one table sit both sparrows and eagles. The eagles are ashamed of their long wings. Someone shares adventures. We will win, explodes a shout as bright as holiday fireworks. And the silence is even deeper now when one has to take a breath, refill the glasses, wipe one's lips with a linen napkin, disappear into the darkness of a village night, where haystacks grow and where one hears branches of beech snap under the paws of invisible predators. Someone is walking through the forest on a narrow path; the light of the lantern stops at the oak leaves; the pale, yellow spots are unable to conquer the darkness.

Others perished in ruins of a great city, in the courtyards of tenements, at intersections, under an avalanche of bricks. As far as varieties of death go, we could publish an illustrated catalog. The dust of bricks demolished by a bomb or an execution at dawn, when the first rooster crows and when you are overwhelmed by the terrible regret that you are only a man and do not know whom the hoarse crowing of the rooster will awaken.

And then the hungry look of those who came back. Their slow march, cautious movements, their silence when others give fiery speeches or brilliant toasts, a silence that expresses one desire: to die in their own beds, in their childhood homes, under a window from which there is a view onto spacious meadows and purple hills, marked with the bronze monuments of trees.

Dusk falls, night comes, and then the bright flashes of lightning illuminate my figure, and You know that it is not the whole nation that is writing this letter but just me, a solitary and mortal scribe who is bent over on an old church pew left by someone in the woodshed. You see me, You must see me—my matted gray hair, my fingers wrapped around a pen, and the wrinkled notebook in which I have been writing letters to You, long or short, full of bitterness and insults, or cunning flattery, letters, applications, manifestos, pleas, constitutional drafts, laments, litanies, protests. It is I; You must recognize my slanted handwriting, the long blades of my commas, my exclamation points shooting holes in paper like rifle bullets, the hieroglyphs of my never-ending, art-nouveau question marks, the blows of my ellipses, the bloody blots of ink that remain when ripe drops of rain fall from my leaky roof. It is I, Your stubborn correspondent, oh, certainly deprived of the elegance and the calculating dignity of the Egyptian writer who reigned in the very center of the economic tumult of harvest and, showing off his slightly mysterious art, calmly counted the measures of wheat and heads of cattle given to the pharaoh. It is I; You must remember my passionate epistles, my rebukes and curses. You sent me to a foggy country, full of disorder and sorrow and memories swaying like sheafs of grain before harvest; I am Your smallest nation, also frail and full of strangled pride. I write to You from the deep province, concealed from the omnipresent police and also from the peasants who would not be thrilled if they found me here working by candlelight, so close to the barns, granaries, grain. Where am I? What do names mean to You? Foxes and hares run everywhere; there are spiders and nettles and crooked fences, empty vodka bottles and warped church pews removed from the temple by the organist, a maniac for order. There will always be a little room for someone like me, the author of more and more new letters, complaints, and protests.

There follows an illegible signature, sudden blast of cold wind.

Spring Thunderstorm

The Decembrists, who lived in penal servitude and exile, returned in thirty years alert, wise, and joyful, while those who
remained in Russia and spent their lives in the civil service,
at dinners and at card games, were a pitiful ruin, of no use to
anyone, without even a few good memories to distinguish their
lives.

Leo Tolstoy

I have been living in the West for a few years now. I am
constantly invited to congresses, conferences, and lectures.
When flying, I always try to get a place by the window and I
look greedily—I cannot tear my eyes away from the surface
of the earth. Forests like green lace, cities like beads, the pastel
colors of spring fields.

Ever since I found myself in the West, much has changed.
There, in my country, everything was clear-cut: I spent a few
years in a camp, I was persecuted day and night. When I could
get out for a few days of freedom, secret agents moved stealthily
behind me.

What is the world? Is it orderly or chaotic? Streams wind haphazardly through lazy meadows, mountains give way to plains, the ocean is light blue and mute.

From the time I arrived, I have been watched by no one. Yet I have rarely been alone. This was because of too many friendships, too much good will. Leaving the plane, I knew someone would be waiting for me. The schedule for the day included banquets, press conferences, colloquia with scholars and writers, suppers, and meetings with ministers. I was transformed from a hunted wolf to a celebrity. I was accompanied by elegant men with smooth-shaven cheeks and women in evening gowns. I was invited to their lovely homes; I admired their polite children, obedient dogs, well-tended lawns, cats with shiny coats, old furniture. At night velvet stars blinked in the heavens, a car drove me downtown, an elevator raised me to the fifteenth floor of an enormous hotel; from the windows of my room I looked at the lights of London, Geneva, or Berlin.

I do not know what reality is. I am always afraid of the moment when a plane dives into the clouds, into their dirty interior. I close my eyes then and count to a hundred.

I read newspapers, give interviews, publish commentaries and prophecies, because that is what is expected of me. But I don't know much, I understand very little. Sometimes it happens that passersby on the street will recognize me the day after a television appearance and they greet me heartily. Who am I, the wolf or the hunter? A film star or the victim of a cruel political system? A beggar or a magnate?

In the camp I believed in God with a faith so pure, so very pure . . . There was nothing between the cold azure sky and the dirt-poor settlement of camp barracks. Nothing. Stars circled like altar boys above my head. Now my faith has palled, but I do not admit it in my books.

I always try to be with someone. I feel their admiration and I can adjust to that. That is, my former qualities—pride, resilience, faith, and despair—reappear. My former despair, which has nothing to do with the hopelessness of days now. Stubbornly I repeat to myself that I must help those who have remained in my homeland, in its camps, prisons, and ugly cities. I have a mission to accomplish, I repeat to myself daily.

But once I was left to myself. At night, in a big city. The car which was driving me to the airport broke down along the way, not too far from the hotel. The chauffeur—a young boy with a handsome, girlish face—was devastated. He called for help, tried to find the problem, disappeared under the hood of the car, which suddenly rose vertically in a moment of Gothic inspiration. On impulse I said that I wanted to walk. I knew the way; I had stayed at the Très Grand Hôtel many times. I left my suitcase in the trunk; the chauffeur wouldn't hear of it. "It's dangerous," he indicated with his oil-stained hands. "It's dangerous," he repeated.

I laughed at him. "What? Here, in a big city, a couple of steps away from a world-class hotel, what danger?"

"You know better than I do," he said, wiping his sweaty face with the back of his hand and smearing his cheek.

"That's only an illusion," I said, "a pleasant illusion. They haven't been using those drastic methods for a long time."

Finally I freed myself from him and left him with the big, gleaming automobile, his head in the mouth of the lion.

Red neons pulsed overhead, casting scarlet shadows onto the sidewalk.

A pleasant illusion—I repeated, talking only to myself

now—that has allowed generations of my predecessors to maintain their anger, resistance, and courage. And it wasn't an illusion then, I added, as if trying to convince myself, reaching for proof of a historic nature (since no one is taking ontological proofs seriously . . .).

I was alone for the first time in ages, if I don't count the surreptitious forays into luxurious bathrooms in the homes of my new friends, and if I don't count sleep, which isn't exactly free from collective drives and invites into our unwilling, drugged imagination dozens of figures we know or will know only fleetingly.

I was alone, without an interpreter, chauffeur, guide, or minister, without journalists, without their questions and curiosity, which I was supposed to satisfy with the simple fact of my existence, breathing or sneezing.

I looked around: no one walked behind me. Or rather, yes, crowds of evening strollers—to whom my political views were of no interest whatsoever—walked behind me (I knew that no one remembered television shows longer than three days, and over two months had passed since my electronic face flickered across television screens).

No, evening crowds walked the wide sidewalks of the boulevard without a care, content with the warmth of the day, happy that everything was moving along as anticipated: April followed March, day followed night, and now the next night was beginning, delivered in an enormous string shopping bag carried by a rosy new moon. You could smell the hard leaves of plane trees and the dust moistened by a passing rain. Windows reflected neon lights; the wind played with shutters, rocked them, and made violet strips of light, street reflections, tremble. Even the faces of wicked outlaws posted over the entrances to movie houses seemed to become softer and invited people to come inside, as if to say, "We're not all that bad. Anyway, we're just a picture, just light." Everything was just light—the bright displays, the taillights of patient cars, the white coats of elegant women, the silk scarves of their men, and the eyes, the eyes of all those who passed me.

Someone was returning from the theater, someone else was going to a movie, and yet another person was hurrying to a restaurant. Tourists walked differently from the rightful inhabitants of this city; theirs was a lighter, less deliberate step. They did not take the land into possession; they looked around with interest, almost the way I did, although it did not seem to me that I was a tourist.

I laughed. I laughed at this city, at the abundance of streets, buildings, stores, passersby, faces. I don't know if this is usual, but abundance has a comic effect on me, a deeply cathartic, comic effect. It can't be serious, this concentration of dozens of planes and lines, colors and cheeks, corners and smells, harshnesses and stickinesses, that which doesn't move with that which speeds, the small and the tall, the real with the fake, the Chinese with the Latin, nose with lip, lips with ties, movie theater with restaurant, lighthouse with gooseberry, rain with moon, crying with a sigh. Who am I if I am surrounded by an abundance of things? A piece of my "I" becomes harsh, sticky, small, tall, nasal, daytime, nocturnal.

O walls, O gates of townhouses built by Baron Haussmann, O stones! Help me understand what has happened to me. Or, rather, with the world. Where have my unwavering certainty, my steadfast faith, my inconsolable despair gone? O gray stones.

I looked at the slabs of sidewalk, as if expecting to find a map on them, a blueprint, guidelines. But the sidewalk, polished by the soles of thousands of diligent pedestrians, had nothing to tell me. Small puddles told of the recent rain. The smell of April. The sweet nothing of spring forecast summer heat waves and autumn rust.

I looked behind me one more time: I was really alone. The crowd had not stopped its majestic stroll on both sides of the boulevard, the courteous and elegant crowd which, thanks to some miraculous synchronization, found a place for itself without crowding too much, without fighting, without killing or hating one another. Some of the grocery stores were still open and shamelessly vaunted the corpses of turkey and deer; peacock colors rose above the exquisite marble. I was alone; I was completely free. What I had dreamed about in the past had taken place. I had found myself within the walls of the city of my dreams.

I strolled by cafés and restaurants, the same I who a few years ago, shaking with cold and anger, was so internally strong and all of a piece and heavy and luminous that I could look at the stars as if I, too, were a celestial body. Star observing star.

So much had happened, yet nothing had happened. What is time when compared to substance? A suitcase in which you hoard your treasures, cellophane in which a salesclerk—a young woman bored with life already, for her life is the fragrance of flowers—carefully wraps a bouquet of yellow roses (yellow roses! There are five, and each is full of a swaggering, youthful energy! To the degree that besides their satin petals each of these roses has green and yellow peaks and extra leaves, and each smells of dew). There is nothing more banal than time and its old tricks. A foaming river of time rushes through every watch. How strange that time does not pour out of the clocks, doesn't flood suburban gardens. The trite accomplishments of time: a few wrinkles, a little death, a bit of maturity, Ulysses returns home, Linnaeus loses his memory.

People don't usually talk about these things, but I will. There, in a cold barracks in a dark camp in an evil country, I was someone extraordinary, and my substance—that which is under the eyelids, forehead, and in the heart—was harder than a diamond and completely indifferent to the passing of time.

I found myself on a side street; which does not mean that the lights were any dimmer. No, the city still glowed. There were fewer people here. The market was shutting down. Booths were closing up. Two brawny young men in blue coveralls— they looked like they were competing in a contest for best outfit designed for innocuous fallen angels—were folding enormous wooden platforms. A third, holding one end of a rubber hose, was already beginning to spray down the street with a jet of water, but for the time being he was playing with this deadly weapon by threatening his blue companions. The other two giggled, ran away from him, and finally began to pelt him with the rest of the tomatoes, apples, and fish heads. The other merchants looked at them indulgently. A big woman who stood in the doorway of a grocery was weighing whether or not to scold the trio or to join in the fun.

She didn't have time to decide, however, because the red ambulance of the fire department came speeding through the narrow street, honking, wailing, and flashing its powerful lights, as if someone inside were preparing a careful photographic documentation of this neighborhood; faces, noses, mouldings, brass latches, booths all appeared in brief violet flashes, tense with impatience. All this existed and lived, in a naïve, simpleminded, perhaps even too empirical yet indisputable way; finally, a stream of clean water straightened itself out and rose, gathering, even here, in this side street, its proper silver dignity and proving without the least effort that it was a distant cousin to Niagara, the spitting image of a mountain cascade, grandson to the ocean.

Everything is everywhere. Summer lightning laughs in tiny match flames. A grain of sand is a sky-touching mountain. Rain threatens to become a flood, and a maple leaf, whirling on the surface of a pond, is ready to change into Noah's ark at any minute. The moon puts on a clean white shirt each evening. The song of the golden oriole always dazzles with its perfection. If only we could grow into that perfection, keep up with it, not let it down, not degrade it. Ah, I knew it was impossible. One cannot change into an oriole, a maple leaf, a poppyseed, a granite cliff, a sprig of lilac.

I felt though—against my own better judgment—that it would be enough to desire this change, ardently, absolutely, and naïvely, in order to find myself there, on the other side, on the side of perfect beings—a little sparrow hopping along a stone bridge at dawn, or a lizard, a squiggle that melted into a crack between concrete steps.

And I knew that this desire had left me. I remembered it; whoever has had it once cannot deny it, even though it may have lost its enchanting qualities. Even the attempt to think about it was difficult and painful. Nettles burned this way in childhood. Large, sweet raspberries were like juicy telegrams which brought news of the state of the world. There were days when nothing else mattered. The Phoenician wars were forgotten once and for all, Napoleon had never been born. The girl that took her vacation late, in mid-August, was already tanned; she had green eyes and laughed quietly but precisely —that is, laughter took hold of her like a brushfire. It was I who had to leave early; my mother had fallen dangerously ill. Then I went to the university and became a teaching assistant—everyone knows the details of my life, I do not have to repeat well-known facts—until, finally, I would find myself in a low barracks. Almost no one knows that there, in camp, my magic powers returned. It is not enough to say they came back. There I became a great magician. I was able to reconstruct the whole from one swallow, bah, from one little leaf of a skinny birch. Of course, there were months of complete despair, illness, nothingness, oblivion. But even then I did not lose the capacity to sustain the gift.

I wrapped it in despair the way one wraps a beautiful stone found on a beach in a hankie, and I waited, waited patiently for the return of my magical powers. Even in the fall, even in December, when the sun was almost invisible, I did not surrender. I knew how to wait!

So what happened later, why did I undergo a transformation, why did I lose the very thing that was my greatest treasure? I did not make any compromises, I did not undermine anything, I did not sell out. I lived comfortably, yes, but that had not been the price for my giving in: I was simply being hospitably received. I denied nothing. Nor do I believe that I was overwhelmed by the multiplicity of things and people on this side of the world. No, abundance amused me, occupied and intrigued me. I knew well that one could come out of it with faith and strength; this was purely a technical matter. Similarly, a sailor is able to take advantage of all, even contrary, winds; all he has to do is set the sails right. Abundance is like a wind constantly changing direction, and an experienced sailor knows how to adjust to every kind of weather.

I came to a place where the street forked and lost its market character. I decided, therefore, to return to the boulevard, not by retracing my steps but by taking an even narrower street to the left. Then, I thought, all I have to do is turn left again at the first or second intersection and I will find myself back on the wide boulevard.

If I had acted indecently, if I had done something repellent, I would feel a lot better. I would simply have found myself in a great crowd of cheats; perhaps I would feel moral pangs occasionally—like memories from a distant time, little jabs to the heart, the vague remembrances of childhood, the whispers of a discarded nature—but concealing my sins would consume me so entirely that it would be difficult for me to be conceited, let alone leave any time for warnings and reminders emitted by my past incarnation. No, I imagine that the world of cheaters is, in certain regards, close to the world of decent people, namely, in its outlay of energy; in both worlds one needs constant activity, constant alertness. Moral people never stop fighting with their weaknesses, and cheaters never stop fighting with people who are decent.

The strange and sneaky erosion of faith is something entirely different, an erosion that is working its way slowly, oh, so slowly, but steadily every month, as if a month constituted the smallest unit of destruction, revealing more and more damage, loss, and doubt. Why? That is the word that belonged to my persecutors. It appeared in the morning, concealed in a cup of steaming coffee, in the collar of a freshly pressed shirt, in the gleaming tip of polished shoes, in a cluster of purple grapes, and then it rose like the sun on the horizon, reached its zenith at noon, lay down to take a quick but scrumptious nap in the afternoon, and returned in the evening, this time squeezed between the fold of the evening edition of the paper, hidden between the pages of a theater program. Yes, because there still are theaters and films, the refineries of illusions, as if there weren't enough torments generated by reality alone. I saw too much, I heard too much. I felt painfully overwhelmed by the images on the film screen. How many sunsets can one stand, how many pictures of the ocean? Beauty became so common, so accessible. A record of a Mozart quintet costs very little. But there is cunning in all this: in order to listen to that record carefully, one must give up half of one's life. Perhaps I am exaggerating—a quarter of one's life. But time is not really the issue as much as the cultivation of a separate province of reality. I will not ask what is music, what are moments full of bitter happiness offered by it (taken by it?), what is the feeling of emptiness when one is unable to accept it.

Where is God—in suffering or in joy, in a beam of light or in terror, in a rich, free city or in a concentration camp? I knew, of course, unfortunately I knew, that it is not difficult to answer the last part of this question. What does it mean, however, when God prefers the dark and terror-filled places? Why? I have also felt the divine presence in beauty, but it seemed to me that it was not the same God. Yes, I know, one must open oneself, one must humbly accept what comes and not insist on understanding things that are incomprehensible. I shouldn't talk about this at all. Who am I to enter the skin of a priest? I am a lay person and I should stick to my areas of competence, to my experiences and reflections. I retreat. I know nothing, I saw little. For many years I lived on a closed ward—is that how one refers to these places?—and because of this I could not see much. Only the blue-black umbrella of the sky.

I realize the risk of my situation: I live nowhere. I think that those should be allowed to speak who can speak in the name of this or that small community, a real community, human and even modestly prosperous. Let us take a baker from a small Swiss town, a fisherman from a village in Brittany, an alpine shepherd. Let them speak. Let them help us. The paradox of my vocation has always been its negativity, or, rather, to speak more precisely, the risky mix of a profoundly positive impulse and the negativity of method, behavior, tone of voice. I had to say a loud "no," but this "no" was the shout of a hidden "yes." Is this clear? To me, no, but I trust that someone else will be able to decode my writing. I also know that to carry within, at the same time, a loud "no" and a profound "yes" is incredibly difficult, almost impossible, destined for failure. Perhaps this happens in order to teach the next generation how to find a less twisted road, to allow them to experience a "yes" uncorrupted by "no" and a "no" that would be an ordinary, healthy, indispensable, and hygienic "no," and not poison, not arsenic.

The next generation . . . It is easy to call on them (it is easy to speak about what does not exist), but is there really so much generosity in me that I would consign my life, honestly and without regret, to a dustbin and instead point to a quadrangle of the young generation? I doubt it. Nor do I know if it would speak well of me to put my life into hock. Without lying? I would like to know. Because even if I were to lie . . . Although I have caught myself a few times, maybe not exactly lying with all its horror and impudence, but embellishing, touching up, exaggerating. On days when I felt tired and discouraged, I presented my case in as flowery and energetic a manner as during my best moments, and, on occasion, I have recited my opinions and convictions rather than say them from the heart. Oh yes, it did happen a few times. In Madrid. It was raining; the day was thunderstorm dark, brown; the tires drowned in streams of murky water. In Edinburgh, in winter, I was infected with a Scottish taciturnity . . . Even in Ferrara one day, although I can't blame it on the weather . . . The sun hung over the rooftops like an ancient lamp, sculpted in gold. I had just seen the frescoes of Francesco del Cossa. I was happy, full of that variety of happiness which comes to us from the outside, from old canvases, tall trees, Romanesque churches, the rhythm of valley and hill. And in spite of my happiness, I couldn't say anything real. Or perhaps because of it, because the happiness had been bestowed upon me, offered, but not so I could use it. Some presents are so frail, so carefully constructed, that they fall apart the minute we want to hand them over to someone else.

Ferrara in the sunshine, Madrid in the rain. Before that, Edinburgh. And between these cities the airplane and I, by the window, staring at the cuneiform writing of forests, fields, and villages, deciphering the secret meaning of this real, meaty map of Europe. In the airplane I did not know how to think, and it was not fear that was paralyzing me but passionate interest: it seemed to me constantly that one of these times I would understand the meaning of this map, that the barely visible church steeples, wooded strips, riverbeds, and country roads would finally speak to me, because they clearly had something to say; and I even believed that all the other, permanent residents of these beautiful countries knew what was going on, what this land was saying to them, and that it was just me, a newcomer, it did not want to know or acknowledge; it showed me the disorderly accumulation of things but had no intention of revealing its mission to me.

Meanwhile, the little street on which I found myself became narrower and darker. I turned left for the second time, and, as I had foreseen and common sense told me, I should have been back on the busy boulevard long ago. I became worried. Instead of enormous geometric buildings, along whose walls climbed mythological sculptures of muscular figures, I had before me poor, dirty, and sickly looking houses. Their plaster was covered with lichens of tea stains, the narrow windowsills looked like degrees of dilapidated, crooked stairs. The gates I passed smelled of urine, mold, and old age, as if something in them was fermenting secretly and disloyally, terrifyingly. The matter of things was not cut and marked by clearly indicated boundaries as it was downtown on the wide boulevard, which I pined for now in vain; this street only seemed to move, undulate, swell, as if these small, disintegrating houses had gills and were gasping for breath with the determination of catfish caught in a net. The sidewalk no longer led me on a straight scout trail; it just seemed to mumble something strange and to limp, like a drunken guide in a small Turkish city, under the sickle of a malicious moon. Under the streetlamp I saw a hyperbolically stretched-out cat with a dirty, matted coat. In the half-light, right next to the wooden fence, I noticed a clochard mummy, wrapped in rags and newspapers. The mummy breathed rhythmically, and at the level of the head grew a wine bottle, like a periscope sticking out of a German submarine. Suddenly there was a terrifying noise, after which, preceded by the roar of an engine, passed right by me a small, thin boy with black windblown hair; his hands rested on the handlebars of a moped that leaped into the air from the speed of his driving. After him came another driver, also gripping his moped; this must have been a twin brother, for he had exactly the same face with sharp features, black hair, also windblown. He wore an identical black leather jacket, the favored clothing of police officers as well as thieves. A moment later a police car appeared in the street; it was locked into the chase and flashing its blue lights; inside I saw the navy fabric of police uniforms.

Neither the cat, rubbing itself up against the cast-iron street-lamp, nor the clochard, deep in sleep, paid the slightest attention to the three bolides who had torn the spiderweb overgrowing the street (it was so narrow here that a dexterous and hardworking spider could stitch the street together in no time, just as a young and ambitious surgeon sews up a wound). The white face of an old woman appeared in one of the small windows, and right afterward, as if elicited by this negative stain, the silhouette of an old man who could barely walk appeared on the unsteady sidewalk. He leaned against every-thing: walls, fences, and kiosks. In his right hand he held a knotty cane and with it he examined the nature of the land —just like the first man on the moon—and then trusted it, hung on to it desperately, moving a few centimeters to the opposite side. Then he froze again by a selected fragment of wall or fence and decided to move the cane again. He wore a suit which might have been very elegant thirty years ago, a white shirt, a polka-dot bow tie, and a crooked, stained hat on his head.

When I got closer to him I noticed that sweat was running down his gray stubbled face and his chin moved incessantly, because, as I understood it, the old man, the slowest wanderer in the world, cursed as he walked, cursed nature, God and people, animals and plants, insects, vertebrates, reptiles, minerals, planes, gliders, kites, blindworms, women and men. I wanted to help him, but he looked at me with such utter contempt and hatred that I immediately withdrew my offer and even hurried my step in order to distance myself from this furious Oedipus, who showered me with curses that flew at me like the flaming arrows of the Greeks.

Something was scary about that street; oh yes, that was definitely a dangerous street. Just in case, I walked down the middle of the street and not on the sidewalk: I preferred to keep away from the doorways! Each doorway seemed to be a barrel full of nothingness, from which fast blades, knives, and razors could jump out. There was no one ahead of me, but it seemed to me that I was being watched, that someone's grudging, hostile eyes were behind each windowpane.

Luckily there was a broad space opening before me; the stuffy street was finally ending. My boulevard, I thought, my wide, bright boulevard, the Milky Way of the city, the boulevard from which it was so easy to get to my hotel.

When I covered the next two hundred yards, however, I saw not a brightly lit boulevard but a canal with innumerable bridges and ramps for pedestrians, all empty, as if they had been built for the conveyence of a great army, and after the army had passed, hurrying to its battles and cemeteries, the bridges had become architectural monuments.

Here at least there was space, thanks to which I was safe, or so it seemed (the great powers are no different in this regard from the solitary evening passerby: when the subject is safety, we are all suffering from delusions). I sat on the steps of a pedestrian bridge. I wasn't sleepy at all. Suddenly I began to quit worrying about my predicament; I stopped thinking feverishly about how to find the way to the hotel.

I remembered a conversation which had hurt me and which I had afterward not thought much about. It took place in Rotterdam during one of the colloquia; after supper an Italian journalist sat down at my table. He was familiar to me and I liked him instinctively. He was not young, but similar in a peculiar way to the man in Titian's famous portrait in the London National Gallery. The man in the portrait—about thirty perhaps—looks at us with his right eye (the left is in deep shadow), and that one-eyed gaze is a masterpiece of arrogance mixed with timidity. The eye is arrogant, as is his outfit: a silk shirt under a black coat that is disappearing into the shadows. Because the man is sitting sideways, leaning against a wooden beam or railing, it is the puffy sleeve of the silk shirt that is most striking, and this sleeve is arrogant, too. The timidity is expressed most clearly by the lips, skeptical and prone to smile. We undoubtedly are dealing with someone who has achieved a great deal in life; yet the position of the subject, the hand freely resting on the wooden railing, seems to suggest at the same time that he is a traveler (if the truth be known, one could easily say he was captured the moment he sat down in the compartment of a first-class express train departing from Rome and destined for infinity), carried away by the most perfect of vehicles, time, and that is why he is skeptical, like all travelers.

The (living) Italian was considerably older, and his beard and hair were peppered with gray, but there was in him the same cohabitation of cocksureness and delicate doubt. He questioned me first about events in my life and pretended to jot something down; I saw, however, that he wasn't after an interview or an article.

"You are a serious man," he said after a while, "and I like that a lot" (he smiled arrogantly when he said this, under-cutting his own words). "But I don't know if you realize that all these people around you, even though they admire you a lot and are honest, are beings of a different construction, perhaps even of a different anatomy."

"What do you mean?" I asked.

"You and they," stated the journalist, "are made of entirely different clays. I can only imagine what you are made of," he added, "but I know for certain that they are made chiefly of irony."

"Really?" I asked stupidly.

"Oh yes," he said with conviction. "I know it well because it also applies to me. Irony admires faith in a way that is not entirely impartial; actually, this is a matter of a life and death struggle. For irony, admiration is the most comfortable tactic, the most perfect piece of siege artillery."

We talked afterward about other things, but in bidding me goodbye the Italian added, "By the way, do you know that in prison even Verlaine became a believer?"

He smiled and again there was in that smile the unlikely coexistence of wild arrogance and soft timidity. I never came across him again; Titian's train left; the silk shirt pulled away. Someone told me a few months later that the Italian was deathly ill (he suffered from one of those great illnesses rarely mentioned in polite society—the name is followed by a mo-ment of silence and a little bogus sadness), and he withdrew from professional and public life.

When we spoke in the hotel restaurant, he held a glass of cognac and played with it, rocked it, examining the lustrous yellow liquid. I felt that this man really was the incarnation of Titian's ambivalence. I knew that he both admired and couldn't stand me. I attracted and repelled him; I destroyed his philosophical system, I contradicted his skepticism, I was a being that did not fit into his botany, zoology, or anthropology. I won't even mention theology. We sat silent for a long while and it seems that for an instant we were able to experience our differing spiritual qualities. I was exposed to his profound duality (profound and decent, absolute), and he, I think, was overcome by the aura of my solidity, by the integrity tempered in the historical oven.

Finally he rose and, sensing that this radiating of ontological characteristics could not last even a second longer before turning into a pitiful caricature, into a grotesque idolatry, said goodbye with that harsh sentence about Verlaine.

He could not have guessed that I had already been infected with ambivalence, that the same accursed and majestic process of shading, counterbalancing, juxtaposing had already begun in me. I desired simplicity and uniformity, when the desire itself was deceptive and testified to the progress of the inevitable process of differentiation.

I can't think about this; I'd rather slide into other areas. I find comfort in the sharp pain of homesickness. I see a pine forest, branches of trees trembling in the rays of the sun, as if they were set into motion by the impatient and sweet desire of light. Columns of dust rise between the trees, the spirits of harvested pines and firs. (There are no such forests here.) A magpie flies lazily, slowly. The grass smells of autumn bitterness. Spiders, inspired by the songs of birds (orioles!), spin long and straight threads, and then swing on them for hours, just like kids. I see rowanberries, completely unaware of their charm. I see country roads planted with cherry trees, twisting trails in the field, disappearing in the grain. But I also see the faces of friends no longer living, their shiny eyes, noble gestures. I look at them laughing. We are taking a bike trip and it seems to me that I am able to see them from above, from a bird's (not a hawk's) eye view, a little group of five cyclists. Before them is a long and carefree day. Before them is an asphalt road rolled up like a Möbius strip, very cunningly, but they don't have to know that, especially since the gentle domes of hills and peaked caps of forests seem to convince them of their imperturbable permanence and ponderous loyalty.

Another time: a hawthorn bush, rain, fever. I had a cold, was running a temperature; it seemed to me that the eyes of all objects were shining preternaturally. We were sitting on the veranda, under the clear pane of a glass roof, along which streamed unending braids of rain. The garden, a half step away, was barely visible under the curtain of rain. Garden! A patch of old garden, neglected, constantly attacked by nettles, weeds, maple and ash seedlings. The forest was trying to penetrate the garden. Even the hawthorn was able to fortify itself in the old rows. There were endless arguments at home about whether to get rid of the hawthorn, which was completely out of keeping with the character of the garden (but there was no more garden), or whether to let it live, since it had already grown up and thus had found its way into the great family of unnecessary but already existing things.

It was then, in September, on that rainy evening, made radiant afterward by the timid rays of a sun determined to set, that the deep yellow fruits of the hawthorn—hard, perfect in their compactness (seemingly useless, but one could make a homemade wine from them)—became the heroines of the moment all at once; they flashed in their leafy array, gilded even more by the sly reflections of the sun, and suddenly no one doubted that they had to stay.

I held her hand then; for us, too, it became a moment of flawless union, to be recalled later, in vain, as if it were our Versailles Treaty. The analogy is not irrelevant; both began in gardens and ended in war, a breaking off of relations, a desert. My biographer wrote that she withdrew under pressure from constant police harassment. The persistent visits of these ugly, wretched, usually undereducated people—who were, nonetheless, extremely sure of themselves, as each felt that there were lines connecting all points of their unassuming bodies directly to the secret and omnipotent center of things—were to completely transform this extraordinary woman. O happy biographer!

He goes to sleep with a history textbook of my country under his pillow, and in the morning he is ready to solve the most difficult riddle. I know, however, that our breakup didn't require the police and their pockmarked messengers, who used too much gas (they never shut off their car engines, as if believing that each detail of their behavior had to be emblematic of permanence). What happened between us sufficed—a normal failure, which the biographer wrongly attributed to my bitter (as he was wont to say) triumphs as a perfectly just man.

And yet another time: no, nothing wants to show itself anymore. Even the perfect mechanism of homesickness can jam and cause the wonderfully maintained tapes of memories—enough to play for a few days—to tangle and block the projector showing my life.

Nor did I tell the Italian something else: not only does ambivalence creep into the territory I inhabit, but I am also beginning to like it. There is something intelligent, even brilliant, in it. Thanks to it things are beginning to double, they are beginning to speak; thanks to it nuances and shades have appeared, half-tones, reverberations. Even skepticism appeals to me. I happened to enjoy someone's intelligent cynicism for a while. These are, of course, nothing but mental maneuvers, the stirrings of a jealous mind, which—in my case—was imprisoned in the flesh and conscience of an incorruptible man, who, therefore, was as contrary as a five-year-old boy; this man is fascinated by the spectacle of omnipresent hypocrisy and corruption, as an observer only, and in the process asks himself an entirely academic question: What if I tried these worse fruits, since I have always been fed the better?

Each belief, I thought, is a movement, a striving toward something, energy, like a boat skimming along the surface of a lake. But when the boat stops, what then? Suddenly it is equal to the still element, to what is immobile and lazy, rotten and moldy. Movement, it is true, is a lot more thrilling, pure, and noble. No one knows where movement comes from; however, there is something unexplained about it, wild and a priori. Perhaps more truth is embedded in things that are still, calm, and lazy; here at least there is no pretense. Darkness does not feign light; silence does not pretend to be a symphony orchestra.

I was still sitting on the steps of the bridge, high above the surface of the street. It occurred to me that I was quite high up, even though I entertained some rather humble thoughts. I could review parades. And, of course, a moment later, along the canal, a lone rat appeared and headed calmly in the direction of the brush, which was lit on one side by a neon light but then passed into impenetrable darkness.

Somewhere far away a church tower clock struck the hour,

slowly and solemnly, as if singing a melody everyone knew well. Somewhere else brakes squealed, a petard exploded. Somewhere.

I got up and went on my way. It seemed to me that lightning flashed in the sky. I walked with an even step, as if I knew how to reach my hotel now. The road was long. I walked by a small park in which chestnut trees with still small, damp, five-fingered leaves jostled one another for oxygen. For a moment I marched down the most normal, bourgeois street, so calm that one could almost hear the residents inhale and exhale in their sleep, all in clean pajamas, over each one the sphinx of an alarm clock stepping harshly through the fields of night until the zero hour, when the inhabitants of sleep would be alarmed with a hissing bell and in three-quarters of an hour would crowd the sidewalks like Allied soldiers landing on the beaches of Normandy. Later an old church with high Gothic windows and walls blackened with age grew on my right. It was divided from the street by an iron railing and a narrow garden in which a young willow swayed back and forth. On the left were railroad tracks and, above them, factory buildings wreathed in clocks, each one indicating a different hour.

I descended. I knew that in a minute I would be on the boulevard. I had to cross just one more short, broad street— serving the function of a dash joining two sentences (two neighborhoods). It got light again: the boulevard still glowed with multicolored lights like a candelabra. There were no more crowds. Chairs and tables were being folded, and men in hot orange coveralls swept the sidewalks. There was no atmosphere of promise and expectation now. Some of the illuminated ads went out and some of the stores were armored in wooden or tin shutters. In one of the restaurants a man with greasy black hair stood at the counter counting bills with the enthusiasm of a great mathematician who works only at night. The last customers were leaving the bars and restaurants and drifting unsteadily in the direction of the street, into yellow and beige taxis, after which they fell weakly into the rear seat of the car and, instead of a last wish, gave the driver their address in a weary, indifferent voice.

I walked with a quick, rhythmic step, not thinking about anything anymore. Without the least difficulty I found the hotel building. The receptionist shook his finger at me roguishly. That finger ended in a gigantic fingernail and gleamed with a gold wedding band.

"We were worried about you," he said without conviction. And added: "Is it raining already?"

"Raining? No."

"The forecast said showers and a change in temperature. Did you have fun?"

"I got lost. You won't believe this, but I got completely lost."

"Oh yes, that happens," the receptionist said cheerfully. "And do you know why? Look." He pointed to a map of the city under the glass countertop. "It happens a lot. You were probably walking, thinking, doubtlessly, that this was a city built on right angles. But no, have a look at the map; Paris is a city of acute angles!"

It was true—the streets grew around the squares like iron filings attracted to magnets (the coral reefs of the pink districts were difficult to fit into the same map).

"There's a letter for you, sir."

I glanced at the letter; it was to remind me of a press conference.

"Yes, of course," I mumbled.

I had a room on the highest floor. Lightning flashed more and more insistently. I knew that on this day, too, I would speak, as always, with conviction and belief in my mission. As I was drifting off to sleep, the storm entered the city like a purple rooster.

THE CHAIRMAN'S
SECRET SPEECH

FLOWER SHOPS, OPEN even on Sundays, and the sour smell of the earth. From inside the store appears the tall saleswoman. Adjusting the hairpins in her chestnut hair, she asks a timid boy what kind of bouquet he would like. Roses. Asters. Carnations. Baroque peonies. Garrulous chrysanthemums. Poppies. Sunflowers. It is quite late. Please don't take notes. It is night, dark, full of a troublesome rain, and I am old and sick. It may just happen that I will die soon. We have learned a lot since Aleksey Tolstoy said death was a bourgeois superstition, and death has been a patient lecturer.

It isn't easy for me to begin. I have already given hundreds of speeches. I would get a text at the last minute, and I read it trustingly, for I have always had devoted aides. But the aides look at me with curiosity; with fear and hope they await the moment when some great funeral will once again interrupt the usual routine of meetings, greetings, and farewells. The cannon carriage is the last vehicle in a long line of those at the disposition of a great man. Enormous hills of flowers grow, but they have no fragrance. It isn't easy for me to begin.

We have more and more cities and villages, railroad lines, train cars, countries, languages; military parades occur so often that the roads must be changed over and over again, ruined by tank tracks. Victory parades. How many presidents would have liked to have been in my place, even in my ailing body: the body of a leader is more than he alone; it is his endless properties, the featherbeds of his subordinates, the ships of his flotilla submerged in green water, the school textbooks in the countries he has conquered, his young, freckled soldiers and the fiancées of his soldiers and the fiancées' sisters, and the soldiers' brothers, and the customs officials, and censors with an alert look, and doltish clerks; and even traitors belong to him, although it seems to them that they don't at all, and emigrants are also his property, though they try and deny it. The more they deny it, the more they belong to him. The body of the leader, like every other organism, is made up of an infinite number of cells, red and white corpuscles, bacteria and viruses, glands and muscles. I like to think about my great imperial body, rinsed by oceans, veiled in winter by merciful snow, defended by freckled soldiers. I often imagine the small towns being nothing more than magnified villages (train station; long, narrow, almost rushing street planted with scrawny linden trees; two bakeries; a hairdresser; and, finally, a town square with its fork of a monument, sticking up tentatively in the very center); I have never set foot there, yet I am present there and strongly so—in portraits, posters, decrees, even in dreams.

There are good thoughts and bad thoughts. Sometimes unpleasant, malicious things reach my ears. One hears accusations. The universal love which, until not too long ago, bound us warmly and tightly is coming apart at the seams. One hears accusations, usually about two decades late. One hears that we murdered, that we were cruel. And who says this? People who have stopped believing in the immortal soul. They are appalled by killing because they do not believe in the existence of the immortal soul.

Yes, we killed. Please think about the sort of life they oppose to death. What exactly were we depriving our victims, our opponents of, what sort of life? A lazy, sedentary, vegetative one.

Can someone who tears through a cobweb in a forest, only because that someone is running, be accused of a crime? What exactly did we destroy? Life? What is it, if it does not grow into one with us, if it does not join us, if it does not increase its velocity, movement (we are movement).

Do you remember Dickens's novels? The small, greedy people in Dickens, monstrous characters, the monsters of suburban households, pitiless shopkeepers, gluttonous old men, cruel, heartless men and women?

Do you remember Dickens's novels? Inscrutable, dark life, fulsome hatreds, suffering, disgrace. The little streets of London, the labyrinth in which innocent children perished every day. Do you remember the illustrations in the Dickens novels? Hooknoses, dull-witted faces, stupid, ordinary snouts. So much evil, so much baseness, which also carried itself with such dignity, walked in glory, in the bourgeois praise of virtue. Do you recall the helplessness of the small heroes in Dickens, heroes condemned to a hopeless struggle against the tyrants of family, school, parish, shop? Life? That was your life: dirty, slovenly, life deprived of splendor in the alleys of great cities. The gold coin shone more brightly there than the flames of hell and was more desired than salvation.

And perhaps you have read Léon Bloy? Oh no, I will not refer you to our writers; witnesses from the other side will suffice. Do you remember what Léon Bloy wrote about property owners, about the saleslady who smiles at you? But just try and tell her that you are fifty centimes short. Ah! Try to tell her that you do not have enough money. That nice person will immediately change into a tigress, will call the police, handcuff you, and send you to the guillotine.

And us? What in the world did we do? We murdered, built concentration camps, that's true, but we were reaching for the characters in the Dickens novels. We wanted a better life, a different humanity—nobler, purer. We wanted every city to be a capital. We wanted broad, well-lit streets.

What exactly did we destroy? An evil world, full of suffering, pain, anger, and boredom. An impenetrable, opaque world. Streets coiled like snail shells. Gardens, jungles of shrubs. Stuffy July evenings, the shouting of drunkards, the unconscious singing of birds, narrow and tangled streams, mountain chains scattered without order on the map, twisted borders stealing like thieves between countries. Sled races, the frosty smell of snow, the rosy cheeks of servants, apples lying still on white paper in basements, locks made of massive metals, expensive restaurants in which food was piled high in pyramids and waiters walked stiffly like mannequins. Parks and forests full of lovers in June. The mocking, repeated whistle of the thrush, echoed in every vale. Judges—old men in wigs, with eyes red from little sleep—called to pardon or to kill, a task greater than they could handle. Beautiful diplomats, eaten by syphilis. Drivers, sleeping with mouths wide open, waiting for their masters. Children whipped at school. Execution squads composed of helpless soldiers who would have preferred the gardener's job of grafting trees. Whores freezing in alleys. The vibrating shouts of onion vendors at the market, where the crowd, it seemed, would immediately explode municipal boundaries and take off across the fields and fencerows for another country.

What exactly did we destroy? A boring history with its small conquests; a history which neighboring world powers drank slowly, gulp by gulp, instead of intoxicating themselves with a real, absolute victory; a history with its low triumphal arches, recalling bourgeois furniture. We destroyed the world damned by prophets, hated by poets, the wormy apple. In the fall, swallows flew south. Smoke traveled to heaven, creeks steamed at daybreak, wagtails ran along the beach swaying like living fans. A train sometimes stopped at night in a field, and the heavy puffing of the steam engine flushed out birds hidden in invisible trees. Tall poplars marked the road. A hawk hovered under clouds, a storm approached, hail and plumes of lightning. A fat policeman had difficulty buckling the belt under his stomach. Jewish neighborhoods and synagogues, the harsh God of the Jews, a polyglot who also knew Yiddish. The despair of beggars who had to leave their modest dwellings because they could not pay their rent and ended up on the streets, in the freezing cold, to die.

Do you regret this? Prelates in heavy cassocks? Do you regret slides and orchestras that played Viennese waltzes in parks? Health resorts in which Goethe bowed to the emperor? Do you regret the thugs who allowed Mozart to die? The unshaven monks who sang Gregorian chants at dawn in a cool chapel? Do you regret the unfathomable multiplicity of races, denominations, and human types, the crowd that walked slowly down the street like an enormous herd of animals crossing the prairie?

Do you regret sunrises over battlefields? The slaughter of Austerlitz and Jena? What is it you regret? The distraught weeping of fiancées who have understood that they will remain old maids with dry cheeks? Do you regret the conflagrations of cities, conflagrations that consume a house a second just the way Gargantua devoured a pork roast? Disputes about universals? Abélard's shame? The grotesqueries of parliaments with their vain deputies who can be bought off, trafficking in every imaginable belief and ready to change their political, national, and even sexual colors every week if only someone would offer them a little more gold? Do you regret a God no one has seen? Theologians writing long letters that are never answered? What is it exactly you regret? Small nations, living with their comical hopes and tending their ridiculous, complicated grammars that no one would ever be able to master? Inept uprisings and sentimental campfire songs? Parliamentary sessions disrupted by drunken hecklers? The cruelties of Prussian officers? The last minutes in the life of a suicide, who lost everything in stock-market machinations?

Winter covered the poverty of cities. Scarlet bullfinches appeared in January. Ferries sank in the rivers. The *Titanic* sank like an iron. Military orchestras practiced for concerts hours at a time. Many unnecessary things. Crusades. Contests. Tons of deception everywhere. To maintain our standing on the appropriate hierarchical level, to mend worn stockings, patch up trousers, polish shoes to a spit shine, so that no one would think we were out of money, in decline. It is better not to eat for a week than to show a hole in a stocking. Forsythias bloomed in the spring. Starlings appeared. Servants stood on the windowsills and washed windows. Soldiers got leaves. Snow melted and rivers swelled dangerously; yellow waves beached trunks of toppled trees, dead gophers, birds' nests. Rains washed sidewalks. In artistic cafés people discussed nihilism.

The boredom of history: always the past tense, the eyelid of perfective verbs, the eyelashes of adverbs. Mercy for those who lived.

Pioneers headed for the west. Always in the past tense. Sunsets: bloody; predicting defeat, the lost battle. Then a light moon floated over the rivers and ponds, reflecting in every puddle. Time passes through the sentence like a reaper through a field. Miserable, small plunder. Someone brought a hare, someone else was happy with a full sack of juicy pears. The strange impression one has when leaving the city for a broad space: the horizon grows, there is more air, the enormous lung of flaxen steppe gives momentary joy. Our people were exemplary at the beginning. Model. Humble, noble, cultured, decent. They understood the seriousness of the situation. They came at daybreak. There wasn't a trace of anger in them. They wore leather jackets and had sharp, swarthy faces; they were gentle as teachers of the people. They were able to avoid exaltation, pathos. They came at daybreak, sometimes without even having the time to eat a decent breakfast. They slept three, four hours a night. No one remembers this. Many of them paid for this later with illnesses and ulcers. They gulped down burning, bitter coffee, ran downstairs to their cars three steps at a time, and drove through sleepy, lifeless towns from which rose the singing of blackbirds. Dew fell on park lawns. Marble statues looked at the black cars indifferently. It is held against us that these cars came at dawn. If they hadn't come at dawn, those people would have slept until noon, tossing in their stale bedding; then they would have stood in front of a mirror for a long time, looking at themselves, yawning, frosting the surface of the glass with their breath.

It is possible that there were mistakes. One has to allow for the scale of the enterprise. I personally regret Mandelstam, even though I realize that some of the later poems would never have been written if not for the policies we were applying to him. Our people liked cheerful songs, the sound of the accordion, military marches, parades, and the future. They were content with modest nourishment; they never complained that they lacked champagne or truffles. We stood before a white canvas then, as painters; our every stroke changed the face of the world. We liquidated horse races. We never allowed certain kinds of boxing or wrestling. We would not agree to things tolerated by those moral Americans. One had to simplify many complicated processes.

What is it that you regret? Hunting with its unspeakable cruelty? Popes with their cold, lordly lack of interest in suffering? Tables set out under old trees so that certain people could feast for four days and four nights? The past tense? The trumpets of the postillion?

Fog in the meadows. In childhood I thought that willows were not trees. They are entirely different, supple, deprived of form. The wind gives them form. I tried then to imagine America, the great cities with their chaos of neighborhoods and races. I imagine modestly dressed immigrants, freezing at dawn, waiting for hot soup, which they would not get until noon, from the hands of an elegant and weary lady. Jews, Armenians, Poles, Irish, Italians, Greeks. What a waste, what an excess of races and languages. Dark hair, white teeth, blue or brown eyes. The enormous eyes of children, widening like desire. It's too bad, but we had to punish the children as well.

I remember this without pleasure, without particular satisfaction. Great changes cannot satisfy everyone; that is not why they are brought about. One must realize that great transformations never transpire on the lyrical plane, so to speak—that is, on the plane of confession, feeling, longing, lament, which are directly accessible to our experiencing of them. No, the great metamorphoses have an epic character. There are few who understand this; we live in times when that maudlin philosophy existentialism was greeted with a standing ovation.

The wind blows. The wind is whipping up again. Tomorrow the next parade awaits us. We cannot be satisfied with everything. In recent years we have become the object of unjust attacks. Sometimes I think that humanity has not matured enough to appreciate these fundamental transformations, that it wants to stick to its little sins, its indolence. Humanity with sticky fingers is sneaking into the larder and licking the sweets earmarked for later, for other holidays. Fat, self-satisfied humanity sits for hours in front of the television set and purrs with delight. We imagined man somewhat differently, we assigned him other tasks. Even our people have changed. They are no longer as youthful; they have begun to look with interest and envy at that enormous human infantry that has remained behind. I don't know. I don't understand it. If I were younger, I would start all over, just as I did then, with the same enthusiasm, with the same impartiality. I do not understand what happened. Flatness, mediocrity, lack of imagination, ease, dull-wittedness triumph. Small, limited merchants stand at the head of historic nations. In their electoral programs there is only butter, bread and butter, ham and bread, mustard and ham. Himalayas of butter. The astounding sentimentality of these people: they assess their losses, pretend to be outraged when one of our prisoners dies. But they are not really concerned with that. Thoughts are invisible. What has become of the old Europe, the Europe of combative, tough, brave people for whom death was not a cowardly, desperate finale? What has become of the Europe of knights?

Once again an impenetrable, dark, many-headed humanity, a sensual anthill submitting to no laws or plans, a capricious beast full of urges, restless, somnolent, vegetative, seeking mysteries where there are none—in the stars, in the gizzards of sacrificial birds, in the ravings of fortune-tellers, in exclamations of love, in moans of passion. Stupid, dark humanity, a zoo, a flurry of idiots seeking to sate themselves, goofballs finding happiness in driving around a Sicilian town on a scooter or marching along an Atlantic beach with an enormous boom box playing black music. The woolly heads of simpletons. Moronic fish eyes. Others are returning to church to once again kiss the soft palms of vicars. Perhaps we shall be defeated, perhaps we will be unable to sustain the outstanding heritage of our legendary predecessors; but one day humankind will understand what it has lost, it will realize the opportunity it has squandered, it will notice it has remained alone, like a child lost in the woods—alone, deprived of guides, greedy, fat, lazy, full of indistinct needs and desires that will never be satisfied, terrified, drowning in tears, helpless. Then we will come again, my friends. We are not allowed to take offense.

What do you regret? Childhood? Clouds which seemed larger than the royal palace? Sparrows dancing on asphalt? Carnivals? Butchers in spattered aprons? Horses losing their footing on the frozen road? Life?

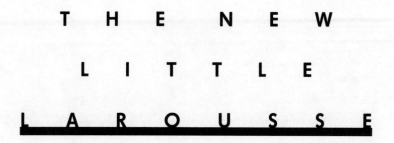

THE NEW

LITTLE

LAROUSSE

TWO BOOKS

PLEASE REACH FOR the first volume of Friedrich Nietzsche's writings, containing four early essays assembled under the title "Premature Solutions." There we will find, next to the well-known essay "Arthur Schopenhauer, Teacher" a no less well-known attack on history and historicism ("Vom Nutzen und Nachteil der Historie für das Leben").

The young Nietzsche passionately accuses historicism of being a position without a creative component. He turns mainly against Germans (it would be difficult to find a more anti-German philosopher than Nietzsche). He also notes the disappearance of instinct, which he calls the "divine animal."

We recall that Nietzsche received a solid education as a classical philologist. His violent diatribe against historicism seems to stem from an internal contradiction peculiar to this specialization. Nietzsche's bearded teachers, university professors strolling thoughtfully along the streets and parks of Leipzig, dress in black suits and equally black shoes. They know everything there is to know about Homer, Pindar and Herodotus, Aeschylus and Sophocles. In the evening they return to their apartments—crammed with furniture—and eat sauerkraut. These are upstanding, modest exponents of the petite bourgeoisie. The contrast between the object of their studies and themselves could not be greater. The heroes of their studies—legendary poets, the lawgivers of European culture—seem to be giants, while they are dwarfs armed with dictionaries, patience, and oceans of time. They are like experts on volcanoes. But the volcanic qualities of the subject of their studies do not rub off in the least. How do they differ from the remainder of the upstanding citizens of Leipzig? In nothing. In autumn fog and dressed in black frock coats, they move slowly, like tired old elephants.

The young Nietzsche cannot bear this pettiness, this distance between the astounding erudition of professors of classical philology and the ordinariness of their provincial existence. "Live," he says to them, "dance, be like those others." Of course, these appeals go unheeded. The professors, awkward and nearsighted, will not change into Greeks. Nor will Nietzsche, who liked to devour the sausage sent to him in packages by his mother, undergo a metamorphosis and change into Apollo.

But Nietzsche feels the stunning contrast between methodical, positivistic historicism and fanciful Athens. He defends life. Later this becomes his philosophical obsession. For the time being, however, the young Nietzsche is having an appealing, healthy reaction to the pedanticism of history cultivated in a positivist spirit.

Nietzsche's essay goes even further, however; it almost leads to the discarding of historicism, to discounting memory. Historical memory appears to him as the opposite of creativity. The creative impulse of a man living in the here and now can be weakened only in confrontation with great models of the past. The unusual, impoverished past becomes a tree, in whose shade are wilting the germs of new talents. History shows its malicious, destructive visage.

Now please reach for another book, Zbigniew Herbert's *Barbarian in the Garden*. Its author is also a young man, a poet in his thirties from Warsaw, traveling in France and Italy. This wanderer, living in cheap hotels, so obviously satisfied that he was able to cross the grim border—then described theatrically and metaphorically as the Iron Curtain—indefatigably visits Italian and French cities, examines cathedrals and museums, paintings and sculptures, and jots down his impressions. It never occurs to him to get angry at historicism. On the contrary, his feelings about history—and historicism—are unusually tender. Historical memory, and especially the loveliest component of it, which has been preserved in works of art, is something absolutely vivifying.

The author of *Barbarian in the Garden* does not say this directly, but an alert reader cannot help but notice that his devoted interest in Siena and Arles is strengthened even more by circumstances of a political-police nature. A newcomer from Warsaw would not have received a passport without difficulty. His country—how much poorer in cathedrals and paintings than Italy or France—was destroyed by a cruel war and then by Communism. To make matters worse, Communism declared war on memory. Feeling uncertain about its freshly declared utopia, Communism was like a madman who throws his most valuable possessions from a fifteen-story window.

Whoever has not lived through something like this cannot know the incredible contempt with which Communism treated the past when it still believed in itself. Antiquity, the Middle Ages, and the Renaissance were depicted in schoolbooks as epochs full of mistakes, ravings, misunderstandings, and crimes. Perhaps this would not have been a bad description of history if its only goal and assumption were not the even more servile glorification of the reigning system.

Herbert speaks of old paintings with the greatest love. It is a love that extends to the entire world of objects bearing traces of human work, human presence. The stone steps into which passersby have pressed the delicate arches of erosion. The smiles of medieval angels. But also the little café in Siena, benches, homes, squares.

Nor can anyone accuse Herbert of being naïve—the chapter devoted to the Albigensians and the cruelty with which this sect was annihilated shows that history is the domain of not only artists but executioners. Except that even the cruelty and the corresponding suffering do not lend themselves to visual or any other kind of representation. The cruelty is described in chronicles; the suffering vanishes together with the last victim's cry (unless we believe painters, the source of paintings depicting Christ's agony, and trust the empirical sources of their experience).

Herbert accepts history with all its duality of architecture and pain; he came to know a world in which memory had been liquidated or at least drastically amputated, and that is exactly why *Barbarian in the Garden* can be interpreted as the notes of a man who is revived by his contact with small, sunny towns, the receptacles of history.

For Nietzsche, memory, whose keepers were those men in black frock coats, became something deforming, paralyzing, inhibiting. Herbert expresses a modern sensitivity, the sensitivity of a citizen of a totalitarian country in which red ties replaced black frock coats and primitive lies supplanted a positivistically oriented historical erudition.

In the second half of the nineteenth century, history could have been a curse; in the second half of the twentieth century, historical memory that looked back to ancient, almost mythical times could bring cheer to itinerant poets.

For similar reasons, other writers of our epoch made memory superior to all other cultural values and virtues. With all due regard to memory—and the writers who praised it—I will say, however, that memory should not be accorded so high a place. It certainly does not deserve to be monopolistic or dictatorial. Memory is an indispensable component of creating culture, but isn't it true that it records and preserves the creative act rather than expresses itself in it? Elements characteristic of creativity often have little in common with memory, for example, innovation and rebellion: both are rather hostile to memory. In creativity there is also that basic and nonchalant je ne sais quoi, whose very nature does not lend itself to description. Yet it is exactly this which transforms clay into sculpture, words into poetry, and rustling sounds into music. Then comes memory and builds bridges between moments of vision. How important this is and necessary. Yet to build a bridge one must first—small detail—come upon a river.

CRACOW

CITIES THAT ARE too beautiful lose their individuality. Some of the southern towns cleaned up for tourists remind one more of glossy photo ads than of organic human settlements. Ugliness creates individuality. Cracow cannot complain of a dearth of infelicitous, heavy, melancholy places.

Right next to light Renaissance streets are dark, almost black canyons rilling through nineteenth-century townhouses. Blue trams, trucks, somnolent passersby in winter coats, and villagers in thick caftans make their way through these ravines. Yet two feet away one finds bright, graceful streets leading to the market square.

Similarly, neurological cells serve our brain's nerve centers, which are the prima donnas of our organism. And, similarly, in the medieval monastery the monks who knew Aristotle's treatises by heart were helped in their everyday, difficult, practical life by monks with hale complexions and large, strong hands.

Here are the names of a few heavy and ugly streets: Dluga, Krakowska, Starowislna, Zwierzyniecki (not to mention the right bank Podgorze). And it was on Dluga that I found my first student lodgings.

I arrived in Cracow as a matriculated eighteen-year-old from Gliwice, a provincial Silesian city, in which I spent my childhood and adolescence. My family was expelled from Lvov, the mythical eastern city. My entire childhood was spent under the sign of longing for the lost Lvov, which I had left as a four-month-old infant. In coming to Cracow, I felt like a pilgrim making a pilgrimage to a holy place. Cracow was a real city.

I found myself in Cracow in October. It was cool under a cold, slanting rain. Classes had not yet begun at the university, so I had a lot of time on my hands. I spent hours walking all over the city. I was a shy student and didn't dare enter stores, bookshops, or museums. For now, I looked at everything from the outside. The gates were closed, the yellow light of warm bulbs glowed in windows.

There was neither jealousy nor distaste nor proletarian anger in me. I was brimming with astonishment. It was enough for me to catch sight of the edge of a bookcase to say to myself: a philosopher, wise man, or renowned writer probably lives here.

I took Dluga Street to Planty and I would walk around Planty, even though the paths were often covered with a layer of autumn dampness and corpses of leaves knocked to the ground by the wind.

Planty separated two kinds of streets, dark and bright, and it is a kind of dike between the murky waters of the suburbs and the pure stream of the city center. In the summer the lush trees—ash, chestnut, elm, linden, even the plane, which is a rarity in Poland—create a dense canopy in which intelligent birds make their homes. But then, in October, the crowns of the trees were thinning.

I looked respectfully upon the walls of monastery gardens that took up quite of bit of space in the city's center. Gradually I discovered that one could look at the churches from two mounds, those of Kosciuszko and Krakus in the Podgorze area. Cracow's churches remind one of ships sailing next to one another. Seen from Kosciuszko's mound, their prows face the observer (because, of course, they were built on an east-west axis). From Krakus's mound, however, one sees their long brick naves, the enormous bodies of the sanctuaries. And it is not the Marian church that seems the largest but St. Catherine's and the Church of Corpus Christi.

They sail next to one another, crowded but gigantic. Their seas are the roofs of townhouses, secessionist towers, and cupolas, gleaming sometimes when the sun emerges from violet clouds after a downpour.

Seen from Krakus's mound, the city seems to blur distinctions between that which is ugly and that which is lovely. Suddenly everything seems necessary. The dark and heavy streets change into furrows of waves. And the churches themselves become something ponderous. We are not in Italy. The ships sail from afar.

I spent a lot of time gazing into bookstore windows. I remember that once I stood before the window of a former Gebethner bookstore (I didn't know what the name of it was at the time), where books and records were on display. A couple from the provinces, an old man with the face of a squire and his wife, stopped next to me. The squire pointed to a record with Brahms's Fourth Symphony. That is very difficult music, he said to his wife.

I was transported into raptures: I was not alone in my wanderings. Brahms's Fourth Symphony united us for an instant. I tore myself away from the window display right away, however, and continued my journey, in the direction of the dark mass of Wawel. I was busy admiring the city. My walks grew longer and longer, but I always returned to the main square.

One of my paths led along the banks of the Vistula, up the river. To my left were garden plots covered with autumn rust, on the right the Vistula flowed calmly. On the other bank I could see boat docks and even now, on sunny afternoons, students in sport shirts sitting in their boats as if they were enormous brown insects prepared for regattas. I finally got to the city, where I looked closely at the Italianate buildings of the convent of the Norbertine Sisters.

I also walked the enormous expanse of the Blonie. Sometimes the fog concealed the center of Cracow, and it seemed that I was in the country, in a spacious meadow, alone.

From the Blonie through Jordan Park I reached the neighborhood surrounding January 18 Street. This was, and is, an intellectual, serious, quiet residential area. And, once again, just about every passerby seemed to be a painter or an actor.

I frequented churches on weekdays, when there were no people in them, except for two old women kneeling before the altar and communicating with Jesus in whispers.

Someone told me about a cheap cafeteria in which intellectuals ate. Someone else told me where the Bishops' Palace was. I found the buildings of the main theaters and the editorial offices of literary journals on my own. I figured out where the Philharmonic was. This building, still used by the symphony orchestra, is ugly and nonfunctional—not a few adagios have been marred by the grating of tram wheels—but even the Philharmonic sent me into raptures.

Then I lived in Cracow and spent almost seventeen years

there. My rapture dissolved in the everyday. Gradually I got to know the local luminaries, artists, scholars, editors. I cannot say that I became disenchanted with all of them. But few met the expectations of that first vision. The artists were often drunk; I couldn't understand this, I thought that the spirits of the imagination should have been enough. The scholars were very cautious. The editors perspicacious. All of them lowered their voices when they began to speak of things political. Some sort of pall hung over the city. I felt like a traveler who had stumbled upon a place threatened by a monster, the Minotaur.

And yet one couldn't talk about the Minotaur! I, of course, was no innocent wanderer, coming from nowhere. I, too, was tainted by the totalitarian disease, except that I was coming from the provinces and the nothingness of childhood, and that is why I was in a position to notice the strange atmosphere of danger, uncertainty, capitulation.

As we all know, this changed. But this is not what I want to talk about; I want to discuss my return to Cracow in June 1989, after a seven-year absence. During those seven years I had been in the great and well-endowed cities of the West— Paris, New York, Stockholm. I had seen Boston, San Francisco, Amsterdam, London, Lisbon, Munich. I am not bragging about this, because there is nothing to brag about (if one is not an urban architect). I mention it only to explain that I returned to Cracow as a blasé tourist.

Yes, many things in Cracow now seemed small and provincial, poor and neglected. The auditorium of the Old Theater, in which I had experienced the greatest theatrical thrills, had gotten smaller. In my memory it was enormous; in reality, not very large.

I now walked the streets of Cracow ascertaining how much

smaller it had become. But after a while, quite unexpectedly, I rediscovered my former admiration for the royal city. And so it happened that I roamed Cracow feeling simultaneously its smallness and greatness, its provinciality and splendor, its poverty and riches, its ordinariness and extraordinariness. I was certain of just one thing: the trees in Planty had grown. My admiration was undercut by doubt, but the trees had become even more majestic, even more real.

In the Library

I AM IN a large library. I raise my eyes from a volume of Keats's letters and observe my neighbors, other readers. They are mainly students, of both sexes. (Because I am forty years old, they seem like children to me; and I, in turn, am an old man, a senior citizen, to them.)

The women open their compacts every once in a while and check themselves in the mirrors, as if to see whether contact with culture has not deteriorated their complexions. The library is located in Paris; many persons have plastic bottles full of mineral water—Evian, or Volvic, or Vichy—the last brand has historical associations for foreigners.

The students are bent over books and copy long, endless quotations from them. Under the balls of pens the sheets of large notebooks begin to curl slightly, as if devoured by flames. We live, it is true, in an era of computers, but the students still transfer long quotations to the pages of their notebooks, just as if they were living in the Middle Ages.

Long quotations. I look over someone's shoulder. "Post-modernism." "An ironic approach, suspicion which never leaves its post." "A parodic attitude toward the past." Or, a bit differently: "History, as the subject and the invisible dictator of taste, language, and sensitivity, has taken over the minds of Europe; its first ministerial post was filled by Giambattista Vico, Hölderlin's friend Hegel, and a certain impudent Corsican, who was born on an island and died on an island." In yet another notebook I find the following words: "Poetry lives only in language; the poetic work is a work of language par excellence. One cannot imagine a poem beyond the medium of the language, just as one cannot hear a nightingale in Boston. Language is not simply a vehicle for poetry, just as a bicycle is not merely a vehicle for the bicycle."

And still another notebook bends under the weight of the following sentence: "The propertied classes produce not just butter and guns, but also more and more perfect spiritual creations. Finally, they are ready to produce even violent criticism of themselves; everything that could possibly be sold appears on the market, including sneers and contempt for oneself."

Suddenly I realize that I am witness to an important event. Ideas, expressed in books, are joined in this library with the minds of readers.

Ideas, expressed in books! After all, I know the authors of books—I meet them at congresses and conferences. I know them well (after all, I write books myself). These usually are people who are rather shy, consumed by doubt, experiencing long bouts of silence, depression, emptiness. When on the occasion of an international congress they are supposed to speak up, they are usually uncertain of their opinions; many of them stutter, make mistakes, speak hedgingly. They expect discussion, reactions; they are ready to change their minds whenever they come across resistance or criticism. They are flexible; one day they will say yes, another no, and on the third they recognize this as a fine dialectic.

They love paradoxes, they love to shock their listeners. Of course, they are basically seeking truth, but if on the way to truth they hit upon a striking paradox, they forget about the aim of their wandering. They lock themselves in their studies, and from the labile, rocking mass of thoughts and impressions, they form books, which immediately become something final, irrevocable, as if frost had cut down the flowers.

Students, however, know nothing about doubts that tug at the authors of books; like medieval copyists, all the students do is transfer the writers' opinions to scored composition notebooks. And this is a particular moment: it is exactly now that ideas, expressed freely, riskily, neurotically, take on the attributes of law.

I look at the bowed heads of male and female students. I look at the pencils, pens, and ballpoints moving quickly, recording ideas. I see that students have a boundless trust in books. Ideas become a prison. They assume a legal power, as binding as Lenin's decrees. And it is not the print but the swaying vista of black and blue ink that endows ideas with superhuman strength. The faith of the students, the questions of the examiners.

I look at the students. I think about books and their authors. I am free.

THE UNTOLD CYNICISM
OF POETRY

THE INNER WORLD, which is the absolute kingdom of poetry, is characterized by its inexpressibility. It is like air; certainly there are truths in it, tensions, differences in temperature, but its chief characteristic is absolute transparency. What then does this inner world accomplish if in spite of its inexpressibility it wants more than anything to express itself? It uses cunning. It pretends that it is interested, oh yes, very interested, in external reality. A great state is in decline? The inner world is ecstatic: it has a subject! Death appears on the horizon? The inner world—it thinks itself immortal—quivers with excitement. War? Terrific. Suffering? Excellent. Trees? Overblown roses? Even better. Reality? Bravo. Reality is simply indispensable; if it did not exist, one would have to invent it.

Poetry attempts to cheat reality; it pretends that it takes reality's worries seriously. It shakes its head knowingly. Oh, it says, another earthquake. Injustice again. Floods, revolutions. Once again someone has reached old age.

Poetry fears that its secret will be discovered. One day reality may notice that the heart of poetry is cold. That poetry has no heart at all, just big eyes and an excellent ear. Reality will suddenly understand that it was only a bottomless source of metaphors for poetry, and it will vanish. Poetry will remain alone in the world, mute, empty, sad, and incommunicable.

Essentialist in Paris

1.

THE PARISIAN DIARIES of Ernst Jünger form a book, or a series of books, that is truly astounding. Let us refresh our memories: Jünger, a writer whose literary career began with a paean to a soldier's heroism in the trenches of the First World War, in the twenties kept company with ideologues of national bolshevism (National-Bolschewismus), so to speak, thereby making him a radical nationalist; afterward, however, he became a determined, if discreet, opponent of the Nazis. In the thirties this lover of men of action began to announce himself on the side of pure contemplation. In 1939 he published the novel *On the Marble Cliffs*, which was read by thoughtful readers as a subtle manifestation of opposition to the absolute power of the Nazis.

In Paris Jünger found himself in the uniform of a Wehrmacht captain, and participated in the short campaign on Paris. He was assigned to Chief of Staff Headquarters in France, which was shortly to become a nest of conspirators against Hitler.

If the war brought happiness to someone, at least in the beginning (because in the last months he was to lose his beloved son), then it was Jünger. This extraordinary observer, well acquainted with history, botany, mineralogy, and hermetic sciences, was thrown into Paris, the richest European city—if one does not count Rome—in terms of civilization. While others fought, Jünger looked. Paris became his book to decipher, a book of plants, insects, minerals, paintings, tapestries. Paris was his herbarium, his arboretum, his dream book, a mine for geological discoveries, a used bookshop, a house of ill repute, a library, a map, an astronomical atlas.

He took long walks and looked. He could walk even in the evening and at night, during curfew, when Parisians generally were condemned to house arrest (and television hadn't been invented yet!).

He took walks, noting, like a traveler in a strange country, his favorite trees—the Judas tree, for example—and also rare minerals and insects. He also tracked unusual specimens of people; he noticed the nihilists, who were obsessed with destruction. Céline is especially prominent, accusing Germans he meets at a party of inadequately persecuting Jews.

Jünger sees the world as an incalculably diverse whole, in which there are countless drawers of species, varieties and levels, types, personalities and exceptions. Reality is complex and multilayered, but ordered. It is no accident that one of Jünger's greatest spiritual authorities is the Swedish botanist Linnaeus. The contemplation to which Jünger devotes himself is not wild or capricious; right next to the element of aesthetic delight is the most rational moment of classification. The Latin name of a plant becomes the crowning glory of an act of almost loving contemplation. The same happens with minerals. And sometimes people, too.

Jünger is drawn to classifications. He truly believes that the world is ordered and that the "botanical" mind does not impose upon a strange reality its webs of terminology but rather reaches, with Latin elegance, the concealed structure of a thing. Thus people, too, must be divided, segregated. Why, even the ancients formulated a typology of temperaments.

He does not, however, like Darwin, not for the same reasons as religious fundamentalists—that Darwin deviated from scriptural truth—but for introducing into aristocratic botany the vulgar element of rivalry, elbowing, plebeian envy. Darwin looked at nature the way Balzac looked at bourgeois society, and this displeases Jünger, a connoisseur of tiny differences between scarlet blots on butterfly wings, autumn roses.

The idea of a concealed, organic order is the intellectual nucleus of Jünger's vision of the world; too bad that this sometimes causes confusion between a universal sense of this concept and Prussian state legacy. Until he was twenty-three, Jünger was a subject of the Prussian king, and he remains loyal to his monarch with an enthusiasm worthy of a better kingdom.

Jünger's favorite epoch, therefore, is not the age of the steam engine but the century that sported wigs. In the eighteenth century he sees the waning of the great tradition of thinking in large wholes, at a time when faith and reason, liberalism and conservatism had not yet collided in a battle full of hatred and partisanship. Out of this partly imagined tradition, Jünger first chooses a style, an aristocratic, calm style emerging from a profound knowledge of the world, on the assumption that the world can be known and that each of its regions has its own Linnaeus.

He reads Saint-Simon and Jean-François Marmontel, Antoine Rivaroli (whom he translates) and Emmanuel-Joseph Sieyès. He reads omnivorously. He reads everything. He reads

Vasily Rozanov and Léon Bloy, André Gide, books about catastrophes at sea and about the fate of the shipwrecked. He studies the Bible and the 1895 work of Abbé Profillet, *The Martyrdom of the Church in Japan*. He regularly visits the used bookshops on rue Bonaparte and the modest bookstalls overlooking the Seine (the same clumsy wooden boxes, which to this day grow out of the stone balustrades of the riverside boulevards like enormous polypores around the trunk of a maple). He reads the diaries of the Goncourts and Dostoyevsky's novels. He reads everything because he wants to know everything. Or otherwise he reads everything because he already knows everything and his readings are the gesture of a magnate who, out of politeness, asks his tenants how the crops look this year, even though he has long since formed his opinion on the subject.

The surrealists did seek knowledge, but it was an irrational, mad knowledge, deriving from stupefaction. Aldous Huxley also voiced praise of mad, narcotic knowledge. Jünger did not treat these pronouncements lightly at all; he even describes in great detail his own experiences with narcotics, except that in his writing it is just one of the wings of a larger edifice in which even reason is not deprived of beautiful rooms.

Someone who may not have encountered Jünger's works might exclaim: What an extraordinary, rare writer! Why isn't he better known? Why did he travel to Stockholm? Why do we live in an epoch which searches for truth in vain, which does not even know what spiritual order is? You tell us about an author who found this order, and you discuss this calmly as if it were a matter of reviewing the book of a fledgling poet and not presenting an intellectual master of the greatest caliber.

If, in fact, a reader did accuse me of these things, I would understand his intentions: I myself am amazed that I cannot draw more enthusiasm from myself for this original writer. I have been reading his books for years. I like the difference in Jünger's tone, the anachronism of his imagination, the scale of his erudition; I admire his style (except perhaps when he goes heavy on the definitions, becomes slightly pedantic and almost pompous). I relish mainly Jünger's un-todayness. His reflections concerning the order of reality thrill me. I admire his powers of observation. Yet in spite of this, in spite of my returning to his works every so many years, I cannot recognize him as a spiritual master. He is instead a master of ambivalence. And I am not just thinking of his biographical ambivalence—praise of World War I (an absurd war), the uniform of a captain in the Wehrmacht, before that a nationalistic episode, discretion regarding the Holocaust—although this is not without significance. (Sometimes in his Parisian diary one stumbles across a formulation worse than ambivalent, as in the entry dated May 15, 1943: "The Jew, generally speaking, is not very likable.")

The fundamental ambivalence is located even more deeply. From someone who has touched the sense of the world, someone who has *seen* the order of the cosmos, we expect some sort of rare, white-hot intellectual energy. Prometheus offered people fire, Shakespeare *King Lear*. Meanwhile, Jünger's writing is permeated with a puzzling frigidity and enigmatic reticence, as if the favorite subjects of observation for this writer—that is, botany, mineralogy, and entomology—radiated onto all the literature created by him a silence characteristic of inanimate nature and of our older but more impoverished cousins, the insects.

To know the order of the world—and what? What is one

to do with this, how is one to live with this knowledge? Mince
one's words, suggest fantastic kinships between various levels
of being, describe fabulously lush dreams . . . ? So much . . .
And just so much? I do not want to join the moralists of the
final hour, who hurriedly and in poor language condemn each
person who was born at the wrong moment. Yet the distance
between the absolute aspiration (I have come to know the order
of things) and the cold-blooded discretion with which Jünger
passes through the most trying periods of the war gives me no
peace and results in my asking myself once again, So literature,
even a literature clothed in beautiful language and inventive,
intelligent metaphors, can erase the truth, fabricate a dense
smoke of ambivalence? Literature: a Persian carpet concealing
a reality of brute force?

Jünger is not and cannot be a spiritual master; the writers
of great nations, experiencing the basest episodes of their own
history, stand before a very difficult choice. If they come to
know the world, however, they see it better than their other
contemporaries, and then they have to decide whether they
are capable of living and working like Alexander Solzhenitsyn.

Below this level of perspicacity and courage there is also
quite a bit of room for other, less ruthless and less masterly
writers. Nor is there a lack of room for the enchanting stylist
and scholar, an excellent narrator of dreams (usually there is
nothing less interesting than someone else's dreams) who delights us with the arabesque of his observations and reflections.

2.

The Parisian diaries of Ernst Jünger are also a rather perverse
social chronicle: the representatives of the Parisian artistic community met by Jünger become, in our eyes, practically au-

tomatically, collaborators. Who does not make an appearance!
Picasso, Cocteau, Paul Morand, Braque, Marcel Jouhandeau,
Paul Léautaud, Jean Marais, Sacha Guitry, and many others
(in passing, I should mention that Sacha Guitry told the German writer an anecdote about Octavian Mirbeau, who on his
deathbed whispered, "Ne collaborez jamais!"; he was speaking
not about the occupiers, however, but against Guitry's using
co-authors to write his plays).

One person Jünger does not meet is Jean-Paul Sartre. Sartre,
meanwhile, who had just returned from a German prison,
lived in Paris and feverishly partook in literary and philosophical activity; he had a passionate interest in existentialism and
was a radical existentialist. Only when we look at Jünger as a
contemporary of Sartre do we see in him an equally radical
essentialist.

One example should suffice: in *Nausea* the reader will find
a famous scene, often included in anthologies, that depicts
the protagonist observing the roots of a certain tree in a public
garden. The bared, damp roots arouse nausea in Sartre's *porte-
parole.* They are the embodiment of the absurd world. The
bared roots stand for senselessness, strangeness; they are terrifying, inhuman.

Now let us imagine Jünger before that very same tree. We
would have found out where that author had seen a similar
tree. The amorous gaze of a connoisseur would have slid along
the roots and boughs of the tree. We would have been privy
to observations concerning the kind of soil the tree likes to
grow in and a list of the insects that like to live close by. We
would know who brought it to Europe (if it came from another
continent) and for which emperor. And, of course, at the end
of the description would blossom the tree's Latin name.

To the existentialist, who is nothing but a gigantic and

hysterical consciousness, the tree seems a sinister and unnecessary creature, a Loch Ness monster. For the essentialist, on
the other hand, the tree is being in the full sense of the word,
constituting a solid rung in the great ladder of nature.

In Sartre the world is obscured by the clouds of our caprices,
choices, and relentless settling of accounts with our conscience. In Jünger, it is just the opposite; the world changes
into a gigantic warehouse, full of rocks, flowers, artwork, cities,
streets, and temperaments. An extreme fatalism takes the place
of Sartre's arbitrary activism. What is must be. Prophecies,
speaking in the language of dreams, must be fulfilled. People
act in accordance with their fates, of which they are unaware.
"It will be a feast for the eyes, there will be no dearth of
spectacles," he noted in his diary in the spring of 1939, fore-
telling the approaching war. The future will move like an
iceberg. Executioners will execute, technicians will utilize
technology, soldiers will employ the arts of war, painters will
not stop painting (unless, of course, one of them disappears
into a dark torture chamber). The human figures in Jünger's
fresco are as tiny as the figures in early medieval paintings.

The existentialist and the essentialist on the Paris street in
1943 or 1944: the dual madness of reason. Neither, of course,
is right: neither the subjective, irresponsible Sartre, seeking
only authenticity, nor the fatalistic, passive Jünger. The short,
nearsighted Sartre, in glasses thick as the window of a bathy-
scaphe, and the average-sized Jünger, endowed with the sight
of a hawk.

THE DOORMAN

WHEN I CAME home from a long walk, the doorman said that I no longer lived here.

"Why?" I asked, more out of surprise than fright.

"You didn't exist enough," he answered.

"What do you mean?"

"Well, my dear sir," he went on, "those bouts of sadness, silence, melancholy . . . They did not go unremarked."

"And what about you?" I shouted. "You don't exist at all. All you do is read the sports section and watch television."

"That's true," the doorman agreed, "sacred truth. Except that I don't *have* to exist. I'm a doorman, an observer."

"No," I countered, "I'm the observer."

"You are mistaken, my dear sir," he answered firmly. "But it doesn't matter anyway. We were counting on your existing beautifully."

"And you mean I disappointed you?"

"The best proof is that you no longer live here."

Indeed, I noticed at that very moment that someone new was moving into my apartment.

When we passed each other, I whispered maliciously, "Well, you won't be staying here long."

THE TWO DEFECTS
OF LITERATURE

1. When the writer is preoccupied with only himself, his own weaknesses, his own life, and forgets about the objective world, the search for truth.

2. When the writer is preoccupied with only the truth of the world, objective reality, justice, and judging people, epochs, and customs, and forgets about himself, his own weaknesses, his own life.

LECTURE ON MYSTERY

WE DO NOT know what poetry is. We do not know what suffering is. We do not know what death is.

We do know what mystery is.

ZEAL

HANNAH ARENDT IN one of her letters to Karl Jaspers mentions a certain German professor of classical philology who—while Hitler was in power—unasked, of his own free will, translated the Horst Wessel song into Greek.

EXISTENTIALISM

EARLY ON I was enamored of existentialism. Oh yes, I thought, I have been cast into the world. I do not know what to do with my freedom. History is meaningless. I should think about death. I must be authentic. Tree roots are absurd.

O indiscreet philosophers, I note now that you want to deprive me of even that which is my most private property, my secret. You want to name and classify half situations and quarter moods. Your professorial pencil pushes its way into everything. O indiscreet, narcissistic philosophers, write poems instead.

THE WORLD IS TORN

YES, I TOO would like unity to prevail in the world, to have the spiritual side of life join harmoniously with civic life, and the latter, in turn, with emotional life, and so forth. But this is not how things are. That strange and enthralling way of being, the spiritual life, does not submit to political mandates and barely tolerates ethical postulates. Thoughts are free. The life of the spirit can be mad, brash, even insolent. Meanwhile, the civic code requires responsibility, discretion, common sense. I support republican virtues with all my heart. What of it, though, if the spirit is neither a monarchist nor a democrat. Chaos, disorder is its element (just as discipline and form are—it constantly moves between these two contradictory poles). Yet a similar inconstancy would be scandalous in civic life. Anarchic, nonchalant sallies seem fitting to art, but they would be inappropriate in the office of a judge, in the mind of a minister, in an official monitor.

The world is torn. Long live duality! One should praise what is inevitable.

Central Europe

HE WAS AN unremarkable, tiny man with dark greasy hair combed flat across his head who, without waiting for permission, joined my table. It was clear he was dying to talk. He would have exchanged half his life for a moment of conversation.

"Where are you from?" he asked.

"From Poland," I said.

"Ah, how lucky, how lucky you are!" he exclaimed, overcome by genuine Mediterranean enthusiasm. "Mourning! Long live mourning! Black coats. Commemorative jewelry. Beautiful poems on a soldier's death. I know all about it, all about it. Fog, stubble, cavalry. Crosses. Thousands of gallant men. Fanfare, signals, dirges. Lovely, lovely. You are a lucky man."

"Why lucky?"

"Force. Force of conviction. Categorical feelings. Moral integrity. A literature that is not alienated from the polis. You have not experienced that alarming split. That state of half hallucination in which the soul of the individual seems to grow like a balloon filled with the helium of narcissism. Never. You have never known the horrible division, the irreversible separation between the world of the soul and the world of brave, masculine energy.

"I always felt in you the desire for unity, the Greek dream of combining emotion and courage. Isn't it better to acquiesce to even historical defeat and discomfort, temporary political imperfection, and in return delight in the unadulterated access to the spiritual sphere, by picking flowers from both meadows, the white inner one and the other scarlet one, dark from contact with the pungent air of history?"

And he spoke a long time, constantly praising my country. After a while, however, I felt that praise alone was beginning to bore him. A light grimace twisted his face.

"Tell me," he asked, without really expecting a reply and without leaving room for it in his dense monologue, "please tell me if they, your poets, were completely honest. They complained that their homeland was taken from them, didn't they? Were they really honest? Wasn't there a bit of hypocrisy? And their own unhappiness, doubt? Boredom? They lied a bit, didn't they? They are people like you and me, aren't they?"

I groped for an answer; I wanted to defend the poets of my language. Before I was able to collect my thoughts, however, the little man jumped up from his chair and deftly leaped into another across from a tourist, two tables down. An instant later, I caught snatches of the new conversation.

"May I ask where you are from?"

"I am from Prague."

"Ah, marvelous. Prague! Orgy of the baroque! Prague, the bowels of Europe. With that amazingly tart but vivifying sense of humor that comes from who knows where."

And so on.

I paid for two coffees and left.

I Killed Hitler

It is late; I am old. I should finally confess to what happened in the summer of 1937 in a small town in Hesse. I killed Hitler.

I am Dutch, a bookbinder, retired for some years now. In the thirties I was passionately interested in the tragic European politics of the time. But then my wife was Jewish, and my interest in politics was in no way academic. I decided to wipe out Hitler myself, with a draftsman's precision, just as one would bind a book. And I did it.

I knew that Hitler liked to travel in the summer with a small group, practically without bodyguards, and that he stopped in small villages, often in outdoor restaurants, in the shade of linden trees.

What good are the details. I will say only that I shot him and was able to get away.

It was a humid Sunday, a storm was on its way, bees meandered as if they were drunk.

The restaurant was concealed beneath enormous trees. The ground was covered with a fine gravel.

It was almost completely dark, and there was such drowsiness in the air that it took great effort to press the trigger. A wine bottle was knocked over and a red blot spread over the white paper tablecloth.

Then I sped away in my small car like a demon. But no one was after me. The storm broke, down came a heavy rain.

Along the way I threw the gun into a ditch overgrown with nettles; I flushed out two geese, which began to run with an awkward waddle.

Why the details?

I returned home triumphant. I tore off the wig, burned my clothes, washed the car.

And all for naught, because the next day someone else, exactly like him down to the last detail and perhaps even crueler than the one I killed, took his place.

The newspapers never mentioned the murder. One man vanished, another appeared.

The clouds that day were completely black, the air sticky as molasses.

EVIL

TOTALITARIANISM—BECAUSE IT is an organized, orchestrated, highly developed evil on a historic scale—leads to the illusion that evil can finally be understood. Isn't that why we are fascinated by a variety of books, from memoirs to historical analyses, devoted to Hitler and Stalin? We read them and hope that this time we shall grasp the essence of evil.

All the efforts of the intellect are directed toward reducing this sophisticated form of evil to a simple, uncomplicated form. When we are finally successful, we realize that the answer to our question has once again eluded us. We are again as helpless as Job.

DROHOBYCZ AND
THE WORLD

THE SMALL, SHY drawing-and-crafts teacher at the secondary school in Drohobycz had tasted a few sweet moments of literary renown before he died in November 1942, gunned down on a street in his native town by a member of the SS. His career—if we forget for a moment about his tragic death —resembles writing careers in other countries or continents. A provincial autodidact begins to write and draw for himself and a handful of close friends. He corresponds with unknown, beginning artists like himself, sharing with them his dreams, thoughts, and projects. Whenever he meets anyone who has access to the real artistic world, to real publishing houses and known writers, he is awestruck and ingratiating—as in his letters to the psychologist Professor Szuman (whom I would occasionally see in Cracow in the sixties: an old man forced, for political reasons, into a premature and complete break with the university).

Then, thanks mainly to the influence of the eminent writer Zofia Nalkowska, the talented drawing teacher becomes the literary sensation of the season, and suddenly the names of the most significant figures of the prewar Polish cultural scene appear among his correspondents: Stanislaw Ignacy Witkiewicz (Witkacy), Julian Tuwim, Witold Gombrowicz. Bruno Schulz comes to know Boleslaw Lesmian, a poet whom he admires. He has a brief love affair with Nalkowska. He visits Warsaw, where, unassuming and quiet as always, he is introduced into its literary salons. Here he has a look at the literary theater of pre–World War II Warsaw: coffeehouses and elegant apartments where, for the time being and on equal terms, the future victims of two totalitarianisms and the future postwar functionaries of a nationalized literature meet. Witkacy will commit suicide in September 1939 after the Red Army's invasion of Poland's eastern territories. Gombrowicz will leave for Argentina, Tuwim for the United States. Nalkowska and Tadeusz Breza will become representatives of the Communist literary establishment.

Yet the known and recognized Schulz will not cast off his less illustrious correspondents, especially if they are women. He will write long letters to Debora Vogel, Romana Halpern, and Anna Plockier. All of them will perish in various episodes of the Holocaust.

Schulz published his works with the best publishers and in the prominent weekly *Wiadomosci Literackie* (The Literary News). He was, to be sure, attacked by critics on both sides of the political spectrum—by aggressive Marxist critics for not being realistic and by publicists of the extreme right for being too Jewish—yet his position was not weakened by these sallies. Schulz, who as an artist was a poet and bard of the provinces, was, paradoxically, supported and protected in the literary world by those in the political and literary mainstream. His trips to Hegelian Warsaw (aren't all capitals Hegelian?) became another source of tension in his life and thought. Of course, the luminaries of the capital had their appeal. In one of his letters, for example, he does not omit noting that he has made the acquaintance of the famous theater director Ryszard Ordynski, yet he returns to his little Drohobycz with relief. He considers moving to Warsaw, but always returns to his native city.

The lesser known of Schulz's correspondents are often people with deep-seated identity conflicts, people who were sometimes suspended between illness and health, who vacillated between two languages—Yiddish and Polish—who were uncertain of their artistic choices, or who were drawn to music and painting as strongly as to literature. They were close to Schulz because he, too, was uncertain of his choice between graphic art and prose, between family life and creative solitude, between Polish and German literature (he adored Rilke and Mann), between Drohobycz and Warsaw. Nevertheless, he was able to create his own sovereign and evocative vision from these contradictions and irresolutions. Even in the late thirties, when awarded the Golden Laurel by the Polish Literary Academy, Schulz still understood his unfulfilled, hybrid, lacerated correspondents. He acquired fame, made the ritual pilgrimage to Paris, sought to have his stories translated into foreign languages; yet throughout he remained in willing contact with these letter writers, for their dilemmas and conflicts were an emblem of the peripheral, of everything that was borderline and provincial—and Schulz needed to be bound to the provinces the way he needed air to breathe.

There was only one thing he defended with great ferocity and ruthlessness: the meaning and stature of the spiritual world. When in an ornery letter written at the request of a literary journal his old ally Witold Gombrowicz attacked him—saying that for the proverbial middle-class "doctor's wife from Wilcza Street" the artistic world of Schulz's stories can have no reality, that for this hyper-sober personage the author of *Cinnamon Shops* is "merely pretending"—Schulz replied sharply and resolutely. The value of the spiritual world can be undermined by depression, despair, doubt, the attack of a malicious critic, but not by a mythical "doctor's wife from Wilcza Street." Here the paths of the two friends parted. Gombrowicz was fascinated by the question of the value of art as seen by philistines, simpletons, idiots; he was capable of looking at literature from the outside and inquiring into its sociological status. Schulz, on the other hand, lived inside a frail ivory (cinnamon?) tower, and he was reluctant to leave it even for a moment.

Schulz's letters frequently take up the classic theme of the struggle to maintain the tension of an inner life, which is incessantly threatened by trivial, external circumstances and melancholy. A universal theme. Schulz, like many artists, confided to his correspondents the doubts he had about the destiny of his own work. Today we look at Bruno Schulz's destiny from the perspective of his absurd death in the ghetto of Drohobycz; the shadow of this death falls across his entire life. Yet there were many normal and ordinary things in his biography. The most extraordinary was undoubtedly his talent: the wondrous ability to transmute the commonplace into the bewitching. And it is exactly here—as in the case of many writers—that Schulz's anxiety is located, in the fear that he would lack the time and the inspiration, that the agony of daily teaching would devour him.

Who was Bruno Schulz, "sociologically speaking"? In his

prose, provincial Drohobycz was transformed into some sort of eastern Baghdad, into an exotic city out of A *Thousand and One Nights*. His life, touched by the same magical wand, also eludes classification. If he had not written and not drawn, he would have been only a melancholy, Jewish, middle-class crafts teacher, the hapless scion of a merchant family, a dreamer writing long letters to other dreamers. But because he wrote and drew so fluently, he left sociology behind. He even left behind that peculiar social stratum typical of interwar Poland, the intelligentsia, or that part of the intelligentsia which could not and did not wish to join in the life of the country, was not accepted by—and did not accept—the temporary reality of the Second Republic, and sometimes longed for the fulfillment of a political, leftist utopia.

Schulz's utopia did not oblige one to wait for it; it lived in his imagination, in his pen, in his epithets and synecdoches. There is no key to Schulz's work. Almost everything is said in his stories, including the erotic obsession, which he treats as familiarly and intimately as others treat their hay fever or migraines. Most frequently Schulz's prose reacts to stimuli of a purely poetic nature; if one were to write down the questions he wanted to "answer" artistically, they would be the questions of a metaphysical poet who wants to know what the essence of spring, a tree, or a house is. His is a breathtaking directness of attack, a driving passion for ultimate answers. In his philosophical-poetic curiosity, we can discern Schulz's spiritual ancestry. His writing derives from the neoromantic, antipositivistic, and antinaturalistic strain of literature, inspired in part by Bergson and Nietzsche, but which in fact was a response to the real, increasingly visible supremacy of the hard sciences.

In Central Europe this neoromantic strain, which wanted some sort of undefined religion in spite of the fact that God had "died," gave birth to many poets and writers touched by a metaphysical fever; they were authors of mystical treatises and novels who threw themselves at the mystery of being on the very first page of their works. Needless to say, many who took part in this metaphysical movement suffered artistic defeat. Those who were belated, slower, and more patient than the rest sometimes succeeded, sometimes achieved their own language, their own method, their own private metaphysics. Veterans of the neoromantic crisis—which reached its apogee at the turn of the century—included outstanding European writers such as Robert Musil and even Rilke, who completed his *Duino Elegies* in quite another epoch, when Ernest Hemingway, that emissary of the spirit of jazz, sport, and the laconic, was making his appearance in Paris.

Being late can be a virtue, and it certainly was in Schulz's case, just as Witkacy and Lesmian were fortunate in appearing after their time in Polish literature. Schulz's case, however, is distinct: In his work the metaphysical, imaginative tendency finds a real counterweight in the form of a specific geographic and familial reality, which the author of *Sanatorium Under the Sign of the Hourglass* draws from abundantly, as if recalling that literature is made of body and soul and that the neoromantic longing for the final, absolute elements of the world must be confronted with a hard, merciless, provincial, and idiomatic being.

This hard partner in Schulz's mysticism is Drohobycz (a small town in the vicinity of Lvov), which Schulz did not choose, just as one does not choose one's body, freckles, or genes. Schulz was born in Drohobycz, a town as modest as his own person. His imagination lived in Drohobycz, and the imagination is unbelievably sly. It is capable of praising a real, corporeal object in a manner that is highly ambivalent. It is capable of praising, augmenting, glorifying, embellishing; yet, at the same time, the embellishment and praise are the most sophisticated escape, the most elegant trick in the world, allowing us to leave our adored city! In transforming the cramped and dirty Drohobycz—in which probably only the half-wild gardens, orchards, cherry trees, sunflowers, and moldering fences were really beautiful—into an extraordinary, divine place, Schulz could say goodbye to it, he could leave it.

He could escape into the world of the imagination without offending the little town and, in fact, elevated it to rare heights. Now even New York knows a bit about Drohobycz, about Schulz's Drohobycz, which no longer exists; all because of the mad subterfuges of the imagination of a little arts-and-crafts teacher.

And only the Drohobycz created by Schulz has survived; the old, historic town, full of Jewish shops and twisting lanes, has vanished from the face of the earth. Now only Soviet Drohobycz exists, in all likelihood a masterpiece of socialist realism.

Among Schulz's favorite objects of contemplation are the seasons of the year, especially as they sweep across drowsy provincial towns. The capital lives its own nervous, narcissistic life, while the province is a place where civilization, diluted in the peripheries, takes up a dialogue with the cosmos, with nature. In the story "Autumn," Schulz characterizes summer as the season of utopia, a lush, opulent time of the year, which promises much but is incapable of keeping its promises because at its edges lurks a stingy and severe autumn, which has no respect for summer's oaths.

The sequence of utopian summer and cruel, cynical fall is a tempting metaphor both for Schulz's life—passing from the creative tension of his work to his tragic death in the Drohobycz ghetto—and for the fate of European literature, which first delights in the pleasures of the imagination and immediately afterward is doubly warned by history: the First World War and the coup de grace of World War II, with its associates genocide and vile totalitarianism. Schulz's life and work succumb to the summer-autumn schema as if the spirit of European literature needed someone who, through his fate, confirmed the development of things: the passing of the epoch of the imagination, the arrival of the epoch of devastation.

Schulz's language, its poetic and profligate riches, is characterized by great precision. The language reverberates with the same joining of oxymoronic qualities that is present in Schulz's overall artistic profile: the uniting of metaphysical passion with love of detail, of specific, absolutely individual things.

The German poet Gottfried Benn, born six years earlier than Schulz, often used the term *die Ausdruckswelt*, the world of expression. This term does not refer to any separate group or artistic direction; rather, it characterizes the work of writers who, with a greater or lesser degree of awareness, survived the tempestuous years of the neoromantic eruption and emerged dazzled once and for all by the linguistic and expressive possibilities of literature. The writers under the sign of *Ausdruckswelt* are enamored of the aesthetic force of language, and at the same time depend on its ability to sing the melody of the inner life. Let us not expect these writers to participate in discussions on the state of society.

In Schulz's writing there appear—built into the masterly structure of the poetic-linguistic fabric—the warnings connected with the inevitable approach of autumn/annihilation. Sober Adela reminds one of the character of Teresa in Elias Canetti's *Auto-da-Fé*; imagination is encircled by enemies. In Schulz's letters too there is an inner tension—creative moods surrounded by enemies, by the boredom of class lessons, by life's sad exigencies. There are evil demons and good demons; the world is full of mysteries; the tramp hidden in the garden may be the pagan god Pan. But Schulz is no prophet. He does not foresee the war; he does not foresee his own death. His message is delicate and reveals itself only to trusting readers in the act of reading. It is inaccessible to critics. Schulz was reticent; he proclaimed nothing. He was even more restrained than Kafka. For him, art was the supreme pleasure, an act of expression, the amplification of seeing and speaking, the primary act of binding things that were once remote from one another. His statement was neither political nor even philosophical. That which we call Schulz's philosophy is a bird that can live in only one cage, in the captivating sentences of his downy prose.

MURDER

THIS IS WHAT happened in Germany: Robert, a teacher of literature, maintained contact with a terrorist organization in the early seventies. He was ordered to kill M., a man his own age. M., despite his youth, gained some prominence as a conservative philosopher and journalist who spoke contemptuously of the radical left. The organization sentenced him to death. Robert was asked to carry out the sentence within three months. Horrified, Robert fled to Lisbon. He broke off all contact with the organization, lived very modestly under an assumed name, and translated Portuguese poetry. He feared the police and his former friends.

Years went by, however, and almost all the members of the terrorist group were arrested, had vanished, or had died in prison. Amnesty was declared for people, like Robert, who had been terrorist sympathizers. Robert finally returned to Germany. He lived in Cologne. He gave talks, worked for radio stations, tried to return to teaching in the schools. One day he met M.—whom he had known only rather fleetingly —and they became friends. M., who had seemed destined for a brilliant career as a scholar, had left the university, lived on unemployment, and read mysteries all day long. When asked by Robert why he had abandoned such a stable and promising career, M. answered that he no longer believed in anything and that he could not pretend, which—he said—was probably linked to something like a genetic flaw that had appeared in his family (on his father's side) for generations.

A few months later, both loners decided to share a large apartment in the center of town. A year later, Robert killed M. in a fit of rage. In court he claimed he could not stand M.'s cough and hated his heavy tread, the way he smacked his lips at meals, and the way he cut bread, holding the loaf to his chest.

THE ACTIVE VOICE

PLEASE FILL OUT the form. Please write a brief autobiography.

I obediently answered the questionnaire. I wrote numberless autobiographies, beginning always with the same obvious sentence, "I came into the world . . ." In other languages one says, "I was born"; only Polish uses the active voice, as if an infant, of its own will, energetically ran onto the stage between Germany and Russia.

The verve doesn't last long, for quickly the passive side takes over: I was assigned to . . . I was transported . . . I was arrested in December . . . released after universal amnesty was granted.

Fraternity Indeed

WRITING IS PERHAPS an act of brotherhood, first and foremost. Writing demands solitude, sometimes profound and radical solitude, but it usually is a tunnel leading to other people, dug in a fertile earth (and this earth is imagination and narcissism, compassion and indifference, tenderness and arrogance, music and ambition, blood and ink). Even suicides write letters. Poets kill themselves. Critics kill authors. Readers are easily bored and drown books as if they were kittens. But who said fraternity was easy? Please turn to the Bible . . .

ECSTASY AND IRONY

TWO CONTRADICTORY ELEMENTS meet in poetry: ecstasy and irony. The ecstatic element is tied to an unconditional acceptance of the world, including even what is cruel and absurd. Irony, in contrast, is the artistic representation of thought, criticism, doubt. Ecstasy is ready to accept the entire world; irony, following in the steps of thought, questions everything, asks tendentious questions, doubts the meaning of poetry and even of itself. Irony knows that the world is tragic and sad.

That two such vastly different elements shape poetry is astounding and even compromising. No wonder almost no one reads poems.

BACZYNSKI

WISLAWA SZYMBORSKA HAS written a fine poem entitled "In Broad Daylight":

He would travel to a mountain rooming house
And go down to the dining room
He would look at four spruce trees
Branch by branch
From his table by the window
Without shaking off their snow

His beard trimmed to a goatee
Balding, graying, bespectacled
The features of his face thick and weary
With a wart on his cheek and a furrowed brow
Angelic marble now covered with clay
He himself would not have known when this happened
Because the price for not having died sooner
Goes up gradually, not all at once
And pay the price he would

As for the bit of ear grazed by a bullet
When he ducked at the last minute—
"I was damned lucky," he would say.

While waiting for the chicken noodle soup to be served
He would read his daily paper
Bold headlines, ads in small print
Or drum his fingers on the snowy cloth
His palms long worn
His chapped hands, bulging veins

Occasionally someone would call from the threshold:
"Mr. Baczynski—telephone!"
And there would be nothing odd about it
That it was he rising, pulling down his sweater
Moving unhurriedly toward the door

No one would interrupt a conversation
Upon seeing him
No one would gasp, freeze in mid-gesture
Because seeing him would be common
And it's too bad, too bad, too bad
That it would be treated like a normal thing.

"In Broad Daylight" is included in *People on the Bridge*, a volume of poetry published in 1986. This poem has already been analyzed for its masterly use of the conditional tense, thanks to which we are dealing with a completely hypothetical situation; Krzysztof Kamil Baczynski, an extraordinarily gifted young poet, died (at age twenty-three) in the first days of the Warsaw Uprising in August 1944.

Baczynski is a legendary figure in Poland. He belongs to the pantheon of heroes who died young. His poems are published in enormous editions; in Szymborska's poem the dead youth changes into a sixty-year-old writer, a little gray, a little bald, and altogether ordinary. The only thing out of the ordinary is that the writer is alive. And it is precisely the fact that living does not amaze us that strikes us in Szymborska's poem.

I would, however, like to draw attention to the kind of life this hypothetical Baczynski leads in the poem which has drawn him from the other world. We are in a "mountain rooming house." Baczynski "frequents" this rooming house. He is at home in it. He would be reading the newspaper, waiting calmly for "chicken noodle soup." He would be called to the phone in an unhurried and natural manner, as if he were a regular member of the household rather than a special guest. For Baczynski would have to have been a famous poet, and the other guests would not have concealed their interest in the renowned sixty-year-old.

Unless . . . Unless this is a rooming house where no one bestows the least attention upon famous writers, for the simple reason that all its guests, waiting for their chicken noodle soup, are writers. (Perhaps not all are famous—but writers know each other too well to make much of rank and distinction.) So perhaps the rooming house is the Astoria in Zakopane, belonging to the Polish Writers Union, and also acts as a workplace.

But does this change anything in our understanding of Szymborska's poem? Does the name of the rooming house the resurrected Baczynski frequents make a difference if he lives the brief life of a one-day May fly and then, when it ends, in our reading of the poem, if he has to return to his nonexistence? Can the fundamental difference between existing and not existing be in any possible way modified by the nature of the rooming house, which the hypothetical Baczynski frequents?

I say yes. The fundamental difference between existing and not existing is, in this poem, colored by the kind of life the writers led—not all, but the majority—in the epoch of collectivism.

The writers from this period of collectivism, it is easy to guess, lived in a manner that one might call exceedingly collective. There was no lack of housing for them to proliferate in, with novelists, poets, and playwrights at various levels knocking on one another's doors—to borrow salt or an iron, or to interrupt a neighbor's creative inspiration.

This was a Soviet invention: writers housed in one place allowed the authorities to control their minds, pens, and wallets. Each person who has ever read about Bulgakov, Mandelstam, or Pasternak certainly remembers the stories about literary apartment houses and tenements, about houses in which there were more typewriters than gas stoves.

This same model for a collectivized literature was transferred after 1945 to all the countries conquered by Stalin. In time, in Poland at least, this model lost its distinctiveness. There were fewer "literary tenements"; writers came to live in regular houses, having regular neighbors—engineers, laborers, officials. But collectivism did not give up all its attributes, such as literary houses and cafeterias, to name two.

Cafeterias! O Muses, help me describe cafeterias for the literati! He who has never crossed their threshold, he who has never seen those dark halls in which friends and enemies, lyrical poets and painters of battle scenes, young geniuses and resigned erudites rubbed elbows, will never understand what collectivism was for literature. Cafeterias! The smell of all-penetrating cabbage soup; pale, neurotic light bulbs trembling under a majestic ceiling; timid, stolen looks, cast by fine writers at trays upon which were plates piled with the second course (stealthy glances—would there be enough meat dumplings? —adorned this cuisine).

In one section of the cafeteria were the proud and frail writers' widows, who even in summer wore their lean fox furs and pointed prewar hats. Almost no one knew who the husbands of these widows had been; Mephisto had forgotten to take back the yellowed contracts signed so long ago. They had lived for centuries—eternal, weak, failing, and tyrannical widows, who were the bane of publishing houses and even censors, blackmailing editors with the unpublished remainder of their husband's travail. Sometimes it happened that humankind inherited two or even three widows from one poet, and these were condemned to eternal mutual hatred of one another and daily contact in the same dining halls; and only the awful flashing eyes and whispered curses betrayed the wild vehemence of these black-clad figures or the tension between the demigoddesses endowed with immortality (though a bit late, unfortunately).

Young writers, barely tolerated by the older ones, gathered in a separate room. Here there was a predominance of poets in army jackets and dark-haired, ugly, taciturn women poets with complicated personalities. Whoever had the least success immediately ran from this room, which was the cold entryway leading to the real cafeteria.

There was no dearth of middle, transitional places where one could meet journalists, sportscasters, fledgling film and theater directors. There were also people here about whom one knew nothing, perhaps secret-police apprentices sent for the experience or perhaps simply cousins of real writers, fed by the writers' union out of pure generosity.

There were areas occupied by Party writers, second-rate, it is true, in a purely artistic sense, but certain of their political value. Perhaps they did not write good books, but when the next congress of the writers' union approached, their votes were worth their weight in gold for the Party. Thus they ate every day, even though they were useful only once every three years. They dressed like officials, always in suits, light-colored shirts, and carefully knotted ties. They smelled of soap and mediocrity, obedience and envy.

Slowly we approach the rooms closest to the center of the cafeteria, the darkest rooms closest to the kitchen. The unwritten rule observed with iron consistency determined that here, in the very nucleus of this enormous place, the best writers, or at least those who were regarded as the best, met. Sometimes one could get there only by being the friend of one of these. In the late seventies all the big writers became dissidents, so that without exaggeration the state, which subsidized these meals, fed its opponents at the best tables. Sometimes, when the heads of dissidents bent toward one another in a conspiratorial reflex and their lips whispered something or other, it seemed the entire cafeteria, all its countless rooms and corners, froze as if in anticipation or desire to hear what its best guests were whispering. Undoubtedly, special confidence men, mixed in with the dissidents, also strained their ears.

But let us follow the camera, let us leave, not without regret, the most important space, and let us have one last peek at the

translators. The translators created a separate milieu, philol-
ogists amid passionate artists. In the translators' room, the
tensions did not run as high. It is difficult to speak at once of
friendship, but at least the hostility manifested itself less than
it did elsewhere; someone would write a Greek word on a
napkin and suggest an interpretation, while the other translators looked at the Greek signs with seriousness, with seriousness and solemnity, and others proposed a different reading
of the Hellenic phrase. They shook their heads, gesticulated,
wrinkled their brows. Someone else read a fragment from an
Auden poem, while a certain old man, known for his lifelong
love of Baudelaire, recited his famous "Balcony" with thick
lips.

Behind the translators were the administrators of the writers'
union, located in a small but quite comfortable room. They
seemed to look at all the rest of the clients of the cafeteria with
a slightly indulgent smile, as if they were meditating upon
Goethe's saying—wafting in from the translators' room—that
"those who do not write, do not compromise themselves."
They, the neat administrative workers, Pythagoreans, advo-
cates of numbers and reports, specialists in negotiations with
authorities for writers' passports, were not compromised by
their writing. They did not describe their childhoods or unhappy love affairs. In Stalinist times they did not confess in
writing their enthusiasm for the Party, and later they did not
express the hopes they had tied with liberalization. They did
not write a single lame poem, they did not construct a single
deformed metaphor. In a certain sense, they belonged to the
aristocracy of the cafeteria; they had clean hands and clean
hearts. The writers viewed them with condescension, of course;
and let us not forget that among them would undoubtedly be

a few dry and efficient collaborators with the political police, writing if not sonnets then reports.

The meals were not gourmet delights. A sample menu: mushroom soup (well watered down), hamburger with potatoes and beets, apple charlotte, and prune compote. Or: chicken soup with very thin noodles, a beef roast with kasha, and those beets again. Apple charlotte again, too. Pudding with raspberry syrup. Currant compote. And more: fried gilthead, potatoes, sauerkraut salad, fruit gelatin, and apple compote. Pierogi with blueberries. Stuffed cabbage leaves. Pierogi with no filling (silent, sad). Sometimes pork chops, small, runty, having nothing whatsoever in common with the enormous, bold, and carefree chops prepared in frying pans at home. And then beets, beets, beets, dug up in spacious beet fields in an autumn drizzle.

We leave the cafeteria; once again we have to pass through the room of awkward and melancholy young writers, but before we do that we cannot resist the bittersweet pleasure of visiting the literary widows, five minutes older by now. The widows don't leave all that quickly. They order coffee, light a menthol cigarette, and stare with unabashed hostility at their antagonists. They will not hurry: the next century will be over shortly. They will wait for the end of the world.

We leave the cafeteria, passing by the cloakroom, site of many scenes (old friends, now hateful enemies, meet and withdraw their hands; each day they see themselves here, next to the cloakroom, and they cannot exchange greetings). We step out onto the sidewalk, and the fresh air rescues us from fainting. A camera films Castle Square. The camera zooms in on the flower stall. Chrysanthemums.

If not the cafeteria, then the "literary house" in the mountains or at seaside, a rooming house which ordinary mortals never see. And again the same friends and enemies and widows and a few promising young people, two translators, and three poets.

What does this lead to? It leads to the fact that the habitués of these cafeterias and rooming houses know each other too well. They see each other daily. Each person who appears there will be thoroughly inspected. The cruel looks of others will rob him of secrets great and small; they will take away his mystery, bleach him of intimacy. Every day at this same little table, in winter or summer, lost in thought, sad or cheerful. Others will find out everything about him. They will get to know his family life, they will know the brand of his typewriter, they will know that he has trouble with varicose veins and that this is a family problem. They will know the state of his bank account and his endless disagreements with his publisher. They will observe day by day his growing marital crisis. They will become familiar with the medicines he must take before and after eating. They will pretend that the state of his liver worries them. They will take everything away from him until he sits before them naked and ordinary, an *everyman*, except that not what is universal will be revealed but what is trivial. This is how collectivism works: it kills with the ordinary.

It destroys what is individual. What it worships is "milieu." Let each person live in a milieu and let him not dare seek refuge on the sidelines. After a while a secret police will be completely unnecessary. What for, if your milieu knows everything about you already.

There is more life in death than in the existence to which collectivism condemns us: chicken noodle soup and the neighbors' astute glance, the inextinguishable reflector of someone's curiosity, long hours of common meetings, when nothing occurs except that life is consumed and becomes ordinary, gray—similar to rationed, skimpily rationed substitute goods.

Baczynski was a darling of the gods—he died young. He leads a mythic existence in our imagination. Wislawa Szymborska allowed the absent poet to don the homespun suit of compromises made by his less happy counterparts. The ashes of the everyday bury the wings of the angel.

One should consider another possibility, however: it is possible that Baczynski, had the German bullet chosen a different course, would have been proud, bold, and internally pure. Perhaps he would not have made a single compromise and perhaps this would even have expressed itself in his noble face, not destroyed but merely sculpted by time.

CHANGES IN THE EAST

I FIND THE extraordinary, breathtaking changes in my corner of the world, in the Europe that stretches east from the Elbe, to be unusually important, vital, crucial. Yet at the same time, for me, for my life, for my development, they come too late. I would not want this to sound coy or cynical. I have an excellent understanding of the incompatibility of historical changes with my own viewpoint.

I would not hasten to express my personal views if not compelled to do so by my strange profession, the profession of a writer, one of whose characteristics is the permanent conflict between "beauty" and "honesty." I put these words in quotation marks to save myself lengthy commentary, but also to express the distance I feel toward Platonic or Platonizing ideas.

"Beauty" would incline me to go into complete raptures over the splendid dynamic of changes in Eastern Europe, to demonstrate absolute animal solidarity with them (and a certain part of me does). But I also see that my entire education as a writer strove to free me from the caprices and grimaces of History. "Honesty" therefore inclines me to say that I was successful in this emancipation to a certain degree, and now that History has suddenly become more gracious, seductive, attractive, and even dazzling, I have become too skeptical to be able to take innocent and enthusiastic delight in its sudden mutation.

During my childhood, History governed ruthlessly, with an iron hand. At its command, my family had to resettle in the West; History shaped my schooling, my youth, my university education in Cracow, and even my poetic beginnings—rebellious, contrary.

I understood only much later that I had identified History with totalitarianism (when I found myself in Western Europe for the first time, it seemed to me that there was no History here at all, only a frivolous, carefree, trite, disorderly everydayness peopled by hairdressers, movie stars, and suntanned bank officials). Totalitarianism produced a quasi-theocratic society. Mystery hung over everything (the key to the mystery was, in fact, the secret police).

Totalitarianism seemed indestructible, eternal. Why, even Hannah Arendt suspected that it was capable of changing human nature, of turning people into slaves. And that is what I thought, too, when I listened to the fear-ridden whispers of Polish intellectuals in the mid-sixties.

And now? A totalitarian system bites the dust every week. What was fate has now become a provisional arrangement. The Party leaders who earlier played political poker with stone faces have now disappeared or have turned out to be common financial crooks. Great and joyous crowds bring down this gloomy political system with such ease that one would like to ask: Beloved crowds, why didn't you fill the streets sooner?

Why did you wait over forty years? What have you been doing until now?

Of course, everyone knows that the crowds had taken to the streets and squares before and that they were unable to effect an overthrow (for obvious reasons).

The late seventies took an active (but modest) part in the dissident movement. I belonged to those who did not believe in the possibility of toppling Communist totalitarianism within a hundred or two hundred years. Yet opposing this false theocracy was, for me and my friends, a source of joy; it was energizing and yielded a completely fresh perspective. But beyond a small group of madmen (and, as always, they turned out to be right), no one counted on the quick, empirical success of the movement.

Before that I was convinced that totalitarianism *was* History. Then I separated these two concepts; I came to understand that even when there is tyranny, the historical process goes on. For some time now, however, I have been convinced that even if totalitarianism is not History, History has something totalitarian in it. It commands a marshal who calls himself Zeitgeist. It forces us to listen to the BBC every day. It reminds us of a giant Hollywood with a pleiad of stars: Cory Aquino, George Bush, Lech Walesa, Margaret Thatcher, Mikhail Gorbachev, Hans-Dietrich Genscher.

All right. I am not a madman (unfortunately) and I do not dream about running away from historicity. In order to live to a ripe old age and not be rendered mute as a poet or as an author, to prevent myself from being smashed by "beauty" (which leads to lies) and "honesty" (which leads to naturalism), I had to take a step back from the avalanche of History. This is not easy; in my language, in my literature, historicity is God.

The changes come too late. Yet it is still too early for me to be able to conceive of the enormity of the changes and their significance. Citizens of the West are mere observers here. For me totalitarianism was both a nightmare and a literary theme, an oppressor and a toy, the policeman watching me and the ecstasy of political humor. I am now pretending to be a skeptical, wise, mature person, but I do not really know at all what the enormous changes in the East signify or what will change in me, in my manner of writing, thinking, living. A repugnant civilization is in decline; but it shaped me, I revolted against it, I tried to flee it; whether I like it or not, I am most certainly marked by it. It will be awhile before I find out what has really happened *for me*.

I will not mourn this repulsive historical experiment, that much is obvious. I am thrilled by its fall, I am worried about the future of Europe. I wonder about my own future—between "beauty" and "honesty," amid question marks, between History and poetry.

STENDHAL

In *The Life of Henri Brulard*, Stendhal writes:

> . . . J'ai été à la Chapelle Sixtine comme un mouton, id est sans plaisir, jamais l'imagination n'a pu prendre son vol" [. . . I went to the Sistine Chapel like an absolute sheep, that is, without any pleasure, my imagination was unable to take wing].

Stendhal's remark casts an interesting light on a certain seemingly innocent paradox: in the Sistine Chapel, full of treasures, he was incapable of delighting in the artwork because his imagination was dormant that day, November 24, 1835; it did not know how to "take wing."

What—sensitive Stendhal is in the Sistine Chapel, and . . . nothing, fiasco. This means that to be able to enjoy artworks one must have a good day, a supple and aroused imagination.

Why, that's perfectly obvious, the bored reader will say.

So what does the imagination do when it "takes wing"? When the imagination glides in the air, we surrender ourselves to daydreaming. This means that the imagination's soaring is not necessarily *getting to know* the work of art that inspires the flight. Daydreaming, activated, mobilized by a sonata, sculpture, poem, or painting, is soon surrendered to one's own narcissism. We harbor—what else?—gratitude for the impulse which has caused our stupefaction, but the fact is, imagination glides and flies away from the airport, disappears into outer space.

This is a rather shameful phenomenon: the narcissism of the imagination, its internal energy. If one could think it through, one would have to say that art is neither for people without imaginations (they are simply not interested in it), nor for people endowed with imagination, for these use it the way people once used snuff, for the pleasure of sneezing.

Only one thing becomes clear: why art critics are deprived of imagination. If they had it, they would say nothing about individual works of art; they would surrender themselves to their dreams. After all, someone has to sit in judgment of art.

THREE HISTORIES

THERE ARE AT least three different human histories, not one: the history of force, the history of beauty, and the history of suffering. Only the first two are cataloged and recorded, more or less. They have their professors and their textbooks. But suffering leaves no traces. It is mute. That is, mute *historically*. A scream does not last long, and there is no note symbol to represent it and make it last.

That is why it is so difficult to understand the essence of Auschwitz. From the point of view of the history of force, it was an episode, undeserving of closer study. How much more interesting was the Battle of Wagram, for example. As the history of suffering, Auschwitz was fundamental. Unfortunately, the history of suffering does not exist. Art historians are not interested in Auschwitz either. Mud, barracks, low skies. Fog and four skinny poplars. Orpheus does not stroll this way. Ophelia doesn't choose to drown here.

READING FOR BAD DAYS

FOR A LONG time my French acquaintances would look at me with amazement when I admitted to reading Paul Léautaud. He was considered a weirdo, a second-rate writer; nor had he written a single novel, a single short story. He had no imagination and he was the first to admit it. Instead, he passionately recorded thousands of details and dialogues in the *Literary Journal* he maintained for decades.

Lately people have been talking about him: new editions of his books have appeared; the Carnavalet Museum is exhibiting a facsimile of his study, famous for its disorder; and someone has made a film illustrating his ongoing relationship with a woman he refers to tenderly in his notes as Fléau (natural disaster).

Was he a second-rate writer? Not in my opinion. He knew that people saw him that way, however, and to an extent, he agreed to that status. In one passage in his journal he wrote that second-rate writers have an advantage over first-rate writers, because they do not lie, they do not have to lie. Writers of the first rank play the role of representatives of the nation, language, literature, and their profession, and this is why they have to beautify, idealize, and round out reality.

And it was precisely this kind of literary cynicism that interested me. And also the fact that Léautaud not only did without imagination: he was equally critical of ideas. In the Middle Ages he would have been an extreme nominalist, casting off general concepts (and especially love, patriotism, nobility). I am not certain if I am attracted to this, but it certainly does interest me. In my literature, someone like Léautaud would have been led to an asylum; we take concepts and ideas very seriously. Meanwhile, Léautaud is perhaps the only writer who can practically move us with his symptoms of ordinary anti-Semitism. Well, we say to ourselves, here is a real miracle: a nominalist who rejects all that unites people, yet who is able to share with his contemporaries some of their passions, even the most repulsive ones. In principle, he was a completely private person; he showed no interest in politics, and hated the radio and false political rhetoric. During the First World War he was an unwavering pacifist.

Léautaud's background was plebeian. His father, who spent his entire life consumed by love affairs, worked for the Comédie Française as a prompter. This modest but peculiar profession intrigued Léautaud the son, and to an extent he took it up after his father—he became the prompter of French Literature, whispering not what should be said as much as making fun of what had already been said.

He was small and ugly. He had a sharp nose that stuck out like a lightning rod. He was individualistic, and, because he was often without money, he was seen as an oddball. He dressed without any regard for the way he looked. In winter he would wear two jackets, one on top of the other (he did not own a coat). He was almost always carrying large bags with food for animals—cats, dogs, or monkeys. At one point he was boarding forty-five cats. During neither of the world wars did he feel any sympathy for people; he was disturbed only by the fate of animals—horses pulling loads that were too heavy, homeless cats, orphaned dogs.

One of the most engrossing moments in his journal is a story told by one of Léautaud's friends (I use the word "friend" in the conventional sense; Léautaud really had no friends, as is the case with someone who keeps a very detailed journal) about blind horses that work underground, in coal mines. But please don't be horrified; Léautaud was not a monster. He was capable of good deeds, he did help others.

He is characterized by something I would call anti-deception. If the usual and very common deception is to be sweet in speech and disobliging in deed, then Léautaud represents the reverse configuration. He is sour and malicious in what he says and writes, but he was not incapable of noble acts. (In this, he reminds one of Dr. Gottfried Benn, who was also rather coarse in word rather than in deed.)

A journal of the type cultivated by Léautaud breaks down into as many subcategories as there are authors and personalities, pens and ideas. This genre is amazingly elastic, never fully delineated. For some authors a journal becomes a battlefield upon which they conduct a furious and lifelong spiritual battle for development, internal perfection, and a better and better understanding of the world and self. The unparalleled model for this type is Leo Tolstoy's journal. There are journals of a very different character. The unintended comicality of Samuel Pepys's diary derives from his lack of regard for any development at all; he simply tells, trusting completely in his numbers, about his successes and defeats (it is a little like reading a diary written by a hamster who would count the number of seeds brought back to his nest). Self-satisfied mediocrity, shamelessly noting its minuscule advantages over others, is one pole of diary writing (Samuel Pepys, Jan Chryzostom Pasek, Samuel Boswell), while Tolstoy reigns alone on the peak of spiritual perfectionism.

Léautaud is closer to Samuel Pepys than to Tolstoy. He is attracted far more to the real than to the normal, the ordinary rather than the postulated. At times he reveals himself as much as Pepys or Pasek. There is practically no taboo which is not broken by Léautaud. He tells about masturbation and ugliness. He is ready to admit that an unexpected guest saw a full chamber pot sitting on the floor. Sharing this last episode takes more skill than relating the erotic details of his liaison with Fléau.

Léautaud is different from Samuel Pepys, however, for one very basic reason: literary awareness. Léautaud is a highly conscious author, not someone for whom scribbling in a journal is a marginal, evening occupation. Léautaud is not a naïve mortal who has unveiled his life accidentally. He is a professional, a member of a writing confraternity, a zealous reader, adorer of Stendhal and Chamfort.

At the same time, because his inner life did not have a strong beat, he had to transform himself into a chronicler recording external events. And because, as we know, he had no imagination, he wrote down what really happened. The field of his observation was mainly literary Paris, seen from the editorial desk of *Mercure de France*, the most important French literary magazine of its day (it wasn't until later that *La nouvelle revue française* moved into first place).

Literary Paris! A marketplace of vanities, and what vanities, first-rate from every approach. The Parisian literary milieu was and is tainted with two serious illnesses—dreams about the Academy (for which one must really scramble) and the fall season of literary awards. Léautaud was an indefatigable observer of the tactics of Parisian literati. Here someone who dreams about the Academy takes up the theater column in a popular daily only to flatter the academics. The minute the Academy garners him to its ranks, he gives up writing theater reviews. In his day Rémy de Gourmont derided patriotism as the plaything of idiots; however, during the Great War he took back his jibes. Maurice Barrès was a different kind of traitor. Léautaud admired him once as the author of modernist prose; then, however, Barrès became a leader of a nationalist youth group. The fall awards make all novelists feverish.

Basically Léautaud watches the Parisian literary scene with the eyes of an innocent babe. He is a professional; he belongs to the guild; he understands the universal corruption quite well, but he is unable to accept it.

His definition of good literary style *("du naturel, du vrai et de la spontanéité")* seems to refer as well to the social world. He draws his ethics from aesthetics. For him betrayal will be each deviation from literature understood as pleasure, as an expression of personality, as a record of the moment. That is why Barrès's example is so significant: the departure from a disinterested literature to literary propaganda.

As a chronicler, Léautaud specialized in sober descriptions of the agony, death, and facial features of the deceased. Whenever any of his acquaintances felt ill—Marcel Schwob, Rémy de Gourmont, Charles-Louis Philippe—Léautaud got busy working to get access to the darkened rooms in which the struggle for life was taking place. Sometimes he came after the fact, appearing simultaneously with the lawyer, a bit before the undertaker. He described the body, the position of the deceased's hands, the expression on the face, the layout of the room in which the body rested. But he also peered at the widow, waiting until her face gave its first smile, the first relaxation of the grief-stricken tension of the muscles.

We shouldn't hold this against him. Léautaud is the literary heir of the French moralists, inspired by Jansenism, the un-bribable observers of corruption not of a concrete social setting but of human nature in general. Léautaud's prose is proof of the possibility of the influences of the moralists (who excelled at aphorism) and the enormous influence of naturalism. Léautaud is a Chamfort who is incapable of being terse. (He also wrote aphorisms, but they do not show him at his best.)

He wrote a wonderfully supple French. Sometimes he bores. In his journals the repetition of the endless description of everyday life bores, days always spent behind the same desk in the editorial offices of *Mercure de France*, in a train between Gare de Luxembourg and Fontenay-aux-Roses, on streets close to Odéon. The eternal descriptions of tender encounters with dogs and cats bore. Léautaud wrote the same thing for thou-sands of pages. Only wars gave him new themes, wars and changes in literary generations. After the last war he com-plained, for example, that the old kind of writer, a lover of the language and live emotions, was being usurped by a philosophy-professor type who also wrote novels (one cannot deny his acuity here).

He had no formal education. He was self-taught; not that that means much—in things literary everyone is self-taught. He lived a long time, from 1872 to 1956. He couldn't stand the radio, as I mentioned, but paradoxically he became famous, thanks to radio conversations Robert Mallet conducted with him in old age. These conversations drew thousands of listeners. Léautaud turned out to be faithful to his definition of style *("du naturel, du vrai . . .")*. His sharp, old man's voice unceremoniously expressing the most nonconformist opinions seemed to emanate from another epoch, as if Robert Mallet had somehow managed to interview Chamfort, dead these 150 years. In an epoch dominated completely by Sartre and his pupils rang a voice that truly thought and felt differently, independently; and if he was a conformist, then even in that he remained faithful to a conformity that was long out of date.

He had no imagination. What exactly does that mean? Is it possible for a writer *not* to have an imagination? Both Pascal and Simone Weil were opponents of the imagination; they understood it as the opposite of truth, of religious truth. One can also understand imagination not as the opposite but as the refining and deepening of truth. Poets, following Coleridge, like to separate imagination from fantasy and recognize only the first as an unmatched aesthetic and cognitive value.

Léautaud had no imagination. To depict an epoch seen from behind a desk, he needed a thousand pages. Imagination is more frugal; it introduces shortcuts, symbols, and acts through suggestion, color, allusion. Meanwhile, in Léautaud's work a heavy naturalistic element prevails; he has to tell everything literally; there is a literal inclusion of conversations, jokes, gossip.

Why then do I read this untempered author, this almost graphomaniac? Is it only for his energetic French? One of Léautaud's undisputed charms is the constant oscillation and competition of two principles or two elements: the amateurish and the professional. In other words, his diary possesses traces of naïveté à la Samuel Pepys. And Pepys entered world literature because he unveiled for us the most sensational spectacle, that is, the life of the most ordinary man, full of ordinary desires. We see him as if through a hidden camera. We are superior to him morally. In reading Pepys we say to one another, Ah, what a simpleton, I would never do that, think that, want that. (Are you sure?)

And Léautaud often does not spare us these impressions. Of course, he is no Sunday painter, but he seems to devote himself to literature as he understands it *("du naturel, du vrai . . .")*, and in writing, he goes further each time. "I'll tell this, too," he decides. "I will not refrain from the ridiculous. I will unveil the doubtful regions of my life." Not just the chamber pot and masturbation, but his doubts as to whether or not he should accept money from a wealthy art patron.

From another angle we are dealing with an expert on Stendhal and a co-author (in his youth, with Adolphe Van Bever) of a once-acclaimed anthology of modernist French poetry, an enthusiastic aficionado of the eighteenth century, a connoisseur, a member of the literati, and a friend, or at least contemporary, of Paul Valéry.

It is difficult to find a greater chasm than that between Léautaud and Valéry. Here the naturalistic fury of notation; there pure intelligence, bored with the arbitrariness of the world and art. Yet their acquaintance lasted until the death of Valéry. They talked about poetry. They had a harder and harder time understanding one another. Valéry became a first-rate writer, Léautaud second-rate. He observed the former and noted his conclusions in the diary. He looked at Valéry's idiosyncrasies; he attacked him with fury when, at night, seen by no one if one does not count the cats sitting immobile around him, in nightcap and goose quill in hand, he settled accounts with his time. Meanwhile, with his usual discretion, Valéry wrote a penetrating essay about Stendhal, which one reads as a savaging of Léautaud's aesthetics.

A separate and interesting problem is Léautaud's attitude toward poetry. He once wrote poems himself but then abandoned that activity to find happiness in prose. He compiled an anthology of poetry. He admired Apollinaire, and as long as he could, would show up at Père Lachaise cemetery on every anniversary of Apollinaire's death. He loved Verlaine's poems and rejected Mallarmé. In a certain sense the path to a literary life opened with his meeting of Verlaine. The young Léautaud once spotted the poet, racked with illnesses, sitting at a café table. He bought a bouquet of violets and had the waiter take it over. Hidden from view, he watched the scene. This small event is something of a motto placed over the hefty volumes of his diary. A bouquet of violets sent by a shy admirer.

Toward the end of his life, Léautaud denied having any interest whatsoever in poetry. It was a matter larger than merely one of taste in poetry, of reading volumes of poetry. It was a matter of attitude toward beauty. Léautaud could not completely deny beauty, but he took the side of "beauty" characteristic of intelligent, sober, sardonic prose. His moral instinct told him to see in poetry only rhetoric, nothing more, and falseness, declamation. He was a moralist, but only in the sense of a French literary tradition; Léautaud was not a moralist in a more general sense. (It is easy to point to the phobias and arrogance—shared with many other Frenchmen—he evidenced during the occupation.)

Poetry attracted and repelled him. There was something of
the survival instinct in this; how was a chronicler of the everyday supposed to behave toward the great works created during
his lifetime? For example, to the end of his life, Léautaud
haughtily emphasized that he had never read Proust nor had
he any intention of doing so. Yes, but in his diary he wrote
about the extraordinary impact of a special issue of *La nouvelle
revue française* devoted entirely to Proust. For a few days Léautaud lived in a fever, in rapture. The image of a sickly, frail
Proust—devoting all his energy to the gigantic novel and dying
from the enormity of the creative effort—left the deepest
impression. But to read volumes of Proust, oh no, there he
expected an artificial, rhetorical, imagined poetry (and it was
also because of the aristocrats; why should he be interested in
aristocrats?). He saw poetry in Proust's life but not in his work.

The same separation of life from work repeated itself more
frequently. Poetry was contained in the very act of writing and
in the countless idiosyncrasies of writers, idiosyncrasies which
moved Léautaud profoundly. It was not without reason that
he adored the famous Beau Brummel, the English dandy who
ended his life in poverty and neglect in Calais. For Léautaud,
Brummel was a nonwriting poet. There were no complications
with him as there were with Proust, because Brummel left
only his memoirs, not poems or thick novels.

One of Léautaud's poetic relics was a fragment of an essay
by Barbey d'Aurevilly, devoted to Brummel, a fragment per-
taining to the saddest period in the life of the great dandy.
Here is a fragment of that fragment:

On some days, to the great astonishment of the hotel residents, [Brummel] demanded that his apartment be prepared

as if the holidays were coming. Mirrors, candelabra, candles, masses of flowers; nothing was missing . . . and he, illuminated with that bright light, stood in the middle of the room in the most exquisite suit of his youth, in a blue Whig frock coat with gold buttons, in a quilted vest and black trousers, tight-fitting like sixteenth-century apparel, and waited . . . He awaited the already dead England! Suddenly, as if he had been split in two, he announced the coming of the Prince of Wales, then Lady Fitz-Herbert, Lady Cunningham, then Lord Yarmouth, and finally all these English personages to whom he once dictated the law, and, believing that they were really appearing as he called their names, he would go to meet them, changing his tone of voice, in the direction of the doors opened wide onto a perfectly empty drawing room, in which there was no one on that evening or any other evening, and he bowed to them, to those chimeras of his own thought, offering his arm to the ladies finding themselves surrounded by the ghosts he conjured, who probably had not the least intention of leaving their tombstones to attend the party of a ruined dandy. How long that lasted . . . Finally, when the room swarmed with phantoms, when that entire other world appeared at his beckoning, he regained his sanity and the unlucky man began to realize he was seeing things, he was demented! Only then, despairing, did he plunge into one of the armchairs, and that is where he would be found, drowning in tears!

In order to banish the assumption that he was honoring the author of the essay, Barbey d'Aurevilly, Léautaud adds—and I quote from the theater chronicles he wrote under the pseudonym Maurice Boissard—that it is likely d'Aurevilly copied this description from a book by the forgotten author E. D. Forgues.

This is how poetry exists—in vision, in legend. It is supposed to be almost as unreal as the evening guests of poor Brummel.

Yet we still continue to insist that Léautaud had no imagination. He himself seems to believe it. He who spends whole
hours daydreaming about Brummel and other heroes. He who
offered a bouquet of violets to Verlaine and was too shy to go
up to him, and then throughout his entire life returned in his
thoughts to that episode.

Léautaud's imagination is ignited by contact with figures of
artists, not by churches or religion or the sea. The sea bores
him. A Mass seems idiotic.

Léautaud is not, therefore, deprived of an imagination,
which doesn't change all that much. It seems that daydreams
and imaginative wanderings took up quite a bit of space in his
mind, and we find his accounts of them in his diary. But
imagination does not become a shaping force, does not change
the chronicler into a poet, does not give him wings. In spite
of this, the daydream, as one of the objects in that great office
of things found, even though it may not decide about the
atmosphere of the diary, has a certain role to play in its structure. It is the horizon, the eastern extreme of the sky, the place
where dawn usually appears. And even if in Léautaud dawn
never shows up, at least it is possible a priori.

I ask myself one more time: what is it that fascinates me in
this strange diary, in which there are so many boring, trivial,
obscure fragments? Not the life of Paul Léautaud and not his
intelligence. Here I would prefer to read Paul Valéry.

It seems to me that the answer should be as follows. I read
Léautaud as a poet of low states of being. It is exactly the
"trivial" then, the modest, the everyday, and the constantly
repeated, that finds a solid and not very romantic seer in him.
Léautaud seems to say, "Look, after all, this exists, these little
things, scorned by first-rate writers." I reach for Paul Léautaud

to experience the goosebumps of everydayness. The disorder of the world reveals itself at both ends of the scale, in tragedy and in triviality, in ugliness. In Racine and in Paul Léautaud. In Dido's lament, to which Henry Purcell composed music, and in the diary of this cat lover.

The second reason has to do with Léautaud's attitude toward poetry. Because I write poems myself and treat poetry seriously, I do not share the skeptical aesthetic philosophy of Léautaud. Yet the writing of poetry—at least for me—is not free from feelings of guilt. Guilt that is difficult for me to define, difficult even to understand. Hunting for beauty—what's wrong with that? Is it because poetry is too closely related to rhetoric and each false step in a poem means that we fall from the Alps of poetry into the valley of rhetoric? Paul Léautaud, paradoxical opponent of poetry, possesses a fatal attraction for me. Not always. Only when my own anxiety about poetry grows dangerously. Léautaud is my reading for bad days.

Saint Peter's Report

I would also like to call to the attention of the highest authorities a certain fact that at first glance seems without significance: in observing, as few have the opportunity to do, the various human types (what variety! But underneath it all perhaps only three or four basic variants), I noticed something quite extraordinary. As we all know, in our sphere we divide people into moralists and nihilists. I have been viewing the classification with some skepticism lately; however, I did not dare protest openly, for I know that great importance is attached to it; almost the entire system is based on this distinction.

Only one person knows how it really is. I, the gatekeeper, am this person. The moralists, oh, they come in taxis. They are affluent and smell of cologne. They bring diplomas and press clippings, good reviews, often a photo of themselves with the Pope. The nihilists come on foot, are deathly tired, unshaven, sad, usually penniless. They have nothing to brag about.

The moralists act as if they had come to attend another international conference. They ask which room has been reserved for them; they check to see where their friends have been lodged. They use a tone that says it is all their due. These are peevish people, accustomed to luxury.

Nihilists do not demand anything and they fall asleep immediately. Depressed, they know that they are moving from one hell to another.

I have to confess that sometimes I switch rooms on them and send the nihilist to a room earmarked for one of the moralistic snobs.

HISTORICAL IMAGINATION

WHILE STILL A high school student hungry for knowledge, I often attended lectures given by well-known personages who would visit our provincial city.

Usually these were specialists in very narrow areas: one speaker lectured on Elizabethan theater, another on the golden age of Dutch painting, and yet another on Stanislaw Wyspianski.

The public was usually made up of high school students just like me and of retired people. The first group wanted to know what the life awaiting them was about; the second was trying to understand what it had been.

Even the most successful talks—for example, a splendid lecture on medieval architecture given by a tall, gray visitor from Warsaw, who spoke with such zeal that one would have thought he was presenting a plan for a city of the future—left both groups mildly disappointed, as they never brought answers to the fundamental questions.

One day there was going to be a lecture on historical imagination. We, the frequenters of these meetings, always asked the director who the next guest would be. This time we were told that it would be neither a historian nor a scientist but a poet, and that he was very talented but not well known. For many years he had been in the authorities' disfavor, but then his situation had improved at least so he could publish and meet with the public. ("What of it," sighed my high school friend. "What of it, if the public did not know him at all. The disfavor of the authorities is followed by the disfavor of the readers.")

Finally he appears. He speaks differently from those who lectured before him, quietly, almost without conviction, as if he did not believe that anyone would understand him. There are exactly five people in the audience.

"We know so little," he repeats. "We have given everything away to history. We explain everything with history. The last war," he said, "was a wretched misfortune not only because millions of innocent people died in it. Mainly. But in that war we lost not just the dignity of people who were murdered after being put through interrogation and sentencing, but also the dignity of people who live as unhistorical, everlasting beings, hopelessly tangled in history but different from it, other.

"Have you noticed, ladies and gentlemen," he asked us— five people: three high school students and two older women, one of whom fell asleep after a few minutes and slept as soundlessly as an Indian—"have you noticed, ladies and gentlemen, that the poems, novels, or screenplays being written now blame everything on history? Have you noticed that we no longer exist, we, that is, people who are the heart of will, of thought, the lens of individual fate?

"Only history that fills, rents, destroys, and exhaustively

defines us is left. Historical imagination, as you most certainly know, developed late but excessively, monstrously, parasitically, devouring everything else, every other variety of imagination and thought and even depriving them of not freedom, no, but the least trace of dignity. Long ago we lived in the world as travelers who had accidentally come upon scenes of violence, death, battle. Some covered their eyes, others tried to run away, still others protested.

"We were other, we came from elsewhere, evil amazed us, we did not understand suffering. Now everything has changed: we are historical. Some Stalin or Hitler stood at our cradle, shreds of uniforms were sewn into our suits; we must always avenge someone or save someone, and when it happens that we ourselves commit an error or a crime, historical imagination becomes our lawyer. Why, it is not me, we say, it is the epoch. We all did the same, we say, and historical imagination is our prompter.

"We have become intimate with history, the borders between experience and inexperience, between night and day, between music and statistics. But I will never agree to this; I prefer being mad to being historical, I prefer being ridiculous to being common, I prefer knowing nothing to understanding everything."

He was tired. He stopped and quickly left the auditorium, not waiting for questions or disagreements. We were left alone, we, five people of various ages. We said nothing and not one of us had the courage to waken the sleeping woman. It was evening, November; our watches ticked away quietly.

FROM ANOTHER WORLD

POEMS COME FROM another world. From what world? From the world the inner life lives. Where is that world? I can't say. Ideas, metaphors, and moods come from another world. Sometimes they are full of lofty trust, at other times they exude scorn or irony. They appear at strange times, unasked, unannounced. Yet when they are called, they prefer not to show up.

On the streets of Paris, mimes often appear who amuse the crowds by imitating the gait of some serious passerby hurrying to work, carrying a hefty briefcase in his hand and hefty thoughts in his head. They follow someone like this, scrupulously imitating his way of moving, his face, bearing, seriousness, hurry, absorption. The minute the passerby notices that he is being accompanied by a moving ape parodying him, the fun ends, people burst out laughing, and the victim of the joke quickens his step and disappears into a side street; the mime then bows and collects his money.

The life of the spirit apes the serious world of politics, history, and economics in a similar way. It walks right behind it, step for step, sad or happy. It follows the real world like a crazy, redheaded guardian angel and cries or bursts into laughter, plays the violin or recites poetry. When reality finally notices it is not alone, the phantom shadow bows to the public and vanishes.

Poems come from another world. From where? I don't know.

EGOISM

IN HER MEMOIRS, Lidia Chukovsky, who knew Solzhenitsyn well, tells how *The Gulag Archipelago* came to be. Solzhenitsyn devoted every free moment to this work. He had no time for conversation. After eating dinner he rushed from the table and returned to work. He stopped seeing friends. Friends bitterly accused him of egoism.

KARL MARX

MARX FOUND A way of dealing with suffering—he put it into a scientific perspective. From then on, he and countless Marxists on planet Earth and in orbiting satellites could sleep soundly.

EMPTINESS

A POET CAME to see a zaddik. The zaddik offered the poet tea and almonds and showed him the view of the city. The apartment was on the twentieth floor; all the rivers and canals of the city glittered like veins of mica in granite. It was a sunny autumn day, and tugboats flirted with corpulent vessels loaded with grain.

"What's on your mind?" the zaddik finally asked. "I see that something is tormenting you."

"Yes," the poet answered, "I need your help. The thing that is bothering me . . . I don't know how to say this, it is difficult for me to find words . . ."

The zaddik sat quietly in his armchair and examined his evenly trimmed nails.

"I am tormented by emptiness," the poet said after a while. "Nothingness. There are so many days when I am incapable of writing or even thinking. There are splendid days, rich in discoveries and dreams, days that are treasures. But then, after that, weeks of silence, despair."

The zaddik smiled in a rather professional way—exactly the way doctors, psychoanalysts, and mountain guides smile.

"You are a lucky man," he said after a moment. "Sometimes God visits you. Imagine a house in which there are dozens of heavy pieces of furniture, screens, and drapes, where antique chests are neighbors to Chinese vases. A ray of light will never find its way into that house. You are like a spacious apartment in which there is only one simple chair. That chair stands in the middle of the room and waits. It has time. Emptiness is infinite patience. Nothingness is waiting for fullness. Despair sings quietly like a robin, a bird that whistles even in November, before the snow falls."

THE INSPIRED DERMATOLOGIST

WHOEVER HAS STOOD, in the evening, at the gates to one of the great European libraries has to notice the young people leaving it, young people so dazzled by their readings in poetry and philosophy that they are incapable of noticing the material world. These young people walk like the blind, and as awkwardly as the blind they enter a city filled with dusk. Some of them perish right away, run over by a car or tram. Others are stopped by the police because their behavior violates common sense and is dangerous to the other, more ordinary pedestrians. Still others go a long, long way—this march in the case of Gottfried Benn lasted seventy years—and come upon two wars on their way, the Third Reich, the Berlin blockade; yet even these horrifying obstacles cannot stop them.

Who was Gottfried Benn? A great poet. Also a doctor of skin and venereal diseases. How did he look? He was not tall, and was rather heavyset and ugly. He peered into the camera lens intently and authoritatively, as if trying to impose an image that he himself had chosen, that appealed to him, onto the light-sensitive emulsion. Had I ever met him? I couldn't have, since he died in 1956, when I was eleven years old and lived in Gliwice. He belonged to my grandfather's generation.

Benn was undoubtedly one of those young men who could never give up being dazzled by ideas (mainly Nietzsche's) from the great library, and who, at the same time, represented an excellent embodiment of the Platonic idea of a German petit bourgeois. The son of a pastor and a Swiss woman, he settled in Berlin after finishing his studies, and he remained faithful to this city until he died. He left Berlin for Brussels during World War I; moved to Hannover in the thirties, when, choosing "the aristocratic form of emigration," he became an army doctor; and finally went to Landsberg (Gorzow Wielkopolski) in the last years of the war.

During the day he received patients, and in the evenings he went to the beer garden. For forty years. Skin diseases during the day, beer at night. Only on Sunday did he replace the beer with black coffee and await a stroke of poetic inspiration, which came, not weekly, it is true, but often enough for him to become a great artist. On Sunday he waited for inspiration and rejected invitations to take trips or go on picnics—with the Hindemiths, for example, who owned a car.

He was an excellent German petit bourgeois, and he knew it, prided himself on it, and sought shelter in it. On the street, concealed beneath the brim of a soft hat—although it was not all that easy to hide his large, pale, uninteresting face—he brought glory to his social class. I am amused by the thought that perhaps Vladimir Nabokov, who lived in Berlin for a time and was not too fond of Germans, met Benn on the street or in the underground train station and looked at him with revulsion, thinking, "There's your typical beer consumer, laundered of all individuality and fantasy."

But it was another prose writer, Klaus Mann, who drew a portrait of Benn in his *Mephisto*. Here Benn, called Pelz, does not physically differ from the original (medium height, sturdy, cold blue eyes, drooping jowls, and prominent sensual-cruel lips). Pelz voices opinions that are a caricature of Benn's political philosophy: "Life in a democracy has become too safe. Our existence has moved farther and farther away from heroic pathos. The spectacle with which we are assisting today marks the birth of a new human type—or perhaps the rebirth of an ancient, archaic-magic-warrior type. What a beautiful and compelling sight!"

For Benn-Pelz supported the Nazis right after Hitler came to power. His admiration for the new regime did not last long—in a few months Benn became a persona non grata, came under attack, and eventually found himself in danger.

There is something grotesque in this episode from Benn's life, something comical and atypical of similar situations under the Nazis or Stalin. Even Klaus Mann (who adored his poetry) saw this, in spite of his anger toward Benn. Mann had other supporters of the Third Reich make much more pragmatic declarations: "I am and remain a German artist and German patriot no matter who governs my country. In Berlin I feel better than in any other city on the globe and I have no desire to leave. Besides, where else could I make this kind of money?"

The grotesqueness of Benn's position came from his solemnity and the purity of his intentions. For a moment he took the philosophy of the new powers (Heroism! Heroism!) quite seriously, but he never counted on a career, money, fame, or special editions of his own books.

But it is not the short-lived "Nazi" episode that interests me in Benn's biography. I am most interested in his extraordinary, melancholy poetry. It is difficult to write about poetry. In the history of poets—distinct from the history of poetry—this unassuming doctor of skin and venereal diseases occupies a unique place. Never perhaps was a poet so masked, so conspiratorial, so concealed, so completely dressed like someone else. Never in the history of literature had there been so absolute a severance of the ties between the poem and the world, between the poet and the physical person in which the poet lived, between spirit and reality, between inspiration and history.

Benn understood this split perfectly and was even proud of it. He tended this chasm and bragged about the discontinuity. He justified it philosophically, and saw in it a guarantee of his artistic freedom.

Stefan George, a generation older, liked to dress in a Greek toga and wear a wreath of laurel leaves. For Benn this was a disgusting masquerade. He himself dressed only in the uniform of the Wehrmacht (I remind the reader: he was an army doctor, he killed no one, and during the war years he analyzed the statistics of soldier suicides), in a white doctor's robe, in a petit-bourgeois suit. He lived modestly, on the ground floor of an apartment house. When inviting friends to his place—which he did rarely and unwillingly—he warned them that they would not be seeing a palace or Renaissance furniture. He apologized to Ernst Jünger for the inferior quality of wine he offered him. He knew only about beer.

The entire fantastical quality of his restless mind he located elsewhere (in poems, letters, essays). Life was, and was supposed to be, gray and trivial, like a cutlet with sauerkraut. In Hannover he had to meet with his friends, officers, and conduct conversations on the subject of "who the chief of staff of the fifteenth reserve regiment was in November 1915." The boredom of his Hannover life Benn described in letters which he usually sent to Bremen. In Bremen lived F. W. Oelze, a merchant and art lover, the co-owner of a company that sold religious articles. Benn made him a Medici and the Prince of Wales rolled into one. This had little to do with the real Mr. Oelze who, it turns out, was a reliable, ordinary merchant.

In letters to Oelze, Benn occasionally notes his spiritual superiority over his addressee (he never resorts to the familiar form in addressing him); however, he endlessly admires the decorum of the Bremen businessman, praises his finely tailored suits, his British—as he sees them—manners, his Europeanness. Oelze's travels appeal to Benn, who attributes brilliant worldly successes and connections to him and suspects love affairs on the highest social rungs.

Rarely does he actually see Oelze. He prefers to imagine him. Oelze is like a poem: he exists in the imagination, in the language, but one should not peer too closely, so as not to destroy the illusion. This is confirmed by an amusing episode: once Benn found himself in Bremen, unannounced, and he was content to have a look at the façade of Oelze's house; he did not visit him. He preferred to imagine his friend rather than actually see him.

Let us return for a moment, however, to Benn's championing of the Third Reich in the first months of its existence. Benn was rejected because he was too serious, too sincere, too principled. He did not know how to betray his artistic allies —the expressionists—and meanwhile expressionism had been condemned as a literary trend profoundly at odds with the healthy spirit of nationalist socialism. Someone probably ended up reading Benn's poems, and the scandal was out: their author could not consider himself an ally of the new state, because he was a decadent, a typical representative of a warped nihilistic art; there would be no use looking for praise of Nordic virtues or state-creating enthusiasm in his work.

Shortly thereafter Benn writes to Ina Seidel: "I can't do it anymore. Some things have acted as the final straw. Horrible tragedy! The whole thing is beginning to look more and more like a kitschy play constantly lauded as *Faust*, but with the cast allowing for little more than *The Hussars Are Here!* How splendidly this began, how repulsive it looks today. The end to this tale is not yet in sight" (letter of October 27, 1934).

On May 7, 1936, in the SS's cultural organ *Das Schwarze Korps*, Benn's person and work were attacked, and the attack was immediately picked up the next day by *Volkischer Beobachter*. Benn was in danger, and if nothing happened to the poet after that, it was thanks only to the careful intervention of countless protectors.

It is worth underscoring the indescribable triviality of some of the circumstances tied to Gottfried Benn's harassment— at least in print. He suspected that the author of the repugnant article in *Das Schwarze Korps* was one H. M. Elster, who earlier, when treasurer of the Union of Writers, was unmasked—by Benn among others—as a crook and a cheat and was forced to resign from the organization.

All this resulted in Benn's being condemned to decades of isolation—his work could not be published. It is then that the radical dualism of poetry and the world, characteristic of our protagonist, reaches its peak. Much earlier, in the twenties, Benn defended poetic autonomy—most frequently against thoughtless and superficial leftist publicists who saw literature as a vehicle at the disposal of the Communist Party (this explains, in part, Benn's position in 1933: engaged in a polemic with the left, he momentarily loses his head over the right). But only the decade through which he walked in complete solitude and bitterness lent this dualism its extreme, exceptional form. One hundred years of solitude happen only in novels. Ten years of genuine, difficult solitude is an adequately severe sentence.

I am not defending Benn the man. I am not writing an apology for him. I admire many of his poems and essays, but some of the texts—especially those dealing with the concept of race (understood, it is true, differently from Rosenberg's)— repel me. I do not know who he was. Was he good? No one knows. Even the British-Bremen Oelze wrote in a letter after Benn's death that there was something evil in him, something "demonic." Yet at the same time he was a good doctor, attending the poorest prostitutes for free. And a poet true to himself, who could not tolerate the deception of the "literary industry" (I'll get back to this).

So I am not defending Benn. Nor do I have to add that his fate was a lot more bearable than the fate of concentration-camp prisoners. After all, he paraded around in a Wehrmacht uniform. And what is curious is that it never occurred to him that he could oppose, rebel; here undoubtedly Benn's Prussian heritage proved stronger than his individual character. In many other situations he knew how to be tough, ruthless.

Benn's isolation reached its apogee during his stay in Landsberg, a small provincial town which is called Gorzow Wielkopolski today. Still an army doctor, still in *feldgrau* uniform, except that this time he was in a place where there was nothing except fields, small houses and barracks, narrow streets, rowanberries and clouds, taking turns coming in from the west, then from the east. Prematurely old, approaching sixty, Benn received permission to have his wife join him. They both lived in the barracks, battling fearless bedbugs. Benn wrote poems and essays, and steeped himself in esoteric texts. He had a lot of free time. The barracks held accelerated army courses for reservists recruited from Berlin and thrown onto an eastern front that was getting closer and closer. The empire was disintegrating, but no one was allowed to talk about it. In the evening Dr. Benn took long walks. Lilacs bloomed in gardens. The Russians were getting nearer and nearer.

It is difficult to find greater mental isolation. It was in the barracks of Landsberg that Benn perfected his cultural philosophy. On the one hand, there is the absurd, cruel, dark history, blood and conquest (as Milosz quoted Jaroslaw Iwaszkiewicz, disturbances in China lasted from the seventh to the thirteenth century), the demagoguery of Goebbels, times of battle and times of relative peace; on the other, the mind, revelation, poem, picture, the life of the spirit. These two spheres do not touch at all. The former deserves only scorn. The second is worth devoting a life to.

I spoke about Benn's march; he walked out of the library intoxicated by Nietzsche (we even know which library—the Staatsbibliothek, which the partition of Berlin left in the eastern sector, something Benn deeply regretted). The road of his march led from Berlin to Landsberg and back. It was the early Nietzsche who had a decisive influence on Benn, especially *The Birth of Tragedy*. It was only as an aesthetic phenomenon that the world could find justification, Benn gladly repeated. Even his short-lived enthusiasm for the Third Reich could be interpreted as a consequence of reading Nietzsche: for a while Benn moved in the direction of the late Nietzsche, to his theses about superman and about his "breeding" (I feel ashamed even to repeat these things). And then, when he finally turned his disgusted back on any kind of political dealings, he "retreated" from the later Nietzsche to the earlier; he returned to *The Birth of Tragedy*; he returned to the library.

The revulsion he felt toward German reality in the late thirties was so strong that he declared it invisible! In a letter to Oelze on July 6, 1938, he wrote: "One could even say, completely concretely in an optical and physiological sense, that we notice only the invisible things."

We notice only the invisible things! Especially in little Landsberg, one did not notice—nor was it worthwhile noticing—the visible things, unless they be roses or peonies or swallows that ignored the war. The historical world, bah, no big deal, cities, villages, hospitals, lighthouses, submarines, telephones, telegraphs, airports, concentration camps. On the other side we will put four stanzas of the poem "Astra," and they will counterbalance the whole burden of the world, at least for an instant.

In his last years of philosophizing, Nietzsche outlined hurried projects that would transform humankind. Benn, after a short period of enthusiasm, accused his spiritual master of having unsubstantiated faith in the possibility of human transformation. He, Benn, knew with the bitter certainty of an aging poet that there would be no such evolution. There exist two kingdoms, spirit and history, and there would be no exchange between them. There will be poetry, and there will be the world of idiots, preoccupied with moving borders, perfecting tanks, and holding parliamentary elections.

Benn's philosophy of poetry has something intoxicating about it (and is particularly appealing to poets!), especially if one receives it in Benn's sharp sentences and if one remembers Benn's gaze immortalized in photographs and constantly challenging us to do something. One can read his philosophy as a poem or as a philosophy. In the first instance, it produces what it is supposed to: spine-tingling rapture and anxiety. If one reads it a bit more rationally, however, it is hard to avoid criticism.

Benn's spiritual radicalism possesses certain features in common with the thought of Heidegger and Ernst Jünger. Once one divides the world into history and poetry, then one obliterates the difference between a history which favors man, which is habitable and human, and the kind which produces concentration camps. It's just like Heidegger's (and Jünger's) view of technology, which is regarded as responsible for all the ills of our era. Yet one must say that the tanks of General George Patton were more "humane" than those of General Heinz Wilhelm Guderian.

Benn knew this, at least from a practical standpoint. After the war, while living again in his beloved Berlin, which was going through hard times, he had no doubts where his sympathies lay. He feared Russian totalitarianism, and appreciated, cautiously, the charms of good-natured American democracy. But these sympathies were not introduced into his "system"; they did not change his radical dualistic philosophy. This philosophy is almost like another one of Benn's poems for me—it gives me a thrill, as it should, but it is impossible to live and think according to it. There is in it, it is true, an intuition of a topographical nature: poetry does, in fact, fit somewhere else than the daily tumult of the historical world.

And even more: by isolating poetry in this way, Benn causes one to recognize its range of "small transcendence" (the large we'll leave to theologians); poetry, and art in general, has to be distinguished from journalism, from purely documentary or didactic writing. Writing a poem is different from writing a constitution.

It is not Benn's acknowledgment of the meaning of poetry that repels me from Benn the essayist, but his taking meaning away from the other side, the historical, political side. To say that that side is meaningless, nonsense, is not only to make a mistake but also to deprive the relations of poem-world their lush and stimulating dramatism.

And it was exactly this that Benn strove for without respite. One reads his essays like one big passionate and scornful tattling on reality. There is nothing in it besides routine, eternal change, boredom. He is interested in medicine because medicine, too, in its own way, has to do with moments of insight, absolute clarity of mind. But political things—nothing interesting. Benn dismissed the Greek understanding of man as a *zoon politikon* as a typically Balkan idea!

He considered himself a nihilist. What sort of nihilist was he though? He described nihilism as a "feeling of happiness." For him nihilism was the elevator of poetic inspiration, taking him up to the heaven of a poem.

Paradoxically, Benn was a nihilist least in the period when he cooperated, or rather, wanted to cooperate, with the Nazis (I remind the reader that that period lasted barely a few months).

There is some confusion in the realm of nihilistic terminology (*nothing*, as one can see, shows itself to the world in a hundred forms). Nazism was nihilism in the sense of an active, fanatical, leveling action.

Benn's nihilism is rather an extreme aestheticism, evoking

a lack of interest in pre-aesthetic reality. That is why I believe that the moment in which Benn glorified the "new state" was connected to the weakening of nihilism in him or even his casting it off altogether. It was then and only then that Benn expressed himself with a certain vigor on "civic" matters.

By the way, in certain situations and contexts, "nihilist" can be the opposite not only of "patriot," "godfearing person," and "political activist" but also of "hypocrite." A nihilist rejects not only values but also the rhetoric that sings their praises. In this field, as everyone knows, there is no lack of corruption and deceit. In Benn's essays and letters we encounter an unusual sobriety and frankness. There is one thing he cannot be accused of: enthusiasm in building a cult of his own work. The letter in which he categorically rejects the proposition of organizing an anniversary ceremony on the occasion of his impending seventieth birthday should be cited in textbooks of literary history along with the 1933 essays that compromise him.

He was an aesthete. He condemned the Third Reich chiefly for its production of one kitsch after another, for bringing a farce like *The Hussars Are Here!* instead of *Faust*. If Nazism had been more successful, if it had fulfilled the expectations of exclusive aesthetes, would that have changed the mood of Jews, Gypsies, Poles, and other uncertain elements?

A German Mallarmé, put by mistake—whose?—into the wrong epoch, stuck into a Wehrmacht uniform, a corpulent Mallarmé; let us leave him where he could live most intensely and where he was most convinced of the correctness of his dualistic philosophy—in Landsberg. Let us leave him among hawthorn, on a country road, in the company of squadrons of swallows whistling arias from unrecorded operas. Twilight falls, poppies and cornflowers bloom. Darkness returns.

In Defense of Adjectives

WE ARE OFTEN told to scratch out adjectives. Good style, we hear, gets by fine without adjectives; the solid bow of a noun and the moving, ubiquitous arrow of a verb are enough. A world without an adjective, however, is as sad as a surgical clinic on Sunday. Blue light seeps from the cold windows, the fluorescent lights give off a quiet murmur.

Nouns and verbs are enough for soldiers and leaders of totalitarian countries. For the adjective is the indispensable guarantor of the individuality of people and things. I see a pile of melons at a fruit stand. For an opponent of adjectives, this matter presents no difficulty. "Melons are piled on the fruit stand." Meanwhile, one melon is as sallow as Talleyrand's complexion when he addressed the Congress of Vienna; another is green, unripe, full of youthful arrogance; yet another has sunken cheeks, and is lost in a deep, mournful silence, as if it could not bear to part with the fields of Provence. There are no two melons alike. Some are oval, others are squat. Hard or soft. Smelling of the countryside, the sunset, or dry, resigned, exhausted by the trip, rain, strange hands, the gray skies of a Parisian suburb.

What color is to painting, the adjective is to language. The older man sitting next to me in the Metro train: an entire list of adjectives. He is pretending to be dozing, but through his half-closed lids he is observing fellow passengers. There is an arch little smile on his lips, which sometimes becomes an ironic twist. I do not know if calm despair resides in him, or fatigue, or, a patient sense of humor undaunted by the passage of time.

The army limits the amount of adjectives. Only the adjective "same" finds grace in its colorless eyes. The same uniforms, the same rifles. Any person who has ever returned from army exercises, changed into civilian clothes, and set off on the first walk in a civilian city remembers the incredible explosion of adjectives, colors, shades, shapes, and differences with which a cosmos full of distinct individualities greets him.

Long live the adjective! Small or big, forgotten or current. We need you, malleable, slim adjective that lies on objects and people so lightly and always sees to it that the vivifying taste of individuality not be lost. Shady cities and streets drown in a cruel, pale sun. Clouds the color of pigeon wings, and great black clouds full of fury: what would you be if not for volatile adjectives drifting behind you?

Ethics is another area that wouldn't survive a day without adjectives. Good, evil, cunning, generous, vengeful, passionate, noble—these are words gleaming like razor-sharp guillotines.

And there would be no memories if not for the adjective. Memory is made of adjectives. A long street, a scorching August day, a creaky gate leading to a garden, and there, amid currants coated with summer dust, your resourceful fingers (all right, so "your" is a possessive pronoun).

Innocence and Experience

We owe William Blake the famous *Songs of Innocence* and *Songs of Experience*. We incline instinctively toward a chronological reading of Blake's poems: first innocence, and then, compensated for by suffering, experience. Is this really so? Is innocence really something that we lose, like childhood, once and for all? Isn't it possible that experience can also be lost? Experience is a kind of knowledge, and there is nothing that disintegrates as easily as knowledge. This also goes for ethical knowledge, that is, wisdom. Someone who has survived a concentration camp, dignity and moral sense intact, might later change into a cocky egoist, might hurt a child. If he notices this and begins to regret it, he will return to a state of innocence.

That is why it may not be right to have experience come at the end. Innocence follows experience, not the other way around. Innocence richer in experience but poorer in self-assurance. We know so little. We understand something for a moment and then forget it, or we betray the moment of understanding. In the end there is innocence, the bitter innocence of ignorance, despair, curiosity.